# SELECTED TALES OF PRICE WARUNG

# Selected Tales of Price Warung

Selected and Introduced by Lucas Smith

Published 2020



Stories selected from *Tales of the Convict System* (1892), *Tales of the Early Days* (1894) and *Half-Crown Bob and Tales of the Riverine* (1898) by
Price Warung (William Astley)

ISBN: 978-0-646-81927-3

Bonfire Books
www.bonfirebooks.org

Cover image: Tim Ozman
Illustrations: John Goldberg
Cover and Layout: Rachel Shershoff

# CONTENTS

# INTRODUCTION

## I.

ASIDE FROM MARCUS Clarke in his 1874 gothic master-piece, *For the Term of His Natural Life*, no writer did more to forge the myth of Australia's convict heritage than William Astley, who wrote some seventy short works of fiction between 1888 and 1898 under the pseudonym Price Warung. Robert Hughes in *The Fatal Shore* mentions only Warung and Clarke as worthy illustrators of the convict period in fiction, "followed by a horde of penny-a-liners" hoping to capitalise on the public's taste for tales of criminal depravity. The story of sadism and hopelessness that they propagated, which like all myths contains much truth, is still alive today. Common conception is its own kind of truth and perhaps more relevant than reality.

Astley was born in Liverpool, England in 1855 and came to Melbourne with his parents at the age of four. He worked as a journalist for various rural newspapers including the Riverine Herald in Echuca, where he collected material for a series of poignant and humorous stories about early steamboat traffic on the Murray River. These stories, reminiscent of the work of Joseph Furphy, were his only departure from depictions of the convict system's grimness.

Warung's period of popularity in the 1890s was brief but allowed him to gain prominence as a literary and political figure. He maintained correspondence with Sir Henry Parkes and Australia's eventual first Prime Minister Edmund Barton, among many other notables. He published five collections: *Tales of the Convict System* (1892), *Tales of the Early Days* (1894), *Tales of the Old Regime* (1897), *Tales of the Isle of Death* (1898), and *Half-Crown Bob and Tales of the Riverine* (1898), but never wrote a novel; he is our Chekhov to Clarke's Tolstoy.

Together with Clarke, he is responsible for our colloquial understanding of the convicts as victims (although usually not innocent ones) of an inhuman system. He never flinches from the brutality of transportation and English establishment hypocrisies are flayed in his work just as sadistically as the backs of the recidivists on Norfolk Island and Van Diemen's Land. Life for most convicts, who worked in households or as assigned men with relative freedom, provided they fulfilled their duties, was more mundane. The historian Russel Ward, among many others, has detailed how Australian convicts often enjoyed higher-quality food and working conditions than the labouring classes in England, where meat was only had once or twice a week. However, the image persists of the striped backs, the broken bodies, and the unrepentant gangs bent on revenge, but although based in fact, these hallmarks were a small aspect of the transportation system.

By the centenary of Phillip's landing, around the time Warung began publishing his tales of the System in the *Bulletin*, there were still a few 'old crawlers' left but memory of them was fading. The two most notorious detention sites, Norfolk Island and Port Arthur, had closed in 1855 and 1877, respectively. But the so-called 'Convict Stain' was a major concern for colonial Australians, uncertain of their place as an outpost of the British Empire after transportation began to be phased out in the 1850s. In the 1880s the convict hulk *Success* was fitted out in Hobart as a tourist attraction with convicts in effigy and all the iron and leather instruments of torture and control. When the ship visited Sydney, as Hughes writes, it was promptly "scuttled in the dead of night by indignant citizens who did not wish to be reminded of the Stain." In Tasmania in particular, the Stain lingered. The novelist Christopher Koch has written of pages being torn from the Hobart library's records up until the 1950s if someone found something shameful in their genealogy. Although "colonial" or "convict" no longer stick as insults, the penal settlement founding of Australia is one of the few things that most foreigners know about us. All in all, nearly 200,000 people, mostly males, were transported in chains to Australia from the British Isles, primarily to New South Wales and Van Diemen's Land between 1788 and 1868. After the 1840s, the flood of undesirables had slowed to a trickle that went exclusively to Western Australia, and included many Irish political prisoners, but the last transportee didn't die until 1938, and direct memory of convict parents and grandparents lived on far longer.

We should be wary of romanticising the convicts. The majority were not innocent victims of circumstance, as was sometimes claimed by the convicts themselves, naturally, as well as by others, but career criminals—although there were a few Irish and Canadian political prisoners, and a few others stitched up for their particular skills or caught by the dragnet of an imperfect justice system. Worse than exile was the "social death of transportation," the impossibility of escaping the Taint. Having little alternative, the bulk of convicts, slowly but surely, and with little glamour, turned their lives around as they were absorbed into the new colony. They and their descendants formed the backbone of the Australian colonies until they were outnumbered by free settlers in the late nineteenth century. The convicts themselves left few written records; many were illiterate or unwilling to reflect on their experiences, or else concerned to protect their own or their family's reputations.

## II.

Warung is far from the supreme stylist of colonial Australia. He is often sub-Dickensian in his sentimentality, and rigid in his characterisations. Nevertheless, his realism, irony and humour, as well as his diligent research, exhaustively undertaken from both archival research and his associations with "the old ghosts of Old Sydney", make him worthy of reintroduction to a contemporary audience. To our knowledge, this is the first edited selection of Warung's work to be published since labour historian Barry Andrews' selection of 1975.[1] Why reissue these stories now? Much of Warung's work is available for free online, but in poorly formatted and edited print-on-demand editions. This selection was chosen to represent a cross-section of his work; the lurid convict tales, the laconic riverboat yarns and the anti-System diatribes. They are taken from three volumes: *Tales of The Convict System*, *Tales of the Early Days*, and *Half-Crown Bob and Tales of the Riverine*.

"Parson Ford's Confessional" is reflective of the Australian convict attitude towards the personages of organised religion, as encapsulated by an anecdote from Russel Ward:

> Symbolic of the convicts' hatred for the kind of religion offered them was an event which took place during Hunter's governorship. When in 1798 he compelled the convicts to attend religious services, incendiaries burnt down the church. He offered to any informer, even one serving a life sentence, a free pardon and passage home, plus a reward of £50. But the group loyalty of the government men was equal to the occasion.

---

1   Andrews, Barry (ed.) *Tales of the Convict System: Selected Stories of Price Warung.* University of Queensland Press: St. Lucia. 1975.

Freed from the grim and technical language of the penal system, Warung's most fluid and picturesque writing occurs in the riverine stories. There is whimsy, such as the wattle powder that falls on Mate Nell's head, and literary allusion: "though there was no albatross to daunt him…"

The characters speak in rough "old-time bullockese" and the proud Australian levelling culture comes through in their disdain for "legislators". Where Warung's convicts are violent towards authority, his riverine folk are merely contemptuous. Both follow codes of honour, if not strictly adhering to the spirit of the rules, as in "The Incineration of Dictionary Ned". "The Last of the Wombat Barge" is a fable against scab labour. "How Muster-Master Stoneman Earned His Breakfast" is a story of pointless brutality on the part of both convict and overseer. "The Pegging-Out of Overseer Franke" shows the power of true *noblesse oblige* against the pointless exercise of authority.

Warung's convicts are rarely without their own sort of honour, and in the longest tale included here, "The Secret Society of the Ring", the plot hinges on the honour of the convict Reynell. In promising to "be true" to the commandant, the sincerely tender-hearted Maconochie, Reynell violates the honour of the secret society of the Ring. There is a strong element of tragedy here, although in Reynell's brash and mockingly obsequious excuse for his life of crime we see a little of the Aussie sense of humour:

> I have to let the devil out of me somehow, sir, and as her gracious Majesty—God bless her! —won't employ me against her enemies, I have to make enemies of my own. And the law's a grand enemy to fight, sir! It'll take such a beating!

In reality, as in the story, Maconochie was the convicts' best hope of relieving the burden of their existence and even offers many the tantalising glimpse of eventual release. His system of marks earned for work and good behaviour, redeemable for better rations and ultimately for freedom, was meant to allow his charges control and direction over their own lives. Unlike previous commandants on the island, Maconochie speaks to his charges as fellow men and rules with carrots, reserving the stick only for egregious violations. And yet the Ring has sworn itself to oppose its gaolers, and the Ring honours its pledges. Better death than to be coddled by a sentimental commandant. Hughes writes that in "The Secret Society of the Ring", Warung

> pulls out all the stops and sounds like an antipodean mixture of Maria Monk, Juliette, The Castle of Otranto and Melmoth the Wanderer, overglazed with Poe; the Ring's nocturnal conclaves are lit with blazing light from the eyesockets of a skull, producing 'a diabolic effect upon weakened nerves," including the reader's. As for the language, 'were you to clothe with literary form the mouthings of the creatures led by Hebert, as they danced round Lais and Phryne enthroned as Goddesses of Reason on the desecrated church altars of Revolutionary Paris, you would scarcely parallel it in point of blasphemous horror'.

By contrast to some of the other men and women of the *Bulletin* school of the 1890s, Warung has attracted little attention from academic writers, who tend to list him as an also-ran, among the vast number of occasional contributors and sensationalist writers of the print-mad colonies. By 1900, the *Bulletin* had an official circulation of 80,000 but was read by, and to, many more, including some as far away as London and San Francisco. Written for an immediate and popular audience, in a pre-radio society where printed literature was among the few forms of entertainment, Warung's work sometimes feels hurried, melodramatic and moralistic. Like most writers, he is best when he lets his plotlines and characters speak for themselves.

One of the few academics who has taken an interest in Warung is the American Edward Watts, who sees in Warung's portrayal of the relationship between convict and overseer a kind of institutionalised shadow-play, reminiscent of the old Soviet joke, "we pretend to work, they pretend to pay us" – in this case, "we pretend to obey, they pretend to reform us." In this symbiotic degradation, Watts sees the effect of an emerging industrial society losing touch with its own traditions.

> Astley [Warung] portrays a far more profound intellectual malaise wherein the values that had sustained Western traditions have vanished in a modern world dominated by impersonal institutional alienation. The result of this loss has contaminated both the oppressors and the oppressed. His inclusion of both groups throughout his fiction is especially significant: Their equilateral spiritual vacuity demonstrates Astley's inclusiveness and universality. Astley thus reaches beyond the narrow frame of the System to address the same deeper loss in Western culture recognized by such literary contemporaries as Joseph Conrad and Thomas Hardy.

"Absalom Day's Promotion", the most morally complex of Warung's convict tales, is one of the few with entirely invented particulars. Watts calls it a fable and makes comparisons to Nathaniel Hawthorne and Stephen Crane, seeing in the executioner Johnson's unwillingness to hang so many prisoners on the same day, a subtle rejection by Warung of the "romanticised proletarianism" he was so instrumental in promoting. Johnson merely objects to the numbers, not to capital punishment itself. Absalom Day's pivotal decision at the end of the story reveals "a nihilistic condemnation" by Warung

> of the inability of man to supervise the survival of

what little there is of value left in the late nineteenth century. When Astley's fiction is reread in light of this insight, his role as "historical writer" diminishes and his significance as a literary naturalist thoroughly aware of literary traditions, scientific theory, and philosophical insight expands. The System therefore comes to be seen as a process wherein the best of humanity is ground out in a Darwinian struggle for survival won by the worst.

Watts argues that Warung has been unfairly marginalised, even drawing a faint comparison to the infamous neglect of Herman Melville prior to the 1920s. This is a conviction that few will share, but certainly he is more than a penny-a-liner and well deserving of further study. Perhaps this lack of attention from the academy is a blessing, as it allows for a fresh reading today, untainted by departmental biases.

### III.

Astley was well-respected among the men who roused the foment of Australian labour politics in the 1890s. A journalist in the newspaper *Worker* commended him as "able and willing to hit hard and straight and corner most of the pugilists who fight for capitalism." Many of his readers would have seen a simple allegory of convict/worker versus overseer/boss. To labour partisans, the convicts were the victimised heroes of Australia's founding.

Warung was also an Australian patriot and nationalist. The danger as he saw it was that England itself would stifle nascent Australian democracy and the uniquely favourable position of working men here. In 1888 he wrote in the *Bathurst Times* that England threatened to "enmesh these colonies in the gilded net of Imperial federation." The Labour Party, as it then was, also came under the opprobrium of his pen when it entered New South Wales' parliament in 1891.

"Entering the House to restore its ideals, you have adjusted yourself to many of its contemptible standards." In 1893, Warung took over the editorship of the *Australian Workman*, the official organ of the Trades and Labour Council. In his journalistic career he alienated the bulk of prominent labour figures, holding them to stringent, if not impossible, standards of conduct. Naturally, he came under suspicion himself, of accepting a substantial loan for the *Australian Workman* in exchange for withholding support for a Labour candidate in the 1892 Hawkesbury by-election and of having an extra-marital affair. Both proved to be unfounded claims. By 1897, he had left the newspaper and labour politics and turned his energies towards campaigning for Federation.

His combativeness was exacerbated by a chronic nervous condition for which he became a habitual user of morphia. Bouts of pain and anger fuelled the "delicious simplicity" of his convict fiction, in which every convict is "an odd compound of Uncle Tom and Dick Turpin and every prison official a distillation of Legree, Torquemada and Charles Reade's Mr. Hawes," as one reviewer of *Tales of the Convict System* put it. A series of disputes with his main publishing outlet, the *Bulletin*, failed business ventures and poor health drove Warung to madness, and an early demise in 1911 at the age of fifty-six.

He maintained throughout his life that his stories about the Australian transportation and penal system were barely fiction, and although that may be so, Barry Andrews concludes that Warung was motivated primarily by emotion and that his vision is ultimately sentimental and idealistic. One-dimensional characters like Warung's sadistic overseers and pure-of-heart convicts seldom outlive their time; the sentimental pieties of the late nineteenth century seem alien to our technocratic society of wage adjustments, policy levers, independent arbitration and the like. Not to mention that our criminal populations are housed well out of sight of the bulk of the public, and, we like to think, in better conditions than that of our forefathers.

## IV.

There is a bad joke about an English tourist clearing immigration at Sydney airport:

"Do you have any criminal convictions?" the official asks. "I didn't know they were still required," replies the Pom.

We no longer live in a time where to have a criminal ancestor is considered a mark of shame. As Mary Gilmore wrote in "Old Botany Bay" we are them and they are us:

> *I was the conscript*
> *Sent to Hell*
> *To make in the desert*
> *the living well.*
>
> ...
>
> *I split the rock*
> *I felled the tree*
> *The nation was*
> *Because of me.*

The reticent Gilmore uses "conscript" rather than convict. In *The Fatal Shore*, Hughes misquotes this, writing "convict", a subtle reminder of the changing mores surrounding the convict legacy.

The vision that Warung showed to the men and women of the 1890s of their parents and grandparents is just as relevant to us. The legacy of the "government men" can be seen in such phenomena as "tall poppy syndrome", and curiously, in the Australian's readiness to accept management and regulation, both at work and from government, which he may grumble about, but does little to alter. We have our rebel legends, but by and large, we are a remarkably docile people. It is said that in the convict system was bred Australians' famous sense of camaraderie, of mateship and solidarity. But conversely, could it not just as easily have bred our comfort with systems, rules, bureaucracy and over-government, the famous Australian suburban conformity? American-style libertarianism never flourished here. In the early days of Australia, to go west or inland meant to die. What is the tortured hand-wringing known as the culture cringe, which persists to this day in our prestige outlets despite such evidence as Les Murray, Arthur Boyd, Bruce Beresford (to name but a few), but sublimated shame at our criminal origins?

The cultural legacy of the System remains by nature inchoate and ephemeral, as it was even in Warung's own time. As he wrote in his preface to *Tales of The Convict System*, "No man can put his finger on the date when it ended, for the reason that it glided imperceptibly into the vigorous and splendid, if still imperfect, present." Folk memory of convict times shows signs of fading amid the onslaught of globalisation and technology. Australia is currently home to large numbers of people from all over the world, few of whom have any compelling reason to recall our convict past. In order for the post-Whitlam narrative of multicultural Australia to succeed, the convict story had to be discarded. But this leaves modern Australia in search of a core that unites. The ongoing transition to cosmopolitanism, by turns painful for some and joyous for others, has yet to fully unfold. This book is published with the hope that it will contribute to keeping the memory of Australia's origins alive, honouring the suffering and sacrifice of the men and women, convicts, emancipists, overseers, soldiers, sailors, yes, even hangmen, who forged us out of the bush and sea.


Melbourne, April 2020


Lucas Smith *is a writer and graduate student and the co-founder of Bonfire Books.*

# A NOTE ON THE TEXT

The stories in this volume are taken from three of Warung's five published books: *Tales of The Convict System, Tales of the Early Days,* and *Half-Crown Bob and Tales of the Riverine.* Original censoring of expletives e.g. "d——d!" have been kept. In the first paragraph of "The Ring" a dash has been removed between "curiously confused". Warung frequently uses the American 'z' in place of 's' in words such as "epitomize". These have been kept as well as "manoeuvering" for "manoeuvring." All footnotes are Warung's original except where indicated by 'ed.'

# FURTHER READING


Andrews, Barry. "'Dynamite, Barricades, Brimstone': Price Warung's Political Themes" *Labour History*, no. 22, 1972, pp. 1–12.

Andrews, Barry. "Introduction". *Tales of the Convict System: Selected Stories of Price Warung*, by William Astley. Brisbane: University of Queensland Press, 1975. ix-xxxii.

Andrews, Barry. *Price Warung*. Boston: Twayne, 1976.

Hergenhan, Laurie. *Unnatural Lives*. Brisbane: University of Queensland Press, 1983.

Watts, Edward. "William Astley and 'The Mystery Which Men in Their Ignorance Label Eternity'" *Antipodes* Vol. 4, No. 2 (Winter 1990), pp. 99-104

# PREFACE TO *TALES OF THE CONVICT SYSTEM* (1892)

THE SERIES OF stories from which the contents of this book are selected, and which have appeared, with an occasional intermission, in the weekly issues of The *Bulletin* during the last two years, are true in essence. There is not one in which the motive has not been suggested by, or based upon, fact. They have been submitted to Australian readers as the first fruits, in literary form, of nearly twenty years' study and investigation of the sources of Australian history, and, however far his work falls short of the standard of graphic story-telling, the writer feels that he can honestly claim that he has sought to communicate to it the quality of historic truth. His principal aim throughout has been the preservation of the appropriate local colour and the historic atmosphere, and not the mere presentment of dramatic episodes To this end he has directed analytic research and systematic industry, and if he has erred in his attempts to describe the subjects of The System as men and women, and not as chattels—things—numbers, the fault cannot be attributed to carelessness or to an indifference to the obligations which bind the historian. In some minor instances the writer has intentionally committed himself to anachronisms. This has been done where the precise indication of a transport-ship, a register-number or a date, might have led to the identification of individual transports or officials. He conceives that the reader is not concerned with the actual personality behind particular characters of his stories, but only with such human interest as he has succeeded in attaching to those unhonoured pioneers of Australian settlement, the convicts.

It has been said by a distinguished Melbourne littérateur that the pages which record the penal chapters of Australian history "should be turned down." We cannot turn them down if we would. The Transportation System has knitted itself into the fibres of our national being. There is not a single Australasian province (and this includes Victoria, South Australia and Maoriland) whose character was left unvitiated by the methods England adopted for the disposal of the criminals she had bred; in three provinces the existing legal systems bear the marks of the convict-mould in which they were fashioned; in two, peculiar land-tenures obtain which, the corollary of the conditions of penal settlement, blight the whole population to-day. The convict past of Australia cannot be shut out of sight. No man can put his finger on the date when it ended, for the reason that it glided imperceptibly into the vigorous and splendid, if still imperfect, present.

TO THE MEMORY OF MARCUS CLARKE

*" The Transportation System . . . . is a monument such as, I suppose, was never before erected by any people, Christian or Pagan, of combined absurdity and wickedness."*

—Archbishop WHATELEY (in the House of Lords, 1840)

# HOW MUSTER-MASTER STONEMAN
# EARNED HIS BREAKFAST

## I.

AN UNPRETENTIOUS BUILDING of rough-hewn stone standing in the middle of a small, stockaded enclosure. A doorway in the wall of the building facing the entrance-gate to the yard. To the left of the doorway, a glazed window of the ordinary size. To its right a paneless aperture, so low and narrow that were the four upright and two transverse bars which grate it doubled in thickness no interstice would be left for the admission of light or air to the interior. Behind the bars—a face.

Sixteen hours hence that face will look its last upon the world which has stricken it countless cruel blows. In a corner of the enclosure the executioner's hand is even now busy stitching into a shapeless cap, a square of grey serge. Tomorrow the same hand will use the cap to hood the face, as one of the few simple preliminaries to swinging the carcase to which the face is attached from the rude platform now in course of erection against the stockade fence and barely 20 yards in front of the stone building.

The building is the gaol—locally known as the "cage"—of Oatlands, a small township in the midlands of Van Diemen's Land, which has gradually grown up round a convict "muster-station," established by Governor Davey. The time is five o'clock on a September evening, 55 years ago. At nine o'clock on the following morning, Convict Glancy, No. 17,927, transportee ex ship *Pestonjee Bomanjee* (second trip), originally under sentence for seven years for the theft of a silk handkerchief from a London "swell," will suffer the extreme penalty of the law for having, in an intemperate moment, objected to the mild discipline with which a genial and loving motherland had sought to correct his criminal tendencies. In other words, Convict Glancy, metaphorically goaded by the wordy insults and literally by the bayonet-tip of one of his motherland's reformatory agents—to wit, Road-gang Overseer James Jones—had scattered J.J.'s brains over a good six square yards of metalled roadway. The deed has been rapturously applauded by Glancy's fellow-gangers, all of whom had the inclination, but lacked the courage, to wield the crowbar that has been the means of erasing this particular tyrant's name from the pay-sheets of His Britannic Majesty's Colonial Penal Establishment. Nevertheless and notwithstanding such tribute of appreciation, H.B.M.'s Colonial representatives, police, judicial and gubernatorial, have thought it rather one to be censured and have, accordingly, left Convict Glancy for execution.

This decision of the duly-constituted authorities Convict Glancy has somewhat irrelevantly (as it will seem to us at this enlightened day) acknowledged by a fervent "Thank God!"—an ejaculation rendered the more remarkable by the fact that never before in his convict history had he linked the name of the Deity with any expression of gratitude for the many blessings enjoyed by him in that state of penal servitude to which it had pleased the same Deity to call him. On the contrary, he had constantly indulged in maledictions on his fate and on his Maker. He had resolutely cursed the benignant forces with which the System and the King's Regulations had surrounded him, and he had failed to reverence as he ought the triangles, the gang-chains, the hominy, the prodding bayonet, and the other things which would have conduced to his reformation had he but manifested a more humble and obedient spirit. No wonder, therefore, as Chaplain Ford said, that it has come about that he has qualified for the capital doom.

Upon this doom, in so far as it could be represented by the gallows, Convict Glancy was now gazing with an unflinching eye. On this September evening he stands at his cell-window looking on half-a-dozen brown-clothed figures handling saw, and square, and hammer, as they fix in the earth two sturdy uprights, and to those a projecting cross-beam; as they bind the two with a solid tie-piece of knotless hardwood; as they build a narrow platform of planks around the gallows-tree; as they fasten a rope to the notched end of the cross-beam; and as they slope to the edge of the planks, ten feet from the ground, a rude ladder. All the drowsy afternoon he had watched the working party, though Chaplain Ford had stood by his side droning of the grace which had been withheld from him in life, but might still be his in death. He had felt interested, had Convict Glancy, in these preparations for the event in which he was to act such a prominent part on the morrow. He had even laughed at the grim humour of one of the brown-garbed workers who, when the warder's eye was off him, had gone through the pantomime of noosing the rope end round his own neck—a little joke which contributed much to the (necessarily noiseless) delight of the rest of the gang.

Altogether, Convict Glancy reflected as dusk fell, and the working party gathered up their tools, and the setting sun tipped the bayonets of the guard with a diamond iridescence, that he had spent many a duller afternoon. If the Chaplain had only held his tongue, the time would have passed with real pleasantness. He said as much to the good man as the latter remarked to the warder on duty in the cell that he would look in again after supper.

"You may save yourself the trouble, sir," quoth, respectfully enough, Convict Glancy. "You have spoilt my last afternoon. Don't spoil my last night!"

Chaplain Ford winced at the words. He was still comparatively new to the work of spiritually superintending a hundred or so monsters who looked upon the orthodox hell as a place where residence would be pleasantly recreative after Port Arthur Settlement and Norfolk Island; and the time lay still in the future when, being completely embruted, he would come to regard it as a very curious circumstance indeed that Christ had omitted eulogistic reference to the System from the Sermon on the Mount. Consequently he winced and sighed, not so much—to do him justice—at the utter depravity of Convict Glancy as at his own inability to reach the reprobate's heart. But he took the hint; he mournfully said he would not return that evening, but would be with the prisoner by half-past 5 o'clock in the morning.

## II.

When Chaplain Ford entered the enclosure immediately before the hour he had named, he at once understood, from the excitement manifested by a group assembled in front of the "cage," that something was amiss. Voices were uttering fearful words, impetuously, almost shriekingly, and hands swung lanterns—the grey dawn had not yet driven the darkness from the stockade—and brandished muskets furiously. A very brief space of time served to inform the reverend functionary what had gone wrong.

Convict Glancy had made his escape, having previously murdered, with the victim's own bayonet, the warder who had been told-off to watch him during the night. This latter circumstance was, of course, unfortunate, but alone it would not have created the excitement, for the murder of prison-officials was a common enough occurrence. It was the other thing that galled the gesticulating and blaspheming group. That a prisoner, fettered with ten pound irons, should have broken out of gaol on the very eve of his execution—why, it was calculated to shake the confidence of the Comptroller-General himself in the infallibility and perfect righteousness of the System. And, popular and authoritative belief in the System once shattered, where would they be?

The murdered man had gone on duty at 10 o'clock, and very shortly afterwards he must have met with his fate. How Glancy had obtained possession of the bayonet could only be conjectured. As was the custom during the day or two preceding a convict's execution, he had been left unmanacled, and ironed with double leg-chains only. Thus his hands were free to perpetrate the deed once he grasped the weapon. Glancy, on his escape, had taken the instrument with him, but there was no doubt that he had inflicted death with it, the wound in the dead man's breast being obviously caused by the regulation bayonet. Possibly the sentinel had nodded, and then a violent wrench of the prisoner's wrist and a sudden stab had extended his momentary slumber into an eternal sleep. The bayonet had also been used by Glancy to prise up a flooring-flag, and to scoop out an aperture under the wall, the base stones of which, following the slipshod architecture of the time, rested on the surface and were not sunk into the ground.

The work of excavation must have taken the convict several hours, and must have been conducted as noiselessly as the manner of committing the crime itself. A solitary warder occupied the outer guard-room, but he asserted that he had heard no sound except the exchange of whistle signals between the dormitory guard at the convict barracks (a quarter-of-a-mile away at the rear of the gaol-stockade) and the military patrol. The night routine of the "cage" did not insist upon the whistle-signal between the men on duty, but they passed a simple "All's well" every hour. And this the guardroom-warder maintained he had done with the officer inside the condemned cell, the response being given in a low tone, from consideration, so the former thought, for the sleeping convict so soon to die. Of course, if this man was to be believed, Glancy must have uttered the words. It was not the first time the signal which should have been given by a prison officer had been made by his convict murderer.

The murder was discovered on the arrival of the relief watch at five o'clock. The last "All's well "was exchanged at four. Consequently the escapee had less than an hour's start. The scaling of the stockade would not be difficult even for a man in irons, and once in the bush an experienced hand would soon find a method of fracturing the links.

It must be admitted that this contumacious proceeding of Convict Glancy was most vexatious. Under-Sheriff Ropewell, now soundly reposing at the township inn, would be forthcoming at 9 o'clock with his Excellency's warrant in his hand to demand from Muster-Master Stoneman the body of one James Glancy, and Muster-Master Stoneman would have to apologise for his inability to produce the said body. The difficulty was quite unprecedented, and Stoneman, as he stood in the midst of his minions, groaned audibly at the prospect of having to do the thing most abhorrent to the official mind—establish a precedent.

"Such a thing was never heard of!" he cried. "A man to bolt just when he was to be turned off? And the d——d hypocrite tried to make his Honor and all of us think that he was only too happy to be scragged. It's too d——d bad !"

It certainly did seem peculiar that Glancy, who had apparently much rejoiced at the contemplation of his early decease, should give leg-bail just when he was to realise his wishes. He had told the judge that "he was —— glad they were going to kill him right off instead of by inches," and yet he had voluntarily thrown off the noose when it was virtually round his neck. Was it the mere contrariness of the convict nature that prompted the escape? Or, was it the innate love of life that becomes stronger as the benefits of living become fewer and fewer? Had the craving for existence and for freedom surged over his despair and recklessness at the eleventh hour?

Such were the enquiries which Chaplain Ford put to himself as, horrified, he took in the particulars of No. 17,927's crowning enormities from the hubbub of the group.

"Damn it!" said the Muster-Master at last, "we are losing time. The devil can't have gone far with those ten-pounders on him. We'll have to put the regulars on the track as well as our own men. Warder Briggs, report to Captain White at the barracks, and—"

Muster-Master Stoneman stopped short. Through the foggy air there came the familiar sound as of a convict dragging his irons. What could it be? No prisoners had been as yet loosed from the dormitory. Whence could the noise proceed?

Clink—clank—s-sh—dr-g-g—clink—clank—dr-g-g. The sound drew nearer, and Convict Glancy turned in at the enclosure gateway—unescorted. He had severed the leg chain at the link which connected with the basil of the left anklet, but had not taken the trouble to remove the other part of the chain. Thus, while he could take his natural pace with his left foot, he dragged the fetters behind his right leg.

A moment of hushed surprise, and then three or four men rushed towards him. The first who touched him he felled with a blow.

"Not yet," said he, grimly. "I give myself up, Mr. Stoneman—you don't take me! I give myself up—you ain't going to get ten quid[1] for taking me." And then Convict Glancy laughed, and held out his hands for the handcuffs. He laughed more heartily as the subordinate hirelings of the System threw themselves upon him like hounds on their

---

1  "Ten quid"—The reward of ten pounds paid by Government on the re-capture of an escaped prisoner.

prey.

"No need to turn out the sodgers now, Muster-Master—not till nine o'clock. Once more his hideous laugh rang through the yards." You had an easier job than you expected, hadn't you, Stoneman, old cove?"

Muster-Master Stoneman had been surprised into silence and into an unusual abstinence from blasphemy by the reappearance—quite unprecedented under the circumstances!—of the doomed wretch. But the desperado's jeering tones whipped him into speech.

"Curse you!" he yelled. "I'll teach you to laugh on the other side of your mouth presently. You'd better have kept away." He literally foamed in his mad anger.

"Do you think I couldn't have stopped away if I'd wanted to, having got clear?" A lofty scorn rang out in the words. "But do you think I was going to run away when I was so near Freedom as that?" And the wretch jerked his manacled hands in the direction of the gallows. "You d——d fool!"

No one spoke for a full half-minute. Then: "Why did you break gaol then?" asked the Muster-Master.

"Because I wanted to spit on Jones' grave!" was the reply.

### III.

Muster-Master Stoneman was as good as his word. Death couldn't drive the smile from Glancy's face. That could only be done by one thing—the lash.

When next the Muster-Master spoke it was to order the prisoner a double ration of cocoa and bread. And, "Briggs," he continued, "while he is getting it, see that the triangles are rigged."

"The triangles, sir!" exclaimed Officer Briggs and Convict Glancy together.

"I said the triangles, and I mean the triangles. No. 17,927

has broken gaol, and as Muster-Master of this station, and governor of this gaol, and as a magistrate of the territory, I can give him 750 lashes for escaping. But as he has to go through another little ceremony this morning I'll let him off with a 'canary'"—(a hundred lashes.)[2]

"You surely cannot mean it, sir!" exclaimed Parson Ford.

"Mean it, sir! By G— I'll show you I mean it," replied the M.M., whose blaspheming no presence restrained save that of his official superiors. "Give him the cocoa. Warder Tuff, give the doctor my compliments, and tell him his attendance is required here. Tell him he'd better bring his smelling-salts—they may be wanted," he sneered in conclusion.

"You devil!" cried Glancy. The reckless grin passed away, and his face faded to the pallor of the death he was so soon to die.

As Muster-Master Stoneman turned on his heel to prepare the warrant for the flogging, he looked at his watch. It was half-past six.

At seven o'clock the first lash from the cat-o'-nine-tails fell upon Convict Glancy's back.

At 7.30 his groaning and bleeding body, which had received the full hundred of flaying stripes, lay on the pallet of the cell where he had murdered the night-guard but a few hours before.

At eight o'clock Executioner Johnson entered the cell. "I've brought yer sumthink to 'arden yer, Glancy, ol' man. I'll rub it in, an' it'll help yer to keep up." So tender a sympathy inspired Mr. Johnson's words that anyone not knowing him would have thought he was the bearer of some priceless balsam. But Convict Glancy knew him; and,

---

2   Muster-Master Stoneman had doubtless in his mind's eye when he made this remark the decision of a Sydney Court which had legalised the infliction, by an official holding a plurality of offices of a sentence passed by him in each capacity, but for the one offence.

maddened by pain though he was, had still sensibility enough left to make a shuddering resistance to the hangman as he proceeded to rub into the gashed flesh a handful of coarse salt. "By the Muster-Master's orders, sonny," soothingly remarked Johnson. "To 'arden yer."

At 8.45 Under-Sheriff Ropewell, who had been apprised while at breakfast of the murder and escape, appeared on the scene escorted by his javelin-men. This gentleman, too, had been greatly perplexed by Convict Glancy's proceedings. "Really it was most inconsiderate of the man," he said to the Muster-Master. "I do not know whether I ought to proceed to execution, pending his trial for this second murder."

"Oh," said the latter functionary—flicking with his handkerchief from his coat-sleeve as he spoke a drop of Convict Glancy's blood that had fallen there from a reflex swirl of the lash, "I think your duty is clear. You must hang him at nine o'clock, and try him afterwards for the last crime."

And as Convict Glancy, per *Pestonjee Bomanjee* (second), No. 17,927, was punctually hanged at 9.5, it is to be presumed that the Under-Sheriff had accepted this solution of the difficulty.

At 10.15 a mass of carrion having been huddled into a shell, and certain formalities, which in the estimation of the System served as efficiently as a coroner's inquest, having been duly attended to, Muster-Master Stoneman bethought himself that he had not breakfasted.

"I'll see you later, Mr. Ropewell," he said, as the latter was endorsing the Governor's warrant with the sham verdict; "I'm going to breakfast. I think I've earned it this morning."

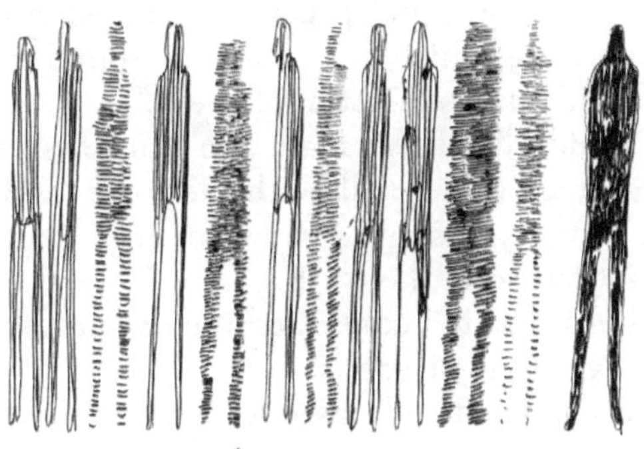

# ABSALOM DAY'S PROMOTION

## I.

THE SOUND OF a bell came floating on the pellucid atmosphere to the ears of the dense, waiting crowd.

"That ain't the 'Tench'[1] clapper yet, surely?" exclaimed a bleary-eyed old ticket-of-leave-man who stood in the front rank, so close to the files of the military guard that his noisome breath dulled the pipe-clayed polish on the nearest private's shoulder-belt.

"Yer ought'r know, ol' chap," sneered an "F.S." (free by-servitude) man." Yer slep' of'n 'nuff in the ol' lumber yard dorm'tories."

"Wot stoopids ye must be as not to know as that's the bell of the *Beagle* as is striking eight bells!" broke in a third person whose assumption of superiority, evidenced in many airs of dress and manner, was based on the circumstance that he was still "free"—a state or condition which, if his physiognomy possessed any value as an index, rather

---

1  Tench (abbreviation of Penitentiary)

reflected on the vigilance of the authorities. And then he proceeded to inform his precious companions that the *Beagle* was a King's ship, "as was a-goin' round the world a-takin' soundin's an' a-collectin' of shells."

"Well," said the T.-L. man, "th' curiowsest thing as they'll see aboard of her will be this 'ere execushun."

Which remark, though somewhat ungrammatical, was certainly not far from, the truth.

"Eight bells, was it?" continued the passholder; "then th' 'Tench will give tongue soon."

His bristly lips had not ceased to vibrate before the sound they were waiting for was borne on the aromatic mountain breeze.

"One—"

The deep solemn tone of Trinity Church-bell—the St. Sepulchre's of Hobart Town—swayed the chattering, jostling, jesting crowd into silence and stillness for a moment only. Before the second toll of the passing bell reached the throng the chattering became excited and furious talk, the jests more biting and brutal, the jostling an angry struggle for a foremost place. The soldiers guarding the vacant space in front of the monstrous scaffold which ran almost the full length of the gaol-facade, were ordered to face about and press back the surging mass with their extended firelocks. The tolling of the bell had communicated a passion like the madness of fever to the veins of the people. The madness of fever, say we? Better, the delirium of blood-thirst. The people of Hobart Town were about to enjoy a rare treat, and their lips were dry for it.

"Execution Mondays" were common enough in the Van Diemen's Land calendar, and it was an exceptional day of the series when only one doomed wretch swung off the platform and into the Mystery which men in their ignorance label Eternity. But it was still more exceptional to have a round dozen of hangings on one day, at the one hour, and in the one place. In fact, there was nothing but a vague tradition to encourage the notion that the event which had occasioned the assembling of the crowd was not absolutely unprecedented in Vandemonian history. The circumstance was, anyhow, quite exceptional in the experience of the existing authorities, and they had been in some doubt as to whether they ought not to divide the twelve criminals left for execution by the last Court of Oyer and Terminer and General Gaol Delivery into two batches of six each. The desire, however, to afford to the criminal element of the population a peculiarly "impressive warning" prevailed, and, accordingly, the simultaneous execution of the twelve was decided upon.

Furthermore, it had been resolved by the Executive Council—present, the Governor, the Chief Justice, the Attorney-General, the Colonial Secretary, and the Archdeacon—that the event should be surrounded with ceremonial details of a unique and peculiarly impressive kind. As the Clerk of the Council was entering upon the minutes the programme for the day as approved by that august body, he paused in his work to nod acquiescence in the opinion expressed by the sonorous accents of the Very Reverend the Archdeacon. "The terrible exemplification," said the dignitary, "which Your Excellency, with the advice of your Council, has prepared, of the majesty of the Law and the heinousness of wrongdoing must beneficially impress the evil-disposed among the people." Vandemonia could not boast of a Bishop in those days, or else this very proper sentiment would have fallen from episcopal lips. It was just the sort of sentiment that the superior ecclesiastical functionary of the colony would be impelled to utter by the obligations of his office as representative of Christ. The Crown, ever mindful of the moral and spiritual welfare of its subjects, always desired the approval of the Church. And, as the Crown paid the Church its stipend and allowances, the approval was never witheld.

"*Ten— Eleven——.*"

The noise caused by the crowd did not prevent the little group of civil and military officials which had gathered round the entrance-gate of the gaol and just underneath the extremity of the gallows to which the ladder was attached, from counting the pulsings of the minute-bell so far. A resonant shout drowned the twelfth stroke.

" They are coming!" cried the crowd. " Look, look! "

Into Murray-street from Campbell-street turned a grim and grisly procession. Up the hill it came slowly—so slowly. A regimental officer marched at the head and gave the measured pace. He recalled to himself as he walked that once before he had done the same thing; but then it was for a *cortege* of honour; now it was for one of dishonour; and his brow compressed and his lips set hard as he cursed the fate which had made him, an English gentleman, the marshal of a massacre, the leader of a felon funeral. Behind him his guard, four deep, with bayonets fixed and ball-cartridge rammed well home. Behind the soldiers one, two, three carts in succession; close beside each walking, first a file of javelin-men, and at a distance of "intervals" as many warders with loaded muskets at the "ready." Behind the carts again, more soldiers and javelin-men, and, last of all, the Sheriff, the Under-Sheriff, and the Gaoler.

And the carts—what of them? Each was drawn by a horse with rusty harness and dilapidated gear, a wisp of yarn being substituted in more than one place for a missing strap or part of a trace. Each was driven by a grey-clad figure on whose clothing stood the prong symbol which proclaimed to all men that the creature within it was a Thing—a Chattel—a Number—anything, rather than a man. Four other figures were also in the cart—no, let us be precise— we should say five. And yet, perhaps, we would not be wrong in saying that there were four only. The fifth other man in each other vehicle was a functionary, and such importance as he had was the reflection of the glory encompassing his four companions. The crowd which lined the streets and which blackened the hill by the Public Offices scarcely gave a thought to him. It was upon the four upon whom it gazed—and gloated. The four were principals in the ensuing drama. The fifth man in each cart was simply an accessory, indispensable, it is true—for he was either the chief or an assistant-executioner—but still an accessory.

The four in each cart were the cynosure of every eye. They had the seats of distinction, for each sat on his own coffin.

One—again to be precise—sat on the fragments of his. Two prisoners in the House of Correction workshops were constantly engaged in making coffins, and, to save trouble and inconvenience in emergencies, the shells were made to average sizes and uniform patterns. Consequently, it happened very frequently that a condemned man found his coffin a trifle too small for him. The law of averages was, however, respected, and the official accounts were balanced by some other wretch finding his a trifle too large. On this exceptional occasion, the particular shell assigned to John Bond, No. 400, per *Asia* (1) was not only apparently too small for him, but was not strong enough to grant him the poor consolation of a comfortable seat to the spot where he was to be hanged by the neck till dead. As he cast his huge carcase upon its lid on entering the cart, his great weight burst one flimsy side from its fastenings, and, the lid slipping, John Bond was deposited prematurely in his shell, or, rather, on its planks. "Why, Jack, you are in a hurry to get in!" laughed James Travis, No. 2320, per *Norfolk*. Travis was always ready-witted. He had begged for the first pick of the coffins that morning. "He wished to get one," he said, "which would just suit him. He liked to be comfortable;" and he had found an opportunity to lie jocosely at full length in his narrow bed, "so as to be sure he fitted it." Finding the measure satisfactory, he hilariously flung his feet into the air. "Taste and try before you buy," said he. "That's been my rule of life, and see how successful it has made me!"

Up the hill came the procession. Most of the condemned laughed at and waved their hands to the crowd. Only one of the twelve sat glum and silent on his sombre perch. This was the youngest of the lot—Absalom Day, who had taken advantage of the comparative liberty he enjoyed as a Sheriff's javelin-man to break into a dwelling house, and, failing in his endeavour to throw the blame on another convict, had been capitally sentenced.

This was only Day's third conviction, and, consequently, he was not absolutely disgusted with life. It was a shame, he considered, to be "top'd off" so young; other men were allowed to live when they had, perhaps, 39 or 40 convictions, including two or three "life" sentences recorded against them. He had expressed his dissatisfaction with his impending fate to Jim Travis. "You're blest 'appy, my son," rejoined that effervescent sinner, "if you only knew it. Them as the gods love dies young." But Day's soul declined to be comforted.

Up the hill it came. The passing-bell tolled in the ears of the Condemned. That was rather unpleasant, certainly. But, then, the bright morning sunshine glanced upon them genially, and the breeze from Mount Wellington puffed piney perfume into their nostrils, and the crowd cheered them, and the atmosphere of distinction was about them. All these things were pleasant; and, pleasantest of all, was not Freedom waiting for them on top of the timber platform yonder? Why should they grieve? Was not the balance in their favour? The door to which yon dangling ropes, when looped, would prove the key-holes, could not open upon a chamber of greater horror than that from which they had emerged in the glorious sunlight of their Execution Monday. Thus, thought the Condemned: all, except Absalom Day.

Two members of the little group of officials before mentioned, mounted the steps of the scaffold in order to gain a better view of the procession's progress.

"Very impressive," said Captain Grove, of His Majesty's ____h Fusiliers, to Chaplain Ford. "Very impressive, indeed!"

"Yes," replied the Chaplain, "it was a happy thought of the Council to order the men to spend their last night at the Barracks instead of in the gaol here. It enabled the Sheriff to organise a very impressive—ah—ceremonial, indeed. Such a spectacle must have the best possible effect upon the convict class." He took from his fob a silver snuff-box, and, having titillated his own organ, tendered the box to the officer. "Have a pinch, Captain? I need a little stimulant on these occasions. My duty is so trying!"

"Just so—thanks!" sympathetically answered Captain Grose. "It must be, I'm sure. I don't like hanging my self. I prefer a platoon at twenty paces, you know."

"Ah, that would be too good for some of our men,'' smiled the parson. "But I think it's time I put on my surplice." He turned to descend when a thought struck him. He looked up.

"By the way, Captain, do you think that beam is strong enough? The weight will be rather much to day. I'd not like any scandal; it would be most unedifying."

To assure themselves, the Chaplain and the Captain walked along the platform and inspected the beam.

"I think it will do," said Chaplain Ford, taking a second pinch. "Have another?"

"I think so. Ah—thanks!" The Captain injected some more of the pungent snuff into his nostrils. "Very good snuff, this of yours, sir."

"Yes, Tandy's best. I import it myself. And, you know," he whispered roguishly, "it doesn't pay duty!"

The Captain laughed, and they descended.

Chaplain Ford put on his surplice which his prisoner clerk—a former mayor of an English city—had brought him from the vestry of the 'Tench Chapel ("Trinity" was so called), and went to the corner of the square, where the soldiers were already forcing the people to clear a passage for the entrance of the procession.

## II.

"I am the resurrection and the life, saith the Lord," began Chaplain Ford, as he led the way to the gallows. "He that believeth on Me, though he were dead, yet shall he live."

The rear-guard of the soldiers closed up round the carts. One by one the Condemned got down. Two by two they followed Parson Ford. They left their coffins behind them; they would not require them again for an hour or so. By their side walked the javelin-men. Behind them, the Sheriff and Under-Sheriff—and the executioner and his assistants.

At the foot of the steps, Chaplain Ford moved aside and mumbled some more portions of the burial-service. "Halt!" called the Sheriff. The Condemned paused. The Sheriff beckoned to the executioner and his assistants to make ready. The chief hangman went into the gaol, came out a moment later with a bundle in his hands, and ran lightly up the steps. He passed along the platform, forming twelve little heaps of calico and cordage as he traversed it. The bundle was composed of the white caps and the pinioning-cords. The Condemned looked on and smiled—all except Absalom Day. He shivered.

"The Condemned will take their stations as their names are called out," said the Sheriff.

"Absalom Day," said Under-Sheriff Ropewell.

Day shuffled up the steps, trembling. Assistant Executioner Sharp assisted him to mount the last, and guided him to the farther side of the drop, where Chief Executioner Johnson received him into his grasp.

The others mounted as their names were called from the dread roll—some bravely, the others with mere bravado; all without assistance. They were ranged in order of age—the youngest, Day, on the extreme right of the platform as the crowd faced it.

A word from Johnson to his subordinates, and the task of pinioning was commenced. The tension of the crowd freed itself by a sigh; the actual drama had begun; the tedious prologue was ended.

Johnson, being an expert, had taken Nos. 6 to 12 of the Condemned to pinion. Assistants Sharp and Muggins, being only pupils in the school of the Law's Finishing Schoolmaster, were allotted but three each. As it was, they bungled their proportion of the work. Johnson pinioned his six in half the time taken by each of the others for his three. The crowd did not complain, how ever. Once the drama had begun, the longer its performance the more prolonged their pleasure.

Johnson stopped in front of the Condemned to "cap" them. The assistants fell back to hand the shapeless calico hoods to him as he wanted them.

By a singular chance, the whole of the Condemned were Protestants. Hence, Chaplain Ford alone was in requisition as the moment of doom drew nigh. He was about to mount to say a few final words—he had seen each man in his cell early in the morning—when the Sheriff stopped him.

"Not yet, Mr. Ford, the death-warrants have not been read. The Under-Sheriff will now please read the warrants."

Under-Sheriff Ropewell stepped up and Chaplain Ford stepped down petulantly. How could he, the experienced prison Chaplain, so familiarised with the proper routine by frequent attendance on similar occasions, have made such a blunder? Chaplain Ford was vexed with himself.

Under-Sheriff Ropewell opened the roll of parchment sheets which he had carried under his arm. He glibly recited the preambles as though he knew them by heart— as was, indeed, probable. By the time a man has read a form aloud a couple of hundred times he should be able to repeat it by rote.

For each of the warrants the preamble was the same. The "orders," of course, varied in their terms.

Beginning, on the left hand, with the oldest criminal, the Under-Sheriff went down the line.

To John Bond, No. 440, per *Asia* (1), he read the order of the Governor for his execution. His crime was murder.

And to John M'Kenzie, No. 8,764, *Elphinstone*, crime . . .; to Charles Argyle, No. 687, *Arab* (2) . . .; to Edward M'Gavin, No. 12,351, *Royal Sovereign*, murder; to Robert Smith, free, attempt to murder; to James Travis, No. 2,320, *Norfolk*, rendering into tallow a sheep suspected to be stolen (he had sold the tallow for 7s. 6d., and the skin for Is.); to Richard Bennett, No. 9,244, *Lord Lynedoch*, robbery under arms; to Philip Grafton, No. 12,755, *Pyramus*, forgery and murder of arresting constable; to Joseph Madden, *Tory*, No. 14,009, murder; to Peter Fyfe, No. 16,150, *George III* (boys' cargo), sheep-stealing; and to Absalom Day, native, burglary with violence. To all these he read the documents of doom.

As the last clause— "These are therefore in His Majesty's name strictly to charge and command you the Sheriff of this Colony and Dependency of Van Diemen's Land that you see the said sentence against the said Absalom Day duly put into execution according to the tenor hereof. And for so doing this shall be your sufficient warrant—" was read, the crowd heaved another and deeper sigh. The drama was approaching the climax.

Under-Sheriff Ropewell finished, Chaplain Ford took up his reverend duty.

"Now, my men," he said loudly, "remember what I told you this morning. God will forgive you all your sins if you really believe in Christ. Even for such sinners as you, there is hope. Grafton, you are not listening, sir." Over the crowd, solitary in the blue vault, hung a fleck of snow-white cloud. Grafton had been gazing on it. His fancy had traced in the fleecy outlines the profile of his dead mother's face. He turned at the parson's words.

"My dear sir," he replied—Grafton's "Educational" rank in the penal records was "C"[2]—"I have heard your remarks

---

2   The several symbols employed by the System to denote the convict's relative degrees of educational proficiency were— "A": Read only; "B": Read and write; "C": Superior.

so often that I am tired of them—and of you. But pardon me this time—I will not offend again." He laughed, and the others of the condemned joined in the chorus of derision— all except Absalom Day.

"Silence!" cried the Sheriff. The Chaplain descended.

Once more the Sheriff spoke. "Men," he asked, "have you anything to say? Now is your last opportunity. You, Bond?"

A thrill penetrated the crowd as Bond flung himself on his knees, and in so doing nearly precipitated himself from the gallows, as, his hands and legs being pinioned, he had no power to balance himself. Assistant Muggins pulled him on his knees with a jerk.

Bond looked up to the smiling heavens. "I wish to say this," he shouted, "that I thank God my time has come at last. I killed Morrison because I wanted to die."

" So do I, thank God! " exclaimed the next man. A dreadful " Hear, hear! " broke from the lips of almost every man forming the doomed row.

When it came to Travis's turn, to speak, he said:

"I'm —— glad I'm going to be hanged, I am. But I don't thank God, for I don't believe there is any God. A God would have given me a chance, and a chance I never had— no, never. Or if He did give me one, the police and the beaks, and the Com'troller took it from me. That's all I've got to say. Good-bye all." He had spoken with a clarion-like fulness of voice that reached the outskirts of the now silent mass. As he uttered his farewell he made a bow of mock-dignity. From the centre of the throng came a loud cheer, and a timid "God have mercy on you!"

The scandal of these proceedings determined the Sheriff to prevent the remainder of the Condemned from speaking.

He motioned the executioner to begin "capping." In a second the pallid visage of Absalom Day was shrouded. The crowd, irritated at losing "a last dying speech" yelled in disappointment.

Johnson took the second cap from an assistant's hand, and was placing it on Fyfe's head when the boy—he was only twenty—spoke to him.

"It's a long time, Dick, since we met, isn't it? An' so you've started in the wholesale butcherin' line, have yer? Well, as you are an ol' pal, I don' min' a-paternising yer!"

Johnson threw down the cap with an oath." You're right, Pete—it is wholesale butcherin'. I don' min' one or two, but a dozen! I'm d——d if I hang so many—so there, Mr. Sheriff!"

And, defiantly, and never giving a thought to the lashes which he must have known awaited him, he walked off the gallows.

### III.

Not so the Sheriff. To say that he was surprised would be to use an absurdly-mild phrase. He was stupefied by the executioner's declaration. The revolt of a hang man was absolutely unprecedented.

"Do you mean, it, Johnson?" he gasped, at last. Johnson did, and said so. "I'll give you two hundred!" said the Sheriff. The Sheriff didn't mean shillings, or sovereigns; He meant lashes.

There was a minute's conference between the Sheriff and the other civil officials, and then the former ordered the assistant-executioner to proceed with the awful business.

"Please, sir, I can't," said Muggins, "I never assisted before."

"Nor I," said Sharp.

But these replies were not occasioned by any delicate doubt entertained by the Pupils as to their own ability to carry the proceedings through to the rope's end. Messrs. Muggins and Sharp were simply desirous of adding to the Sheriff's embarrassment.

The Sheriff was dangerously near his wits' extremity.

"I'll 'sist, sir, if yer can get some 'un else to knot th' ropes, an' yer'll make my ticket a pardon," spoke a voice from the crowd. It was the old ticket-of leave man who proffered his services.

The words suggested to the Sheriff that he should ask for volunteers from the throng. He did so. None were forthcoming except the T.L. man.

The Sheriff grew pale with alarm. The Governor had left town on Saturday evening on a hunting-excursion to Richmond, and he knew that there was, therefore, no possibility of obtaining a formal respital of the men till a fresh executioner could be obtained. To postpone the execution on less authority than his Excellency's he dare not. It would invalidate the sentences. Neither dare he contemplate the fearful but legally imperative alternative of hanging the men himself. To hang a dozen men by proxy was one thing; to adjust nooses and pull levers with his own shapely hands was another. And then a thought flashed into his mind which he told his "lady" at dinner that evening he regarded as a Providential inspiration. Acting upon it he addressed Bond.

"Bond," he said," I promise you life and a free pardon if you will hang the rest."

A terrible second, and Bond's answer came clear and decisive.

"No!"

The crowd was tremulous to its margin with delight. This was something not in the bill.

"Will you, M'Kenzie?"

"No!"

"Argyle?"

"No!"

"You, M'Gavin?"

"I'll see you in hell first!" said M'Gavin.

"Smith?"

"No!"

"Travis, you?"

"Life on such terms? No, sir; T ain't a sneak!"

"Bennett, you? Remember, life and freedom!"

"Bah!"

"Green?"

"What would my old father say if he 'eard such a thing o' me? "

As Mr. Green's father had some years before undergone a suspensory operation in front of Horsemonger Gaol, London, Mr. Green was putting an insoluble conundrum to the Sheriff, which, to say the least, was not respectful of Mr. Green, considering the perturbed state of the Sheriff's feelings.

"Grafton? think what you refuse!" cried the great law-officer.

Grafton thought for fully a minute. He gazed at the sky. The fleck of cloud had vanished. Then he said:—

"Will you throw the permanent billet of executioner in, sir?"

There was a note of general relief in the Sheriff's voice as he replied: "Yes, certainly." He thought his troubles were ended.

"What is the screw, sir."

"Thirty pounds a year, rations, and the usual fee for each—ah—execution."

"Not good enough," sneered the reprobate, delighted at the way in which he had excited the Sheriff's hopes.

Away down the cove the sentry on the quarter-deck of H.M.S. *Beagle* was roused from semi-slumber by the mighty roar of laughter which broke from the crowd at Grafton's reply.

"Madden—you?"

"Mr. Madden's compliments to the Sheriff, and he respectfully declines the honour."

Another roar from the multitude.

The tenth man had now refused life and freedom on the Sheriff's terms. Before Fyfe, the eleventh, could be asked Absalom Day, the only one who had been finally "capped," was observed to struggle violently, as though he were already in the convulsions of death. In his contortions he nearly threw himself over the scaffold. As it would be an act of inhumanity to allow Day to suffocate, even though it was intended to break his neck in a few moments' time by due course of law, and as the System distinctly repudiated, by countless Regulations, inhumane conduct of all kinds, the Sheriff ordered the cap to be taken off. Muggins obeyed, and Absalom Day looked once more upon the world.

Barely had his ghastly face been freed before he gasped out: "I'll do it, Mr. Sheriff; I'll hang 'em, sir, if you'll grant me my life. I don't want freedom, sir—only life, sir, only life!"

"It's my chance, first, Sheriff," said Fyfe. Day shrieked. "Will you do it, Fyfe?" asked the Sheriff.

"Oh, sir, I 'udn't like to take th' billet from poor Day; he hankers so arter it!" laughed the wretch. "Let him do it."


## IV.


Eleven dangling forms, a few minutes afterwards, testified to the fact that Absalom Day had "done it," and had performed his share of the bargain.

That the Sheriff' performed his may be inferred from the following extracts from the HOBART TOWN GAZETTE of the week following the execution:—

Pardon (Conditional).— Absalom Day, native, for meritorious services rendered to the Crown.

PROMOTION.—Absalom Day, native, from Javelin-man, to executioner, vice Johnson, dismissed.

DISMISSAL.—Richard Johnson, No. 4,563, per *Rodney*, from his post of executioner, for disobedience of orders. Transferred to the chain-gang at the settlement to serve the remainder of his sentence.

The details of flogging were not gazetted, otherwise we would be also able to read in the files of the official paper this:—

By order of the Comptroller-General, Richard Johnson, No. 4,563, per *Rodney*, 200 lashes, for gross disobedience of orders. Scourger, Muggins.

We may here observe that owing to the expeditious manner in which the law acted, there was no necessity to proclaim Absalom Day's dismissal from his post of javelin man. Found guilty and sentenced to death on Saturday morning, he had won promotion on the Monday; and as no GAZETTE intervened between the one date and the other, all legal requirements were met by simply notifying his pardon and his elevation from the inferior post to the superior one.

* * * *

The first of the Civil officials to leave the scene of the massacre was Chaplain Ford. In his progress towards St. David's, where he was to hold a christening service, he was stopped by an acquaintance who wished to introduce to him a young naturalist who was voyaging on board the *Beagle*.

"Proud to know you, sir," said Parson Ford, effusively. "I hope we shall be able to show you a thing or two in this colony before you leave."

"I don't doubt it," said Charles Darwin—for he was the young naturalist—who had witnessed the execution; "I have already got some new light on a subject on which I am theorising—the kinship of man with the lower orders of animal life."

"Indeed," said the Chaplain; "how very interesting, to be sure!"

## V.

As demonstrating the effective manner in which the criminal classes were impressed by the edifying ceremony of the morning, it may be mentioned that, the same night, an atrocious murder was perpetrated within half-a-mile of Hobart Town Gaol. The murderer was the ticket-of-leave man who had volunteered "to'sist." He had spent the afternoon in company with an old "Norfolker," and had quarrelled as to the interpretation of a certain ship-signal floating from Mount Nelson. The Norfolker had contended that the flags denoted a vessel from India. The old T.L. man asserted they formed the "Ship with female convicts from England" symbol. As it happened, he was right; and, determined that his friend should not forget the lesson, killed him. The System taught by the agency of Death; so did the "ticket" holder.

# THE LAST OF THE WOMBAT BARGE

## I.

JIM KILLEN, THE puntman, and his mate Tom had just swung back their pontoons after letting the old *Pride of the Murray* and her barges drop through from the wharf, when the exhaust of an incoming steamer was borne pantingly on the languid evening air. Jim put his hand to his ear to catch the sound more distinctly. Like most of the dwellers by the river-side he could distinguish the various boats by the tones of their escaping steam.

"It's the *Little Lizzie*," he growled to his assistant; "s'pose I'll have to let her through!"

"'Taint the *Lizzie*, Jim. It's *Maltby's Hero*!"

"Get alon' with you, you Sydney-side crow. Think I don't know every twist and turn of the little woman's steam-pipe? Listen there now—she's down by the Park, and she always speaks so when she's that far. 'Open the bridge, Jim! open the bridge, Jim!' that's what she says, and none but a derned fool of a cornstalk what don't know a side-saddle from a stern-wheeler would say dif'rent."

"Lor', Jim, don't get shirty, old man," said Tom, who,

being a Sydney-side native, was contemptuously regarded as a "colonial" by Killen (imported by Government at a cost of £20 3s. 4d. in the days of assisted immigration). "You know better 'n me, of course. But what are you goin' to do? You won't let her through to-night? It's after knock-off time!"

"W'en a cove as don't know a steamer from a barge wants to boss this bridge, I tells him to shut up straight. So now, Tom Hopwood, shut up. The *Little Lizzie's* a-goin' through if the skipper wants her!"

And though the dusk was fast settling down into the long, sweeping reach that was crossed by the bridge, and though the steam-whistle of the crane-engine had shrieked the knock-off signal full fifteen minutes before, Jim swung wide the crazy old pontoons into the muddy stream. They swayed on their hempen hinges sullenly and creakingly, as though, too, convinced that it was quite time to end their long day's work.

The men hauled in one rope, slacked the bight of the other, and waited for the steamer. Tom had shirked his pull somewhat, and Jim knew it. But he heeded his mate's ill-temper as much as he did the mutual grinding of the pontoons, or the vexed beat of the river-ripples as they wrestled with the crumbling bank. If the *Lizzie* wanted to go through she should, and if she didn't, well, it didn't matter. So Jim, surly and precise always, and surly and precise in a double degree when it was a case of swinging the bridge after hours, resolved. Jim, like many a better and many a worse man, was, as he himself described it, "a bit weak on the womanines." That's what he used to say when accused of favouring the *Lizzie* by letting her pass the bridge at all sorts of unreasonable times and periods. But there was the *Victoria*, and the *Emily Jane*, and half-a-dozen other boats with feminine appellations, and the *Alice*, and he would never budge from the strict mark of duty and routine for them. And this circumstance—coupled with the fact that when flour was £70 a ton at Wilcannia and potatoes £15, and the great *Cumberoona* and the *Little Lizzie*, both loaded to the pilot-house with produce, were starting at the same moment for the drought-smitten Darling township, he had accidentally jammed a pontoon against the *Cumberoona's* starboard paddle (thereby smashing the box and several floats)—had tended rather to discredit his partiality for the sex.

"It isn't the *Little Lizzie* Jim favours," said "Gus" Pierce, of the *Undaunted,* the satirist of the Riverine; "it's the *Lizzie's* mate!" Gus was right, though it scarcely needed his keen vision to have discerned as much. Any one with the proverbial half-an-eye could have perceived the true cause of Mr. Killen's willingness to oblige the *Lizzie.* Certainly no one who noticed how, on this September evening, the ruggedness of his face softened as the "mate" hailed him, could have failed to understand the motive for his favouritism. For, sure enough, it was the *Lizzie* and her consort, the *Wombat,* that with great animalish gaspings and pantings stemmed the strong river, and forged breathlessly round the willowy bend, through the pontoons, past the half-buried hull of Cadell's old *Lady Augusta,* to her berth under the wharf cranes.

"Thank you, Jim," shouted the mate from the pilot-house; "you're a good soul to let me through to-night. It's worth ten pounds to me." And a flattered smile ironed out the furrows in Jim's countenance as he waved his hand in acknowledgment of the words. High-pitched was the majestic voice, but there was a note of mournful music in it which Jim, with his rude fancy, compared to a curlew's cry. No man's voice could claim that trill surely. The mate of the *Lizzie* was a woman.

## II.

There had been the very devil to pay on the rivers when Capt'n Kingsley—who, after running one season under McCulloch's flag and another under Whyte Counsel's—

had, in the third year, purchased the *Little Lizzie* with her barge *Wombat*, and put his wife to the wheel. It was done as a joke at first, the mates and deck-hands thought, and they entered into the spirit of the freak. They cheered the little woman as she piloted the craft in and out of shoaling channels, by snaggy gullets, and over treacherous reefs. And they "put their money on her" and the *Lizzie*, when it came to racing the *Princess* or the stately *Cumberoona*, for what the more powerful boat gained in steaming, the little 'un more than won back by the deft way she was handled. And they worked with new vigour when wrought upon by the kindly criticism of her glance.

When, however, in the beginning of Capt'n Kingsley's fourth river-season it was made apparent that he was shipping no mate, but that his pretty, youthful wife, a mere slip of a girl she was then, was going to take turn and turn with her husband, the skipper, there was open rebellion on the part of the *Lizzie's* crew, and the deadly antagonism, covert and overt, from the hands of other boats. Men whom the event directly concerned, men whom by the widest stretch of imagination it could not be conceived to concern, joined in the row. The whole river population—from Albury to Goolwa, from Wakool Junction to Wagga, and from Wentworth to Wilcannia—were in agitation. The mate whom Mrs. Kingsley had displaced had almost as much to say on the matter as Sooty Bill the loafer, who never had a wash except when he was thrown into the river in a squabble, and who never did an honest day's work out of gaol.

Unto Captain Richard Kingsley came Captain Freeman, inspector for the Melbourne Underwriters.

"You're frightened of the insurances, are you, Mr. Freeman?" politely inquired the former. "Now, my wife doesn't get drunk. And tell me how many down cargoes come to grief and a river's bottom through a drunken mate at the wheel."

Captain Freeman walked away.

Unto the captain came a deputation of the skippers.

"Lookee here, gentlemen," he said, "I've a little girl down in Melbourne. She can't live with us on the river in Echuca—the weather'd kill her. My wife does a mate's duty, saves a mate's wages, and we keep that child where she has a chance for life. It's my wife's own wish, not mine, and as I haven't paid for this boat and barge yet, I don't intend to cross her."

Upon the heels of the skippers' deputation there came a number of deck-hands.

"Men," said Kingsley, "I'm skipper of my own boat!" They persisted. "Men," he said, "if you don't like my service, clear!"

And they did so. Not that they were afraid of trusting themselves to the "mate's" skill, but the idea of being bossed by a woman galled their manhood. And, as no other men would fill the revolters' billets, Kingsley filled up the vacancies with Chinese. He could not see that in enlisting nine or ten odorous Ah Fats, and Ah Leans, and Moy Sins on his wages sheet, he was placing the axe to the root of his life and his fortunes.

They served him and the "missie matie" admirably. Whatever the pagan was put regularly to do he did with the unerring instinct of imitation, in which consists his intelligence. As deck-hand and rouseabout, as stoker, as cook and steward, as lumper of wood-bales on river-banks, cutter-up of firewood and stower of cargo, John was active and untiring. But when initiative and readiness of wit were required he was almost as miserable a failure as a "new chum," who berthed on a river-boat to earn tucker "till his remittances arrived."

Capt'n Dick stuck a sounding-pole in Ah Ling's hands one afternoon on an up-river trip.

"Ah Ling, you put stick in water, and when water comes to this mark you call—'By the mark—three. And to this mark—four, and to this mark—five, and to this mark—six. You savee?"

After half-an-hour's patient instruction, Ah Ling "saveed," and the skipper relieved his wife at the wheel. They were in a long, deep reach where the ten-foot pole should not touch bottom. Dick thought he'd test his pupil.

"Sound, Ah Ling!" shouted the captain. "Sound!"

With a coolness that indicated a mastery of his business, the Chow dropped in the pole and boldly sent forth the awe-inspiring cry of "By-y'-mark—Fwee!"

"Three! Heaven!" There was no shallow ridge or bottom thereabouts, but a great snag must have shifted into the boat's course—and the *Wombat* was down with produce seven feet! In a second the skipper had his wheel hard down, and the engine-room telegraph had been signalled "full speed astern," and the bargeman shriekingly ordered to "stop way." Dick recovered from the fear of seeing his crafts snagged in mid-stream just in time to hear Ah Ling repeat the last words of his lesson—"By-y'-mark—six"—and to hear his mate, Nell, who had rushed forward, laugh, with a laugh that was half a sob—"Go ahead, Dick, it's over the pole. This gaudy old parrot doesn't know any better!"

Another day Andy McBean, the *Lizzie's* engineer, and the only white man who had remained on board after the Chinese invasion, told his stoker, Sun Lee, to watch the steam-gauge, while he, Mac, made up, by a short nap, for the loss of sleep during the night when they had been running during the small hours.

"Water get down here, Sun," said Mac, pointing to a safe point on the tube, "you come and shake me."

Mac coiled himself in the shade of his woodpile, and slept the sleep of the just man and the tired engineer for a couple of hours. Then he was awakened by the hiss and the bite of scalding steam. Sun Lee had been relieved on the night-watch, but if his boss slept in the day-time why shouldn't he? So he allowed his silky eyelids to droop over the almond orifices through which his soul looked out on the world, and he too slumbered sweetly while the steamer plodded along the Twenty-mile Reach, and the water in the boiler evaporated, and the tell-tale in the gauge got lower and lower. Sun Lee and his brother heathens were nearer heaven at the moment Mac woke up than they were ever likely to be again, unless some other steamer's boiler blew up. "The closest shave I ever knew," breathed Andy to himself, as he flung open valves and cocks with trembling fingers, which did not lose their tremulousness until they had encircled Sun Lee's dreamy eyes with grimy rings of puffy flesh.

A close shave indeed! So close a shave that the skipper and mate henceforth had to do double duty because they could not trust any single pagan further than they could see him. For the mechanical routine which an educated donkey would have gone through with ease John was invaluable, but as to all else he wasn't worth his ration of rice. Kingsley would have thrown the individual and collective Chinese overboard but for the "missie matie."

## III.

She stuck to the Chows when Kingsley's better judgment would have sent them adrift.

"Dick, there's Katie, and I don't like to be beaten, dear. I'll work double, but go back to the old plan I won't. I'll not confess we're beaten. We save forty pounds a month by having them aboard. That'll buy us a new barge next season. And, Dick how the rivers 'ud laugh at us having to own up we're wrong."

So six-foot Dick, with the broad shoulders and the bronzed face, was wheedled by his fatherly love, and his wife's cooing, and his skipper's pride into continuing a foolish policy. He was manly enough to face a crowd of drunken deck-hands when they rushed from the wharf-side on to the *Lizzie's* deck to avenge the insult to their class implied in the engagement of the Chinese; manly enough to face them and strong enough to thrash them. Nevertheless, his love and his pride made him weak, and he kept to his plan. He worked double-tides himself; was skipper, deck-hand, mate, and bargeman in turns. And worked his wife, too, double-tides. The rougher work she could not, of course, manage, but her little hands grasped the wheel almost continually when steam was up. She would stand in the pilot-house for nine and ten-hour watches, clad in neat blue serge with bright brass buttons. Beat the sun ever so hotly, or blew the wind ever so blastingly, she kept her post. In her long spells of duty she learnt the river so well that no other mate possessed an equal knowledge. She knew all the landmarks and guiding points, and where the water shoaled, and where the current would lodge the snags. She threaded with delicacy of touch the boat's way under overhanging gums to dangerous landing-places, and up shallow channels to wood-piles, and when she was at the wheel, the boat seemed to steal from her something of womanly felicity of movement, and went in and out of the pinches and bends with a more graceful swaying of her stem and a softer beat of her paddles. By the close of Kingsley's fourth season, his mate Nell was the most accomplished steering hand, bar Bill Davies and Ted Barnes, on the three rivers. Even the river-men who hated Kingsley for his alliance with Celestials admitted as much. When six steamers and nine barges were stuck up by the falling water at Campbell's Island, Kingsley's mate put the nose of the *Lizzie* right up the channel, and with swift nervous balancing of the wheel, drove her through devious cross-cuts and over treacherous spits of sand that masked ghastly snags beneath their glittering whiteness into deep water.

"D——d if she war't take the craft over wet grass nex'!" cried the *Riverina's* mate, Jim Morris, with an honest chord of admiration ringing in his rough voice.

And if you think anybody on the rivers desired greater praise than that, you don't know the Murray boating trade!

* * * *

The close of the fourth season brought them, though Capt'n and Mate Kingsley knew it not, the beginning of the end. Fate had dealt out to them some first-class cards, but she had made the shuffle with her hand covered with a poisonous glove.

During the summer off-season when the rivers were down, and the boats laid up, the Kingsleys visited Melbourne to taste the rare joys of a sweet home life for a few months. After one happy day spent on the St. Kilda beach beneath the ti-tree clumps, in and out of which the father and mother played hide-and-seek with their laughing child, the captain strolled into the baths. He rolled himself luxuriously in the pungent waves, as was his wont in the greenish Murrumbidgee after a warm day's work on Hay wharf, and showed the other bathers a trick or two of fancy swimming. But they looked strangely at him as he leapt out of the water, with a curious shrinking made visible in their glance. For upon his head, and limbs, and body, like miniature moons surrounded by rose-flushed halos, were white spots encircled by pinkish aureoles. All over him, from the broad forehead that he had held aloft as a frontlet of manly pride in the face of all men, to the curving ankle which it would have defied the skill of Phidias to mould in marble, the horrid blotches appeared.

He saw the things himself. As he gazed upon them, scarcely alarmed as yet, and with no dawning of the horrible truth glimmering its way into his brain, his strength went from him—the strength that had nurtured the copious hairiness of the massive chest whereon the spots clustered more closely—and he fell, a log, on the deck of the bathing platform. One only of the bathers drew near him—a young doctor. "Keep back all!" the latter cried, and then ordered blankets to be brought. With careful touch he covered Kingsley up, and then, striving vainly to overcome a natural repugnance, whispered to the barely conscious man: "Where do you live?" Dick told him, muttering with a feeble discordance, and prayed: "What is—the matter with me?"

The doctor rose up, and motioned the staring bathers and attendants away. They obeyed the gesture—some who were half-attired gathering up their garments and dressing as they went. The doctor knelt again by Dick's side. "Are you a man?" he said. "Can you take—a blow?"

"Yes," answered Dick, "if you—don't hit—my wife—a d child—as well."

"The blow will hit all you care for."

He paused, and the air was heavy with the respirations of the two men before he went on.

"You are a white leper—and a dead man."

## IV.

The old order of things partially resumed its sway on the steamer *Lizzie* and her consort, the barge *Wombat*, with the beginning of the Kingsleys' fifth season. A white-man crew superseded the spawn of the lazar-house. But Jim Morris, late of the *Riverina*, was skipper, while Mate Nell retained her post. The rivers did not object to that arrangement when they were told that Capt'n Dick had been smitten by a mortal sickness and would never finger wheel-spokes again. Upon the news, the great heart of the river manhood gave one sharp, short beat of gladness, and then another of shame at itself, and then went on pulsing regularly in sympathy with the little woman.

The rivers did not know how awful was the doom that had overtaken their erstwhile enemy. Nebulous popular belief shaped itself at last into the notion that Dick's masterful brain was thrown out of gear by a sunstroke; and it was good for Mate Nell that nothing of the ghastly truth penetrated to the quick intelligence of the boatmen. Deck-hands would have fled the Lizzie as a thing accursed, and stevedores would have refused to handle freight. For the river-men would have concluded—and justly—that had

Capt'n Dick kept himself from contact with the leprous brood the hideous canker would not have rotted his splendid virility. When a white man clutched poles, and ropes, and fenders after Chinese paws had slimed them over, what could he expect but that some of the slime would stick?

That is what they would have said had they known. Fortunately, they knew next to nothing. Fate was so far merciful.

Only of all Riverina did Jim Killen, the puntman, know. A worthless son of Jim's had died in Wentworth Hospital while the Lizzie lay at the wharf at the junction township. Nell had nursed the scamp in his last hours with sisterly tenderness. Thereupon Jim had vowed that what he could do for the mate he would do.

"The mate, she loosed my Ned's warp-lines gently, an' he hadn't to let go with a thud," he had said when he spoke of the incident.

Up to the coming upon them of Kingsley's doom Killen had done no more than throw an occasional ten-pound note into the captain's way, by dropping the *Lizzie* through the pontoons after hours, so that the boat might have first chance with the disengaged crane. But in the hour of her extremity Mate Nell thought of the puntman. Dick craved to return to the riverside; he would live in a bark humpy or a tent, he said—anywhere, in anything, so long as it was in sight of a river, and within the sound of a steamer's whistle and exhaust, and where he could sometimes see his wife. And Nell took the puntman into her confidence.

He helped her.

"So Capt'n Dick is goin' with the stream, is he?" he said. "I never liked that Chow bus'ness, but I'll help you for Ned's sake, Mrs. Kingsley. You let Ned's warps drop quietly into the current, ma'am, an' the Capt'n shan't go with a rush, if I can help it."

He built a rough humpy on a thickly-wooded twenty-acre block he had purchased on the Moama side, and there

Dick was brought by night-stages from Melbourne. In the late autumn this happened, in the early winter the rivers were "up."

The season promised to be a long one. The Hay, Balranald, and Wentworth wharves still were burdened with back-block wool left over from last season. Every station on the river and out back was crying out for produce, and stores and sawn timber and the late wool would give return cargoes till the new clip was hurried down. These bright prospects made Dick desperate. He moaned in his gunyah tomb and fretted his heart away quicker than the scaly patches ate into his flesh. The next seven months should have given him fortune, and instead he was being offered death!

Every sound of Nature or of man pained him with a sharper than physical pain. The steam-saws at Macintosh's mills on the opposite bank tore him with their teeth; and again and again he suffered the throes of dissolution as he pictured himself being crushed between the gigantic logs that fed their steel saws. That was all he was fit for—to throw himself beneath the logs. Other men could carve the timber into shiny, golden sovereigns, each of which would melt into some joy or buy some happiness—but for him, the only timber he needed was six pine planks for a shell!

Then the laughing-jackass would stop in his work of snake-hunting to cast a sneer at him from the crown of unstripped gums, and the young cicadae would join the taunting chorus from the teeming grass. And he would deride himself for being their revengeful sport.

Then the rippling stream, on which he dared not look in the day-time save between the interstices of thick foliage, stung him with its jesting whispers. It asked him why he did not drag money from its bosom, and when he did not answer, itself answered for him. It flaunted an iridescent bubble on its surface that momentarily mirrored his dreadful features.

So with everything. The monotone of the curlew was the

wail of his despair; the steam-whistle spoke to him defiantly and dared him ever to disturb the forest glades with its shriek again; the fluff of the wattle showered upon him the jingle of the gold whose hue it had stolen. The distant hoarseness of the men as they called the soundings and the screech of plumaged parrots made him shiver, for they reminded him of Ah Ling—and he knew now the significance of the tiny spot on Ah Ling's neck! And the sky, whether it glared in brassy brilliancy or opened its storm—fountains, tortured him, for the one aspect told him that the hot sun would draw down the mountain-snows, and the other bade him reflect how the swollen tributaries would pour their wealth into the main streams and give the boats another month of activity, when every hour would be worth a yellow coin. Life mocked him at every turn.

So, in effect, he said on the slate, which, his sole means of communication with the living world in his wife's absence with the boat, he was accustomed to leave on the border of his woody prison; and Jim Killen, reading the chalked words with laborious eyes, muttered, "He's a-goin' looney." And when, on the September night in which we saw Jim first, he waited at the head of the cutting after throwing the bridge across the stream for Mrs. Kingsley, in order to escort her through the darkness to the leper's home, he recalled the words so that he might break to her the frenzy of her husband.

"What news, Mr. Killen?" she said, shaking his hand.

"Bad, I'm afraid, ma'am. He's losing his lines in a way I don't like. He's a-goin' looney."

"Oh, God!" She could say no more, but fell trembling; a wattle that, shaken by the pressure, dropped a golden shower on her head.

"Oh, God! That is too much!"

"He put on the slate two days ago, as near as I can remember, these words—'I have cursed God, and yet He lets me live. The very snakes laugh at me when I want them to bite me. I took a tiger-snake to bed with me last night,

and I am alive still. Say the word, Nell, and I shall kill myself.
I won't do it till then because I promised you. But say the
word, darling.'"

"Oh, Mr. Killen, oh, Jim, what shall I do?" wept Mate
Nell.

Jim knit his brows painfully.

"You won't be vexed, ma'am?" he muttered at last.

"Vexed, Jim, my friend! How could I be vexed?"

"Well, I'd say the word, ma'am. It 'ud be most merciful
to you, an' him, an' the little daughter!"

"Never, Jim, never! Better be a leper's wife than the
widow of a suicide!"

"It'll be that in any case, ma'am. But if you won't say the
word, you'll jest have to stop with him."

"He won't allow me!" moaned Mate Nell. "I did not want
to start this season—I wished to stop with him. But he said
we would be robbed if I did not go, and no one could watch
the rivers as I would!"

To watch the rivers was necessary to play the game of
speculation successfully. An exact calculation which would
get a boat and barge loaded with produce down the
"summer-level" Murray in time to meet the first freshets of
the Murrumbidgee or Darling, might win a couple of
thousand pounds, while an error of a few hours would entail
the loss of hundreds. And it took the owner's eye always to
note the fall and rise of the stream, so Dick thought.

They moved on—the man wondering how it was all
going to end; the woman stupefied and as in a dream, the
dilated pupils of her eyes alone showing that she was awake
to the horror that awaited her.

## V.

The next down-stream trip from Echuca, Mate Nell was
mate of the *Lizzie* no longer. She was "bargeman" of the
*Lizzie's* barge, *Wombat,* and the old bargeman had taken

her place on the steamer. And aft on the barge, in a newly-built compartment, went—a passenger.

Nell wouldn't say the word that would have released Dick from his fate, and he wouldn't let her remain with him. To leave him alone was to leave him to madness. So in the dead of the night, before the Lizzie next cleared the Customs for Hay, a tottering spectre, sheeted in greyish cloths, stole from out of the shadows down by the path through George Air's shipyard on to the punt, and thence to the Wombat's cabin.

* * * *

The men wondered at first that they had not seen Capt'n Dick come aboard, but their delicacy forbade a syllable of surprise to reach the ears of Mate Nell. And then Killen dropped a word here and there in mysterious accents, how he had seen Capt'n Dick, "An' he'd take his oath Dick was a gone looney."

Down to Hay, and then to stations below for late wool; up to Echuca again; up to Tocumwal for a short timber trip, and back to the port once more to fill up with stores and wire for which the big 'Bidgee stations were ravenous, went the *Lizzie* and the *Wombat*. Another quick run would have followed with the first-clipping of the new wool, and back again to race the Victoria for the Burrabogie and Huntha-wang clips. First come first to load, was the rule of the two crack stations, and their freight carried an extra pound per ton of "greasy," and thirty shillings for "washed," for balance of the *Lusitania's* cargo-room was booked for their wool, and, filled or not, the ocean freight would have to be paid. Up to Burrabogie, beating McCulloch's boat by half-a-day, and back to Hay, there to top up with Hunthawang bales, and thence home for Christmas. This was the plan.

Golden trips in golden weather, all these passages! Every hundred revolutions of the *Lizzie's* paddles minted a sovereign as the leper calculated on his slate. If the water would hold up till January or February they could then sell the crafts, and, with the proceeds added to the season's earnings, bid the rivers farewell. They would seek thereafter some distant home—and wait calmly for the end! This was Capt'n Dick's notion, for once back on the rivers the swish of the floats as they carried the water, and the throbbings of the pistons, imparted something of their restless vigour to his enfeebled system, and thoughts were struck out of him as masterful and bold as in the old days.

"We shall have a happy Christmas after all, Nell," he wrote on his slate, and passed it through the partition to his wife's hands, just before they left Pollard's wharf, at Hay, on the last trip of the year.

"God grant it, dear!" she whispered as she went out to trim her barge.

The wharf-loungers cheered the little woman as the barge drew by, and wished her the best of good-luck, and the happiest of Christmases, and the speediest of recoveries to the old man. For a moment the cloud lifted, and against hope she hoped and believed their hearty wishes would come true. As Skipper Jim sounded the last whistle, she turned and kissed her finger-tips to the throng. It became a tradition, that kiss. The glory of the river-trade has departed, but the memory of Mate Nell's farewell lingers yet in nooks and corners of the Riverine country.

For Hay never welcomed Mate Nell again.

* * * *

The craft had reached Canoon when the river fell suddenly. That very morn the sun had risen fiery red, and as he ran his course he trailed behind him scorching blasts and steaming mists that wanted only a solitary spark to link the heavens to earth in a chain of flame.

And the spark fell!

In the great reach, fifteen miles below Canoon, Morris found he had to run a gauntlet of fire. Magnificent eucalypti bordered the sorrowing stream with spires of flame, and the tangled undergrowth spread the lurid contagion from clump to clump with an unquenchable rapidity. For miles in their front, miles on either side, and miles to their rear, the torrent of fire rolled on, roasting boat-hands with its heat, barring return with mammoth trunks that fell hissing into the stream, and threatening to stop their egress from the furnace with like impediments.

Every eye on the steamer was strained with a forward gaze, and none noticed that the piles of wool on the barge ignited. The bales had not been tarpaulined, and a fiery shower from a thicket of ti-trees had set the packs ablaze. Nell was the first to see the fire from the barge-bridge, where she held the wheel, and she cried for help.

Some of the steamer hands rushed to save her, but at the moment the *Wombat* reeled and shuddered as she struck bottom. Drawing two feet more than the steamer, she was aground.

Morris put full towage-way on the *Lizzie*. The paddles lashed the cindery current into foam, and the great shaft seemed as though it would burst from its bearings with its Titanic strokes. But this effort had the most fatal of results, for it severed the tow-rope. As a bird freed from a cage, the *Lizzie* sprang forward and left the *Wombat* aground and wrapt in her cerements of smoke and flame.

There was no returning. The shoaling water threatened the *Lizzie* with the same fate if she delayed her advance. Morris lingered until death had nearly completed his leaguer around him and his men also, and then, then, went on— leaving Capt'n Dick and his Mate Nell on their funeral pyre.

Perhaps it was fancy, perhaps not, but Morris, looking back, thought he saw a woman's hand project itself from the smoke as if waving a kiss. "For little Kate," Morris whispered. "For little Kate!"

# DICTIONARY NED

## I.

EMERSON SAYS SOMEWHERE that it is an achievement of high eloquence to confer an expressive nickname, but no particularly fine quality (oratorical or otherwise) was needed to attach a bye-name to Ned—

Ah—now I'm stuck! It has never dawned upon me till this moment, that in all the years I knew Ned to be spoken of I never heard his surname once. Perhaps none of the men who referred to him constantly as the biggest "cure"[1] in that region of "cures" and "queer cards," the Riverine district—where each square mile has its tale of some human soul going to wreck on its sea of grey plain—knew his surname. Perhaps he hadn't one to know. Most likely, indeed, was this the case. His earliest recollection went back to the time when he was tending Parson Marsden's black poleys on the venerable Principal Chaplain's grant at Bathurst, so, as likely as not, Ned was one of the hundreds of infants that were cradled in Parramatta factory, and were sent into the world worse than motherless, and with a choice among fifty fathers. All the same, I am sure none of the fellows who

---

1   A curiosity or curious person (ed.)

spoke of Ned to me knew his surname, else it must have slipped out sometimes. But it was always "Dictionary Ned."

Now I was saying that any one without the faintest touch of eloquence could have given Ned that name—would have conferred no other on him had the selection of a hundred appellations been offered. Even a Victorian shire-councillor, who is the least oratorical person in existence, would have called him "Dictionary Ned." The congruity of the term was so obvious that a blind man could have seen it.

The name had its origin in the fact that Ned always carried a dictionary—a wonderful sort of one. It was based "upon the labours of Johnson, Worcester, Webster," and Heaven knows how many more, "and incorporated the latest results of the most modern and scientific lexicographers." Further, it was illustrated by "one thousand superb engravings from drawings by the best artists" (I am quoting from the title-page), and as though that was not enough to furnish to the humble student, it supplied, at the forepart, an "Analytical History of the Growth of the English Language" (in two pages), and in appendices a "Glossary of Scientific Terms, a Classical Encyclopaedia, and a Collection of Proverbial Sayings and Phrases from all Languages." The whole of this overflowing repository of learning had been published at sixpence. And Ned paid ninepence for it on his solitary trip to Melbourne, at Cole's bookstall, in Paddy's Market, in Bourke Street, twenty-five years ago. Cole wasn't a millionaire then, and you couldn't buy books at English prices. You paid ninepence for a sixpenny publication, and fifteen-pence for a shilling one, and a half-crown, and sometimes three shillings, for a two-shilling volume. And Ned, paying ninepence, had therewith purchased a treasure of wealth untellable, of joys limitless, and all the glorious orbs in the firmament of culture swam into his ken when he pocketed the book.

Keats never extracted from Chapman's Homer, Landor from Shakespeare, Lindsay Gordon from Horace, Marcus Clarke from Balzac, one thousandth part of the delight Ned obtained from his dictionary. The only volume he ever possessed, to him it was a library, a literature, a many-volumed life itself. Somehow or other, the intangible charm that the mere study of words as words, as the fossils of human experience and emotions, has for many people, had entranced this illiterate wanderer whose home was always on the fringe of "settled country," who was never at ease except he was "inside," who got astray in a one-street township, and who was utterly lost in the solitudes of a great city. Amongst the thousand-and-one types of humanity that wandered over the Old Man and One Tree Plains, there was the man who had never turned in till he had read a chapter out of his Bible; there was the man who carried a shilling Shakespeare, and the one who kept his mind alive on Byron; there was the fellow who always kept a woman's photograph, and the one who nourished his soul amid deadening wastes by the crucifix dangling around his neck. The consolation that each and all derived from his and their several idols Ned drank in from his pocket dictionary.

He had bought it with the vain hope of making up the deficiencies of his early education. "Never too late to larn, boys," he would assure the scoffers. And though he was wise in the wondrous lore of the plains and rivers, "up to any dodge" in free-selection and station life, knew every trick of bush-craft and of river-craft, and overlanded cattle in the early gold days from Adelaide to Forest Creek, and (earlier still) ship from Bathurst to the valley of the Wannon in far western "Port Phillip," and had held the wheel of the *Lady Augusta* when she ran up to Tocumwal months before Cadell made his first chart of the Murray, he esteemed his precious knowledge, out of which "smarter" men had coined small fortunes, to be worthless compared with "book-larnin'." At every interval of leisure, and during the times of work when the duty of the moment would not be impeded by "study," out would come his book. When other men smoked, or swopped yarns, or drank, Ned studied. There was nothing complex about his methods. He went straight at the business of mastering its contents.

Somewhere about forty years of age when he invested his ninepence, by the time he became bargeman of the *Royal Duke* barge—she was built in the epoch when ferocious "loyalty" dislocated a man's neck—as consort of the *Currency Lass* steamer, he was within a year or two of fifty. And unremitting in his pursuit of knowledge, with all sorts of difficulties he had mastered the dictionary so far as "V," the page that begins with "vital" and ends with "votive." Ten words a day for a minimum, and one hundred for a maximum—when he had a rare holiday he totted up the hundred—he had got off by rote the words and their meanings. And this was without counting the Sundays. He had devoted those to the "Glossary" and to the "Proverbial Sayings and Phrases," and to the horrible combination of letters which the dictionary-compiler, on the authority of the most modern and scientific lexicographers, used to express the pronunciation of the foreign phrases. It was a gigantic task this last, and Ned had done well to devote his Sabbaths to it when he had no other occupation than to boil his white shirt for next Sunday. Mezzofanti himself would have felt the task of memorizing the phrases to be herculean, if he had also found it necessary to recollect the key to their pronunciation. Just think of the labour of getting off by heart not merely the interpretation, for instance, of *L'homme propose et Dieu dispose*, but the weird and mysterious conjunction of letters with which the latest modern and scientific lexicographer expressed the sound of the phrase—"lom-pro-poz—a-dyoo-dis-poz." But all these fearful and wonderful shibboleths were gradually being mastered by Ned—to an accent. He was a beggar to learn, was Ned. As he himself said—"He warn't no slouch at stickin' to it."

That was the curious thing about Ned. All his grinding away at vocabularies never seemed to tinge by the faintest degree of refined colour his vigorous colloquialism. Perhaps, in some distant period, when he contemplated sitting under his own vine and fig-tree—the most errant knight of the Murrumbidgee plains has always a vision of some roof-tree o' his ain—he intended to employ his "dictionary words," but in the days of his scholarship he kept to the rude, energetic speech of his kind.

Nor was it clear why he hadn't begun "larning" before he reached middle age. Once he was interrogated upon the point, but the answer, though apparently at the time conclusive, does not appear a sufficient explanation now that we can look back.

## II.

It was in the following circumstance that the question was put to him, and the answer received. Ned was running shares in a fencing contract on Benduck at the 'Bidgee. Sunday came, and Ned, having washed and ironed the white shirt he had worn at intervals during the week, in readiness for the next Sunday, donned his other "b'iled rag" and the "moleskins," which he called his "go-to-meetin's," though they never went there. His toilette operations were observed with keen interest by one of the fellows who had sundowned it to the men's hut the previous night in expectation of the plum-duff and tot of rum which Benduck, even more liberal than other stations, invariably gave to the Saturday to Monday "whalers." A man of middle height and naturally sturdy frame, already, while still young, he carried himself with the swagsman's stoop, and his watery eyes gave the lie to the story of natural or acquired refinement which the clear-cut features would have otherwise told. Dirty with the indescribable dirt of the man of position who is debased to a congenial gutter, College Bill revolted, as he lay on a sheepskin in the early sunshine, against Ned's sacrifice at the altar of cleanliness.

"Who's that toff?" he asked of the cook.

"'Im? W'y, that's Dic-shun-ery Ned! Never 'eard of 'im?"

"That Dictionary Ned! My word, I didn't know he went in for white shirt and collars! I'll have some fun with him, boys—just you come and watch!"

Now, College Bill was esteemed a bit of a humourist, or rather of a satirist. For a "Bishop Barker" he would compose a quatrain on any subject—a person preferred—suggested by the man who tipped him the drink, and for a bottle of brandy he would write a fifty-line satire and recite it with becoming action. It was whispered among the bosses and "colonial experiencers" that he was a University prize-poem man, but that could hardly be so, for Bill's "Ode to Swipes," the shanty-keeper at One Tree, was quoted all over the Riverine for its originality and force, and since the first University was, there has never been a prize-poem that contained those qualities.

Being what he was, Bill always had a claque, and when he meandered his odorous carcass to the tank-side, where Ned was performing his toilette, he was followed by several others of the sundowning brotherhood, prepared in advance to applaud his satirical efforts at old Dictionary's expense. They were already in laughter by the time that they had covered half the distance between the hut and the tank, for Bill, as he walked, improvised—

*Devoted student! while other "whalers" slumber*
*He studies hard, does Dictionary Ned!*
*But still he's storing only useless lumber*
*In the squash-pumpkin which he calls his head!*

"You're Dictionary Ned, arn't you?" began Bill as he approached. "I'm Bill—College Bill the boys call me. Shake!"

Ned turned at the remark. Perhaps it was the circumstance that his fingers were busy buttoning his collar—he had only the one collar—that prevented him accepting Bill's proffered hand. Anyhow, he did not take it; he simply nodded and said—

"Oh, yer Bill, are yer?—College Bill? I've hern o' yer!"

"Yes," responded Bill, not feeling quite so easy as he should, his reception was so chilling. "No doubt you have. Being brother students, y' know"—he paused to wink impressively at his admirers—"we ought to be acquainted!"

"Ye-es,-yer think so?" drawled Ned.

"Of course, men of culture are not too numerous on the river country."

"So?"

There was a titter, not quite at Ned's expense. Bill was annoyed at it, and grew truculent.

"Do you know, I think you should drop the 'Ned,' my friend."

"Yes?"

"You should style yourself 'Dick.' 'Dictionary Dick' would be not only alliterative, but would be more euphonious!"

The chorus of laughter again went up—now on Bill's side. Wasn't Bill rubbing it in! What jaw-breakers he could use!

Ned didn't reply, but drew his dictionary from his hip-pocket where he always carried it.

"Going to look up 'alliterative' and 'euphonious,' old chap?" Bill continued. "Now turn up 'h'—you'll find the first under 'A,' and 'euphonious' under 'E.'" And the rouseabouts and swagsmen grew merrier. Bill was getting on well with his chiacking of old Ned! Ned, however, was still silent.

"Ned," went on Bill, "the only two men I ever heard of were books in breeches were Macaulay[2] and yourself. Macaulay was a beggar to talk, but you're a beggar to keep your mouth shut. Oh, and by the way, why didn't you take your schooling earlier?"

"I don't usually ring my clapper on'y when I've got some

---

2   English MP and historian. In associating himself with Macaulay, College Bill is significantly elevating his social status (ed.)

toon to play," now responded Ned. "That answers yer first remark. An', as ter the second, it's my turn ter ask questions. Yer can read French, Mr. Bill Boozer—I beg parding—I mean Mister College Bill?"

Over his drunkard's rosiness Bill's face showed a deeper red. And the audience rejoiced exceedingly.

"Who'd 'a thought that ol' Dicshunery war goin' ter take down College Bill?"

"Can yer read French, mister? I've hear say as how yer says as yer could. An' if yer can, jest rip out that for the present company!" He held out in one hand the dictionary open at the "Appendix of Foreign Phrases," and with his other forefinger pointed out the phrases which he wished interpreted. Bill stared, and the carmine of his dissoluteness and of his shame vanished together. Grey-green, like the salt-bush scrub nearby, was his quivering face.

"Look y'ere, coves," went on Ned. "He's a college chap, an' can't tell yer what mau-mo, vais-va, su-soo, jet-ye means! Or is it that he's ashamed ter tell yer?" He paused, and there were muttered requests from the audience to Bill to respond to the challenge and "take up the parable." But he was dumb.

"As he can't, or won't, coves, I'll tell yer. 'Mo-va—soo-jay,' that's a 'bad subject,' the dic'shinary ses, an' a bad subject is a no-good-sort-o'-chap, a reg'lar bad egg, a rotten spud; an' who's that I should like ter know? Ain't that Bill's picter—ain't that the spit o' the chap as comes down 'ere to chiack me, the poor ignorant roust-about as is tryin' ter make up the loss o' what he never 'ad, an' him what chiacks me 'as 'ad it all the time? An' what's he done wi' it now he's 'ad it? Used it, ain't he, ter lower hisself ter the swine as is in the styes—don't he act as decoy-duck ter get shearers to ev'ry knock-'em-down shanty in the Rivereena? He's used his larnin', ain't he, ter prove that Gawd Almighty don't know His own bizness?" He had closed his precious book as the speech lengthened, and, with his final words, raised his right hand as though in defiance of the Supreme Wisdom.

"What do you mean, Dicshinnery?" said one of the group.

"What do I mean? Here Gawd gives that boozer, that cove what'll sell his larnin' for a ball—I forgot as yer fellows call it a shout now-a-days—and his soul for a bottle o' the stuff; Gawd, I say, gives him—him, the swine—'Varsity eddication, an' me, an' some o' yer as well, who thirsts for it, and hungers for it, why, He don't give us our A B C!"

Bill quailed beneath the artillery of scorn that all eyes now levelled upon him, and walked away. In that brief space he had lost a nickname, and gained a choice of two others. He was no longer College Bill, but ever after, according to his company, "God Almighty's mistake,"[3] and "mo-va—soo-jay." More French was spoken in Riverina in consequence of this episode than was taught in its schools. And the teacher was simple "Dictionary Ned," and the manual his ninepenny compilation of the lexicographers' labours.

### III.

A man's hobby is oftentimes his death as well as his delight. This was Ned's case.

The great spurt of pastoral enterprise in South Riverina, which occurred in the late sixties, operated advantageously upon Ned, as it did upon every one else except the shepherds, who found themselves being gradually replaced by "Rylands" and "Whitecross," and the old-style squatter who wouldn't move with the times, and who consequently got "shifted" into back-country and Queer-street in one and

---

3   "GAWD ALMIGHTY's MISTAKE."—Words substantially the same as in the text were addressed by the original of "Dictionary Ned" to a drunken ex-University man, who was waiting on the verandah of the Bridge Hotel, Echuca, for an opportunity to cadge a shilling from a party of English tourists, among whom was the present Sir Charles Dilke.

the same impulse. Ned, when the spurt set in, gave up rouseabout and odd-job work, and took finally to the rivers. One short season as deck-hand proved his trustworthiness, and the next season he was promoted to bargeman. Ten pounds three and fourpence per month, live like a fighting-cock—there never was a boat on the rivers which kept its hands on skimpy allowance, save one—and the best chance, if he wished it, to ullage the cargo: this was his billet. Too honest, however, to ullage, accustomed to live too sparely to revel in luxury, Ned seemingly put his increased screw to no better purpose than the re-binding of his dictionary.

The cloth cover of the treasured volume had become dilapidated, and one day when the *Currency Lass* was moored at Echuca Wharf, he took advantage of a "smoke-oh!" spell to run up to the Riverine Herald Office, then managed by Johnny D—for Angus Mackay, of Bendigo.

"Yer can get this re-bound for me, Johnny—fine now, an' gilt edges."

"I'll send it to Melbourne," said Johnny, gingerly turning over the greasy, thumb-marked pages, "to Detmold. But don't you think, Ned, it's time you had a new copy?"

"A new copy?" echoed Ned. "It's easy ter see as yer not a readin' man, Mr. D—, for all yer run a noospaper. If yer were, ye'd know as a book a lone man 'as used for the matter of ten years, is mother, an' missus, an' kids, an' drink, an' all ter him! A new copy! Blazes!"

And so the old book, round which the tendrils of Ned's heart had grown, went down to Detmold, the famed Melbourne binder, to be dressed in delicately-perfumed leather, with flexible sides, and richly-tooled bands, and gloriously-gilt edges, and all the rest of the finery so delightful to the book-lover's mind and so ruinous to his purse.

During the month following Ned felt all the distractions and all the sorrows that spring from a gap made in one's life when his hobby-horse is stolen from him. No man gets half the pleasure out of his business that he does out of his hobby, and he bears, therefore, the loss of his business better than he does that of the avocation of his leisure. And Ned was disconsolate, and would not be comforted—"moped," as his mate said, "like a native companion, and sorrowed as Jim Dickson, of the Cumberoona, didn't when he became a widder-man." It was a standing joke on the rivers how Dickson had sorrowed when the news of his wife's death reached him from Sydney. He was at Hay, and he hired the galvanized-iron Temperance Hall for a dance that same night. "I've got to dissipate my grief, ladies and gents!" he said to his guests. And if the depth of his sadness is to be gauged by the extent of his dissipation, he was pre-eminent in grief among men. Ned, however, didn't drown his sorrow in Lindsay's beer, he simply moped.

But as the time drew near when he might expect the book, he brightened up. The *Currency Lass*, with her somewhat disreputable consort, the *Royal Duke*, was coming down stream from Burrabogie station to top up at Hay with back-block clip, when just in the narrow bend opposite the town cemetery, the crafts met the *Resolution* and barge laboriously steaming with timber and wire for the up-river runs. The warning signals were exchanged, and the steamers were slowed down. It was an awkward place to meet in. It takes careful steering enough to allow for the tangential force of the current in a sharp bend in carrying a steamer round the curves; it is trebly difficult when it is a question of getting a barge round as well; but the task becomes formidable when the surge and sweep of the current is complicated with the rule of the road and two not too smartly handled boats going in the opposite direction. Still all would have gone well if it had not been for the dictionary.

Linton, skipper of the *Resolution*, was at her wheel. On recognizing the *Currency Lass* ahead, he had sent down to his cabin for a parcel which had been entrusted to his care, and when he saw Ned, as he expected, at the wheel of the *Lass's* barge, he hailed him, and brought the *Resolution's* stern a point nearer to the slowly-moving *Royal Duke*.

"Ned, there! Diction-ary Ned!"

"Aye, aye, Mr. Linton!"

"'Specting anything, Ned?"

All Ned's desolation and expectation went out in his eager tones.

"Yes, skipper! My book—'ave yer got it?" In his excitement he had forgotten his usual cautious devotion to the work in hand. Instead of keeping his barge's head inshore, he steadied it mechanically.

"Yes," shouted Linton in reply. "Johnny D— said you'd growl like h— if it was knocked about in the mail, and as I was first boat he asked me to bring it. Here you are!"

Holding his wheel with his left hand, he drew with his right the carefully—wrapped package from the seat of the pilot-house, and swung his arm so as to gain impetus for the throw.

"Ready, Ned!" he called. "Look out!" He did not notice that in the movement he had shifted the *Resolution's* course dangerously near the *Royal Duke*. Nor did Ned, fearful the book might fall in mid-stream, perceive his duty. He shouted to Linton—

"Hold hard, skipper!" and ran along the wheel-platform so that the toss would be an easy one.

On river barges the wheel-stand is shifted with the disposition of the cargo—now for'ard, now aft; now raised, now lowered. On long trips it is geared; on short ones held in position simply by its own weight and the rudder-chains. Now, from Burrabogie to Hay was but a few hours' trip, and as the top bales would have to be bestowed at the township wharf, the platform of the Duke was not stayed. Running to its flat end to get his precious book, Ned forgot this. When he remembered it, he was between the sheathing of the Duke and the steamer—jammed! A crunch, a shriek, and a horrid splash!

In their beginnings all catastrophes are so simple—are so easily preventable if the initial blunder in the man or the weakness in the thing could only be understood to be the beginning of disaster. The gearing of that wheel-platform to the vessel's sides—and it would not have slipped under Ned's rush to port! A turn of her wheel and the Resolution would have stood up-stream ten feet away from the barge. But the platform of bolted planks was not stayed down, Linton's hand failed to send the gaily-painted spokes revolving, and the result was that poor old "Dictionary" was done for. It was not a very heroic way of dying, perhaps—and for the sake of a ninepenny book, too. But then the book was Ned's hobby, and men go to the death, do they not, all the world over for their hobbies. A king is but a hobby, a woman another, and Ned's hobby had never deceived him—and never smitten him with the despair of broken faith! And of what king or woman can that be said?

## IV.

He lingered for a few days, sometimes partly conscious, sometimes delirious—oftener still pathetically dead to sound, almost to sight. But about ten hours before his death—he "went inside" at sundown one Sunday—he revived to a calm clearness of brain. Among the watchers—there were as many as the hospital surgeon would permit—was one whom Ned was vainly trying to recognize. And the man saw the glance and understood.

"Don't you know me, 'Dictionary'? I'm Bill—College Bill! The fellow you gave it to so hotly on Benduck three or four years ago—don't you remember?"

A flicker of a surprised smile shone on Ned's face, whose tan was changing to pallor.

"Yer—Bill?" he whispered. "Yer've a col-lar?"

A change indeed had come over Bill's appearance. He wore not a collar alone, but a "b'iled shirt," and—heresy!—studs, and his suit of cast-'em-aways was replaced by Geelong-tweed slops.

"Yes, I'm Bill! I pulled up, Ned, soon after you let me have it. I went on one big spree and then gave the drink best. I tried my best to get out of the styes, Ned. And you helped me."

"Ye-es? W'ere are yer—now?"

"At Pimpampa, teaching the super's kids! I'm putting my education to some purpose, Ned, at last!"

There was a silence, broken by Ned.

"Now, Bill—Mister Bill—on yer oath ter a dyin' man! D'yer mean ter keep straight?"

"Before God I do, Ned!"

"Where's my dic'shun-ery?"

This was the first time he had asked for it. The surgeon gave it to him, in its luxurious garb of Russian leather, with graceful scrolls of gilt lines relieving the dark brown. He took it, but it slipped through his nerveless fingers to the counterpane. He gazed on it curiously.

"Ter think as I can't hold the ol' book!" he whispered. "Bill, page 147, please!"

Bill turned up the page. Against one word was pencilled a cross.

"See that?" He pointed to the cross.

Bill nodded.

"Read it—slow!"

"In-cin-er-ate—to burn to ashes."

"I've a few hund'erd—ev'rybody listen, please—in Boyd's Bank.[4] They're yours, Bill—"

"No, no!" exclaimed Bill.

"Wait! What do folks do with their corpsuses—when they don't want ter be buried?" Strange how strong his voice grew!

---

4    "BOYD'S BANK."—The Bank of Victoria, of Echuca, was in the seventies under the management of Mr. A. B. Boyd, now of the Union Bank, Sydney, and was generally spoken of by the name of "Boyd's Bank." It was a popular notion among the river-men that Boyd owned the bank—and the rivers.

"Order their bodies to be given to the hospital!" said the surgeon, with an eye to business.

"Cremate them?" suggested Bill, thinking of "incinerate."

"That's the word! Lor,' what a thing it is to have larnin', Bill! But the word ain't in any dic'shunery, an' that chap there"—pointing to the marked word—"was nearest I could find!"

"You wish to be cremated?" said the surgeon, still professionally alert.

"Yes—cre—cre—oh, dash it, I don't see what they want ter use words not in the dic'shunery for. In-cin-er-ate—that's my ticket."

"And the expenses will be defrayed by the money in the bank! Hadn't you better sign a will?" Still the surgeon.

"Hang a will! Bill's ter have all the spons—yer all witness—after he's burnt me. Boyd'll fix it!" And he mumbled on and on into slumber—and at sundown he went "beyond the boundary."

* * * *

Boyd did fix it—very irregularly, and to the detriment of the Curator of Intestate Estates' commission—as soon as he was satisfied that Bill's claim was bona-fide. And it is gratifying to know that Ned's few hundreds planted his legatee's feet firmly on the upward path. Bill has suffered in all these years only one relapse from decent behaviour. That was when, in '77, he stood for Parliament. But by that time he had won popular respect, and people thought too much of him to give him his way. They rejected him, and he is still, therefore, an honoured member of the community and unqualified for gaol.

And as to the manner of the incineration of Bargeman Ned and his dictionary—why, that is a tale for another time.

# THE INCINERATION OF
# DICTIONARY NED

IT IS A traditional belief with the sturdy people of the Riverine district that theirs was always "an honest man's country"—that in the elasticity of its atmosphere men of the shady sort could not breathe, and their methods would not work. Like many other good old beliefs this particular one had no warrant in fact. What with smuggling and "the rebate system" on the rivers and dummying and "peacocking"[1] on land, I do not think, area for area, a region can be found in Australia where the device that is dubious and the dodge that is dark grew to such luxuriance. Once upon a time of very long ago, that was, of course. At the present day, it is unnecessary to state, the men of the Riverine are as guileless "as they make 'em." The breath of the plains and the rivers is now an exhalation of innocence—of a surety. Such a dodge as is herein related would be of impossible happening now.

The generation of settlers of which the parentage was in

---

1   Obtaining the best pieces of land in such a way that makes the surrounding land useless (ed.)

the Robertson Land Act[2] was, in truth, a very sad one. Morally speaking, I mean. As far as spirits and tempers went it was jovial and companionable, but the admirable comradeship which, on the surface, marked the country, hid feuds, and hatreds, and duplicities that were so far from admirable as to be detestable. Sometimes the disguise was thrown aside, and "the fine free-handed squatter" showed his teeth clenched menacingly, or the "enterprising selector" forgot his manners and threatened and boasted that he and his class would pick the eyes out of every run in the district, and the heart out of every run-holder. Sometimes the one was in fault, and sometimes the other; oftenest, both were in error. And thus, whether the Riverine sky smiled with exquisite delicacy of blue tint, or frowned with occasional sullenness, or glared brassily, the men who worked and schemed beneath it were driven by the folly and iniquity of the politicians to range themselves in one of two opposing armies, and to spend their energies in cutting one another's throats, instead of combining in the eminently useful work of cutting the throats of the legislators.

It was nothing but natural that some persons and things quite innocent of partisanship should get mixed up involuntarily with these class-battles and animosities; bankers, tradesmen, and clergymen with every wish to remain independent of both sides became entangled with one or the other, or both. So, too, the boat-owner, who earned big lump freights from the squatter for wool and stores, but who also made big profits on his own tradings with the selectors and tradesmen. Even the Government officials took sides.

But of all the men, and things, and institutions that, having no immediate relation to the adversaries in the great battle of Free Selection versus Squatterdom, yet became involved with the fortunes of the fray, the most singular

---

2   A series of laws introduced in 1861 designed to break up the power of the so-called "Squattocracy" (ed.)

item was the corpse of Dictionary Ned. And the story of the way it did so is also an illustration of the lack of honour in the achievement of one's ends which widely characterized the Riverine men of the period. The trick by which Ned's corpse enabled the race between the *Currency Lass* and the *Pride of the Darling* to be won by the former was, in one aspect, justifiable. But certainly, in several others, the reverse. And this is the case where the predominant qualities give the tone to the whole proceeding.

* * * *

Dictionary Ned, dying in Hay Hospital, had desired with his latest words to be cremated, or as he termed it "incinerated." "Cremate" or "cremation" were not in his dictionary; "incinerate" and "incineration" were. In this epoch of the early seventies, when the disposal of the dead by burning was mooted, the latter terms were as often used as the former, but both expressions were as novelties, and the thing expressed was more novel still. Accordingly, when poor old Dictionary had "gone inside," the *Riverine Grazier*, of Hay, and the *Riverine Herald*, of Echuca, each put forth a claim for the honour and distinction of burning Ned. Also—for the profit.

Ned was known on the rivers—well and favourably known—and nobody in the flush times of the Riverine thought anything of travelling one hundred miles to do respect to a dead acquaintance. In ordinary circumstances Ned would have had a glorious funeral, and the local publican a rousing time, but when his obsequies were to comprise no ordinary hearse and ostrich-feather business, but the genuine novelty of a cremation, there was every reason to look for an inrush of visitors, intense grief, and deep drinking. Consequently, each of the patriotic and bibulous editors of the two influential papers named, demanded that Ned should be finally disposed of "in his own important and leading centre."

* * * *

Echuca won the point—not, it is to be suspected, by any superiority of logic on the part of its editor, or of body in its local brew, but owing to the fact that Boyd, the Echuca bank manager, had possession of Ned's funds. He wired Mr. Grundy, forwarding agent at Hay, to "send Ned along by first boat. Dispose of him here." Mr. Boyd's word in this particular case was law. It was often law in others, too—and deuced expensive law at that.

Ned, you may remember, was bargeman on the *Royal Duke*, the barge of the *Currency Lass* steamer. And as the *Lass* and the *Duke* were topping up with back clips at Pollard's Wharf at the time Boyd's wire came to hand, it was the easiest thing in the world to slip Ned in his coffin aboard the craft to which he had been attached. As they dropped down into the mid-stream the hands from the other boats in port joined the loafers and lumpers on the wharves and cheered. Every person of standing above the average departing by coach or steamer, was sped by a cheer from the Hay people at that time. A prisoner going to Deniliquin to be tried and hanged, and the judge who would sentence him, a newly-married couple, or, as now, a corpse—it was all one to Hay. How the cheers would spring forth—and the throats would get dry and dusty and be washed out. Disappointed as Hay was at losing the chance of seeing curious, prosaic old Ned transformed by fire into a poetic white salt, it would not refuse him the farewell, as he lay in his shell under the tarpaulin aft in the barge. The sight of that elongated object was touching—and a splendid excuse for drink. Hay folk always disliked drinking for its own sake. They appreciated an excuse.

Between Hay and Nap-Nap the trip of the *Lass* and her barge was uneventful. Somehow, every one on board had expected something to happen. It was no unusual thing to pick up a coffin at a wayside landing for transport to the nearest township or to Melbourne, but there was, when the crew came to think about it, something eerie and peculiar in carrying a stiff'un to be burnt. And the river men were almost as superstitious as sailors.

Without the same reason for hating to have a parson on board that Jack-at-sea has, a boat-hand grew morose when a white-choker was seen among the passengers; though there was no albatross to daunt him as it poised itself on a magnificent length of tremulous pinion, to entrance him with malign glance, there were land-birds which infected him with their mystery; and if the mermaid did not spring from the water to lure him to ruin, still the yellow wave was alive with weird creatures, whose murmurs could be heard in the still night when the boats were tied up, and the moonlight splintered through the gums and acacias on the banks. And so the nervous system of the *Lass's* crew was shaken severely by the knowledge of their defunct passenger's destination.

"'Tis a-temptin' the Arl-maäghty, that it be," said Cornish Jim, the Methodist fireman, who would sing Wesley's hymns in a sweet tenor in the intervals of blasphemy. "I do b'lieve as they maäght ha' wa'ted a bit, and so he be warnted to be buirnt, don't ee' think? 'Twarn't as if Satan 'udn't do it arl in good time!" And Jim spoke in all seriousness the sentiments of all. Nevertheless, M'Farlane's, Nap-Nap, was reached without incident. At M'Farlane's the *Lass* found the *Pride of the Darling* taking in wool and passengers. Though owned by different men, they were twin boats from the same yard, built on the same model, with equal engine-power, but, owing to the *Pride* having been generally worked on the Darling, while the *Lass* was a Murray and Murrumbidgee boat, they had never been matched in a trial of speed. And it was a problem on the rivers which was the better boat. The general impression was that they were much of a muchness, and that any test of superiority would really be decided by their skippers.

* * * *

The *Currency Lass* was commanded by Ted Gowan—one of the early-time chaps who had risen from the position of an ordinary deck-hand, while the *Pride* was skippered by one of the big firm's newer importations. Forrester was a decent fellow enough, and ready to adjust himself to the river conditions. He was, however, like so many new chums, too much disposed to toady to mere wealth, and "the big-frontage man" was to him an object of veneration, quite irrespective of the consideration as to whether the fellow he made much of was anything more than the nominee of a bank, or was in the least degree admirable regarded merely as a man. Consequently, he was "just the sort" to tumble into all sorts of pitfalls on the rivers in an epoch of transition. In the disputes between squatters and selectors he could not help taking sides, while grim old-stagers like Davies, and Dorward, and Lewin steered right ahead, and let the troubled waters close up after them as best they could.

As the *Lass* steamed by the Nap-Nap landing, she was gladly hailed by Dick Pillar, mate of the *Pride*, who was hungry for a tussle.

"Hello, the *Lass*! In a hurry, Ted?" he called. "Can't yer wait for us at the town, and we'll race yer up to 'Chuca?"

"How long'll yer be, Dick?" Gowan said, as he slowed down. "I'll go slow if yer won't be long!"

"We've another score of bales, an' the fadges to stow, an' then to trim her. We'll be arter yer in a hour!"

"Right you are then. I'll wait at Cramsie's an' fix up terms. I'm on for a skim if your skipper is!"

And then Dick bethought himself. Perhaps the new chum cove wouldn't be willing to give up command to him, Dick, as it was essential he should for a race on equal conditions. To pit Forrester against Gowan was to lose the race before the start. Gowan could wriggle his boat and barge across "wet grass" without the thrilling of a nerve, but

Forrester was desperately afraid of the shifting stream and its mysteriously changing currents and snags and sandpits. Would Forrester consent?

Dick put the question before his skipper. He urged how the rivers had always wanted a fair heel-and-toe race between the sister craft, and here was a quite unusual chance to oblige 'em—loading about the same—next to no passengers to kick up a fuss when the pressure-gauge was getting suspiciously high—fair weather—and the race would be over before the bosses (owners) would know anything about it. The bosses did not object to racing per se, but they had, in view of the risk thereto attaching, a repugnance to rapid night-runs, and it was, of course, a prime condition of a contest that there should be no stoppages.

Forrester was dubious. He was not certain, he said, how the bosses would take the thing at all, win or lose. And he hinted—he did not say—that Gowan knew the stream ever so much better than he did.

"Oh, the bosses won't say nothin' when it's all over!" urged Dick. "It's the knowin' of it in advance they can't get over, for it shakes up the insurance people a bit. An' as to runnin', why, sir, I'll stick at the wheel till I drop jest to have a show of puttin' ol' Ted Gowan down."

Forrester was aft when Pillar had approached him, talking to a passenger just come on board from the station homestead. This man, the Hon. Samuel Darke, M.L.C. (Victoria), was a well-known figure in every spot familiar to Riverine men. Half Irish, half Scotch, he was as tall as one of the first breed of Hawkesbury cornstalks, and strong with the strength of the brute. His intelligence, though it smacked of the brute too, as it was more cunning and instinct than reason, had carried him upward from the duffing-yard of the Manaro gully-raker to the proud position of a frontage shark in Riverina, who was spoken of with admiration at Scott's in Melbourne, and Esplin's in Hay, and Petty's in Sydney. Why the heavy jowl, the eyes that wouldn't look straight, the coarse ridge of fleshy nose, and the overhanging brow had not hanged him before the "gully-raker" had merged into the "honest squatter" and influential legislator, suggested questions as to the peccability in the way of bribes of the rural police. He was one of the chieftains of the moneyed host, who had sworn by the altars to beat and bounce the "cockie" out of Riverina, and was altogether so great a man that the British-born soul of Captain Forrester worshipped him immensely. Was he not the favoured of the principal of Britishers' gods, Success?

Now, Darke had overheard Dick's appeal to his skipper, and, conscious of his supremacy, interfered unasked.

"No —— racin' while I'm aboard, skipper! Ye don't come that game wi' me!"

"No, oh no, of course not, sir," and Forrester, forgetting that he was no longer an apprentice in an ocean-liner addressing his omnipotent captain, touched his cap.

"An' I'm d——d if I don't get the marks of that other fellow's wool! If he carries clips of any of my friends I'll take care he gets a fine rap over the knuckles!"

"Yes, sir—just so—Mr. Darke! That's what I feel, sir. 'Tisn't fair to consignors to run risks!" Then, turning to Pillar, he said—

"No, mate! Can't think of racing!" So Dick retired for'ard.

As he passed the engine-room he spoke disgustedly to the engineer.

"My colonial oath! Hanged if I don't start a blooming subscription to buy th' old man a soot of plush an' false calves."

"What's he been a-doin' of, Dick?"

"A-touchin' of his cap to that—Darke!"

"Wot's th' rivers a-comin' to when a full-blown skipper does th' flunkey to an old cattle-duffer? Th' rivers is a-goin' to the devil, an' no mistake."

* * * *

This was at Nap-Nap landing. When, however, the *Pride* had covered the thirty miles or so to Balranald, an alteration in the resolution of her skipper and passenger was effected with unexpected ease. A company of young fellows from the Heytesbury country, in Western Victoria, had just selected on Canally and neighbouring stations, and some of their number were on their way to Echuca to shift down their stores and waggons. They had booked as deck-passengers by the *Lass*, and were all impatience for the arrival of the other boat in order that the race might be entered upon.

Gowan, whose craft's steam was up, wood in, and passengers aboard, sprang from Cramsie's stage to the *Pride's* deck, as the latter slowed in to take up a lot of hides.

"Well, Forrester," he said, "what d' you say? Are you on to make a match of it? First through 'Chuca punt—losers to give winners a spread at Jimmy Iron's?"

"No!" said Forrester shortly, "I'm not on!"

"Phew, you're not, ain't you? What the dickens did you mean then by putting Dick Pillar up to ask me? Have you grown funky on it?"

"No, I haven't. But business is business—and our owners don't pay us to run races and risks at the same time!"

"Our owners! Speak for your own, my boy," retorted Gowan nettled. "I'll speak for mine, who trusts to my judgment and doesn't keep me in leading-strings like some other coves have got their skippers!"

Then he turned to go. As he did so he caught sight of the Hon. Sam Darke.

"Good-day, Mr. Darke. 'Ope yer well! I want Forrester here ter race us ter 'Chuca, but he isn't game."

"I'll take care he ain't game," said the M.L.C., with characteristic coarseness of tone.

"Well," rejoined Gowan, annoyed, "my passengers, though they're only selectors, ain't afraid of a bit of a flutter."

"Oh, oh, you're carryin' some of those—blackmailin'

beauties, are you?"

"I don't know nothin' about blackmailin,' an' as they ain't M.P.'s on the land racket I don't think as they does, either!" shouted Gowan, as he was crossing the gang-plank.

"D—n you! I'll make you pay for that sooner or later!" exclaimed Darke, furious, as all his class were, at the insinuations referring to their well-known land-sharking methods.

"Oh, keep your hair on, Mr. Darke!" replied Gowan; "an' if yer want to make me pay, back that bloomin' *Pride* in a match with me to 'Chuca, an' she's bound to win, y' know, when she's you aboard. You bring good luck wherever you go, don't ye—'specially to the cockies an' dummy crowds!"

Darke, irritated at these words, discovered a perception of a way in which he could take down this impertinent skipper. He turned to Forrester, whose notions of propriety were being grievously shocked by the language of his brother skipper, and said—"Forrester, are yer in racin' trim?"

"Well—yes—sir, if you really wish it."

Darke, without answering, called to Gowan, "Look 'ere, you cheeky dog, if your —— black-mailers 'll back you to a 'underd, money down, I lay two to one on th' *Pride*!"

And while his challenge was exciting a sensation among the passengers and crew of the other boat he chuckled himself into good-humour by the consideration that "he'd got 'em there, he'd risk two 'underd with pleasure, seein' as 'ow the loss of a 'underd would break the ——" This was an occasion when his old-time bullockese was of distinct value as a mode of expression.

* * * *

After a hasty conference the challenge was accepted by the *Currency Lass* party. While the crews of both boats eagerly wooded up for the fray, so as to avoid needless stoppages, a stake-holder was appointed. A colonial experiencer, returning full up of his experience to Melbourne, en route for his mother's Kensington drawing-room, offered his services, but was treated with scorn by both parties. They applied to him with unnecessary indelicacy of phrase the old query—"Who shall guard the guardians?" Peter Campbell, bush missionary, also on his way to Melbourne for a mild dissipation after a fairly successful journey among the Edward and Wakool stations, was also repudiated. Peter was well known, and "they didn't like to throw temptation in his way." And, finally, Cramsie's manager being appointed with instructions to wire the amount to the firm's Echuca agency to be claimed by the winner, the stakes were lodged. Of a composite nature they were! "Cash-orders" on the shipping firms and stations were the main currency of the rivers, and the stakes held a superb variety of autographs of more or less financial solidity. Even the Legislative Councillor, who never travelled without gold—gold payments to dummies and their kin could not be traced!—took advantage of the opportunity to free his pocket-book of orders.

And then the conditions were drawn up on two halves of a sheet of notepaper:—The stakes to be lodged with Cramsie's manager—£200 on the *Pride*'s behalf; £100 on behalf of the *Lass*.

Each boat to have a representative on the other. Day and night running.

First through the punt at Echuca.

The boats to start from the foot of Yuranigh Street, called after Sir Thomas Mitchell's famous black Yuranigh (whose grave enclosure was for some time used by a distinguished legislator as a cow-bale).

No warping over pinches and shallows.

Fair heel-and-toe work all through.

Fuel, cord for cord, taken in at Balranald, and no stoppage for refilling at wood-piles permitted. And—fuel not supplemented from cargo.

Last in the schedule of conditions, this proviso might not improbably prove the most important. Races had taken place in which an unscrupulous skipper had used consignee's casks of tallow as stoking-material for a furnace, paying the same out of the stakes thus illegitimately won.

* * * *

They started from the crazy timber thing called the wharf, after a three hours' spell devoted by all hands on the two boats to adjusting top hamper, getting clean furnaces, trimming the barges. Opposite Yuranigh Street they shut off steam, and waited till Cramsie's manager passed a measuring-rod over the stacked cords of wood. The *Lass's* stock was, if anything, under that of the *Pride*. With much greatness of soul, the Legislative Councillor consented to a dozen sticks of firewood being shoved over to the *Lass*.

Then a brawny young blacksmith from the Camperdown country, Victoria, was dropped on the *Pride* as representative of the *Lass*, and the *Lass* received Peter Campbell, selected by Darke, to watch over the interests of the *Pride* on her rival. Peter's main spiritual—and spirituous—sustenance came from the squatters' class. Hence Darke felt that he was safe with Peter.

And then, as the best available substitute for a pistol-shot—a reverberant cracking of Gory Sam from Tanga's stockwhip—and amid a roar of cheers, a full head of steam was put on. With a crash, and a splash, and a rattle, they ran off level. If the start meant anything, it should be a well-matched race.

* * * *

A wire from Balranald had acquainted the Swan Hillites with the intelligence that at last the twin boats were "at it." And, as they rolled by with a duck-like skimming—they were almost level—the people clustered on the banks at the crossing township shouted hints as to the state of the rivers, which might have been valuable if only they had been understood. And—but why particularize all points? Now one was ahead a tow-rope's length and now the other; each was greatly handled, and each answered to her builder's fame.

But, nearing Gunbower, they set down for the final struggle. Dick Pillar—Forrester was wise enough to give up the wheel and do the mate's work—and Gowan were sleepless, and yet each was fresher, so it seemed to their backers, than when the crafts left Balranald.

At Gunbower the *Lass* hung up for a couple of hours to cool her bearings for the final run in. Pillar would have done the same, but he was over-ruled by Darke, M.L.C. There are problems in applied mechanics that even the massive intellect of a legislative councillor cannot solve. Darke could not apprehend the impossibility of running incessantly with heated plummer-blocks, and how he chuckled and chuckled as the sound of the *Lass*'s exhaust grew fainter and fainter, and utterly faded into silence.

"He would give those (bullockese) selectors somethink to remember him by!" he swore.

But ten miles beyond Gunbower a dreadful message was communicated to him. The wood had given out! Overnight the stock had been drawn upon largely, and now, in the blossoming dawn, it was known that the fuel on board would not suffice for two hours' full running.

Heavens, how he effervesced with bullocky talk! He swore he would stoke the furnace with the (bullockese) carcasses of the (more bullockese) deck-hands!

"I'll be hanged if you do!" quoth Camperdown's son of Vulcan. "Deck-hands ain't wooden you see, Mr. Darke—not being members of Parliament, sir!"

Then he would have had the men's bunks and the cabin fittings broken up for fuel.

"No, you don't!" persisted the Camperdonian. "Not if I knows it!" And the Honourable the Legislative Councillor was beaten again.

But one gleam of hope had he. The *Lass* must be almost in the same plight. And of fulfilment of this he was not deprived, for when, some time after the swift gliding of the *Pride* had given place to a subdued and pulseless motion that was almost retrogressive, she was gradually overhauled by the *Lass*, it was noticed that she too was running at less than half-speed.

As the *Lass* drew near to the *Pride*, Peter Campbell, missioner to the back-blocks, waddled for'ard and shouted. The words were no sooner out of his mouth than—it hurts me to have to relate so painful an incident—the closed fist of a sturdy child of the forest struck Peter's saintly paunch and doubled him up. "Shut up, you old fraud, you! If we're out of firewood that's our look-out, not theirs!" It would have been some consolation to Peter, as he revolved in some inconvenience for some moments, could he but have been sure that his words had reached the Hon. Samuel Darke's ears. As it happened, they did; and Darke and his sympathizers took heart of grace thereby. The *Lass's* people must be in equal trouble with themselves.

* * * *

Unfortunately for Darke's two hundred, the distress of the *Lass* was, however, not quite so extreme as the *Pride's*. The *Lass* had something in reserve.

By slow puffings and feeble paddlings which were ever on the verge of ceasing to propel the crafts a foot further in their course, the two steamers had reached the bend which leads into the reach by Echuca Park. Twenty minutes' fair steaming would see them at the pontoons of the floating-bridge, but how on earth were they to reach the point?

If, during the rapid running, the excitement on the boats mounted with the steam-gauge, there was, as might have been expected, no dropping off of enthusiasm as the steam power grew weaker and weaker. Progress, since Gunbower Mills were passed, was decidedly of an ironical sort, and, had the river been flowing with a masterful flood current, it is quite conceivable that the race would have been declared off from sheer inability to complete the last ten miles of their course. It was, however, sluggish, and the crafts managed, with laborious strainings, to make headway till entering the long park reach. Then even Darke considered the contest not worth fighting. Between the stern-post of the *Pride*'s barge and the nose of the *Lass* there was a good forty yards. It was evidently hopeless for the *Lass* to conquer even that paltry distance and come level. Morally, if not by the precise conditions of the match, the race was won by the *Pride*.

He was saying as much to Forrester and Pillar, when a solid volume of murky cloud burst from the *Lass*'s smoke-stack, and with increased firing the *Lass* and her barge shot forward suddenly.

"H—!" cried Darke. "They've been gullin' us!" Then he became too maddened to indulge even in the unqualified vocabulary of the gully-raker and the puncher.

As for Pillar and Forrester, they confessed the game was up. But how the devil did Gowan manage it? Had he burnt his boat's fittings? That was unlikely! He had no rich squatter aboard to stand the damage. Then, how had he managed? Had he not been running fair but had surreptitiously obtained fuel?

The way of it they learned from the reverend sufferer, Peter Campbell. As the *Lass* rushed past them, they could just grasp his words over the derisive cheering of the victorious party—

"Mister Darke, mon, they're boornin' the corpse!"

* * * *

It was even so. Dictionary Ned, by a happy thought of Gowan's, was granted his incineration: somewhat prematurely, perhaps, but on the final judgment of the river-men when the subject was debated later, in the way he would have most preferred. And he raised just steam enough to force the *Lass* and her barge the *Duke* through the pontoons.

Darke, at first, protested against the stakes being paid over. "Cargo was barred!" he spluttered. "D——n it! if it came to firin' up with cargo, I'd have shoved in half-a-dozen bales of wool!"

"Dictionary Ned wasn't cargo!" contended Gowan. "There isn't a boat on the rivers that 'ud take poor old Ned as cargo, except Locky M'Bean's Goldsb'rough!"

"What in —— would you call him then?" roared Darke.

"Why, an honorary passenger, sir, o' course!" retorted Gowan.

The popular verdict, and the stake-holder's, went with Gowan. And, thereupon, there was the most royal of sprees at the old Bridge, at which the memory of Dictionary Ned was toasted in the most solemn and impressive of silences.

It was Cornish Jim who set the ball of talk rolling once more. "P'r'aps," he said, "th' Arlmaäghty do know 'Is business best aäfter arl!" Jim was like most men. He approved of the Almighty's dealings with him when he was on the winning side.

# THE DOOM OF WALMSLEY'S RUBY

NOT RANDALL'S *RUBY*, but Walmsley's—an older boat than Randall's pretty, gay little craft, so familiar to the Mildura people—a boat of the seventies and not of the nineties, and built therefore when the river-trade was best going into by wise and keen men. With engines of twelve horse-power nominal, she worked up to fifty; with the firewood aboard for the run from Swan Hill to Echuca she could also carry fifty bales wool and "sundries" on a draught of three feet, while hauling her barge with four hundred bales on a draught of five feet. So she was "a neat 'un to handle" (as the river phrase went), and if she could not exactly travel over "wet grass" (the boat to which was accorded the praise of floating upon dewy pastures touched perfection in the judgement of the river-men), she could achieve the next best thing—she could skim the rivers when they were "down" longer than any other boat, and consequently earned for her owner a considerable sum in dealing "in trade," in timber-running, and in bringing in to the port the wool-cargoes of larger crafts which had been stuck on a falling river. A clever craft, and no mistake about it.

Fred Walmsley, owner and skipper, was justly proud of her. She had not an inch of gilt-beading anywhere, or a scrap of velvet on her cushions, and yet she was always pleasant to the eye of her passengers, and restful to their bodies. Fred, as a rule a taciturn, gruff, unpolished sort of fellow, was expansively eloquent and courteous to his fares about his boat's performances. Every other skipper worth his salt on the rivers—with the exception of Locky M'B——'s skipper— was accustomed to affect a delight in his own particular boat, even to the verge of unveracity. Fred, however, was under no necessity to fib regarding the *Ruby*. He talked big about her, but she justified every word, and he was a curious man indeed, who, being borne along by the *Ruby*, did not respond to her skipper's generous enthusiasm as to her "lines" and her "model," the taste with which her coat of white paint had been picked out, here with red and there with blue, the shiny brass of her engine-work and of the wheel, the musical note in her exhaust-pipe, the rhythmic beat of her paddles. Without wife or child, Fred found all the solace of a home in his craft, and gloried in her as other men glory in their home, their pictures, their books, their bank-balance. He would make oath in his rough, ungenial way that he would stick to the little *Ruby* as long as she'd stick to him. He didn't believe, he said, in selling the little craft, which had made the first money for the owner, as soon as a second and larger boat could be bought. That was the river practice, and Fred disapproved of it. It is a curious thing how, in this age that throbs with mercenary passion, and brawls, and cheats, and grows mad with lust of gold, even coarse-bred men grapple to their hearts the most fantastic of affections. Here was a rude river-man, shrewd and keen and not over-scrupulous, a blusterer to his equals, and a tyrant to those over whom he was entitled to exercise a petty authority, who loved the combination of iron and wood called the *Ruby* steamer, as finer-fibred men love their ideal woman, or the inspiring spirits of their art. He loved every plank in her—every bolt and nut. When chaffed about marrying, it was his standing retort that while he had the *Ruby* he didn't care (a quite superfluous word) for any petticoat alive.

* * * *

Of course, other men interested in their vocation, whose energies are concentrated in the routine of life, have said the same thing, and yet succumbed to a rounded cheek and the flash of a long-lashed eye; and while Fred Walmsley was listened to with the respect commanded by his big brawny shoulders and iron fist, he was never believed. It was a popular jest—never, though, indulged in while he was present—that when the "neat-footed gal came along the little *Ruby* 'ud ha' to take second place an' sing small." The amours of the river-men might sometimes be coarse, but while they lasted Cupid had, as a rule, no more devoted or willing subjects. Not one in ten of the boat-hands could boast truly of being unsusceptible to his shafts, and they did not conclude that Fred-o'-the-*Ruby* was constituted with any peculiar impregnability.

"Go 'long! There ain't a chap on the rivers as I couldn't get over if I wanted ter!" retorted Miss Jenny Forbes, daughter of a wood-pile keeper on the Goulburn, to the indirect challenge jocularly issued to her by "a snagger" to try her hand at subjugating Walmsley. "But you needn't think as I'm agoin' to fling the handkerchief to any river chap. A reel squatter is my dart!"

Half in jest, half in earnest she retorted so. And the men who listened to her, and glanced admiringly at her, though they resented her words partly, yet thought most of the squatters they knew would surely think themselves lucky if they could win a girl like Jenny.

They were river-men, all of them—all of them, too, snaggers—hands of the *Melbourne*, the famous old snagging boat which did some of the best work ever done in the Riverine. The time was Sunday afternoon. The *Melbourne* was tied to the bank, and the men, in their white shirts and Sunday Geelong tweeds, lay on the green slopes, luxuriating in the balminess of the time, in their thirty-six hours' freedom from work, and in the smiles of beauty.

* * * *

A beauty Jenny Forbes most certainly was. Straight as a sapling, she held herself with a springy erectness that added height to her perfectly-moulded figure. Dressed now only in a snowy muslin, she would have graced regal velvet, for as she moved, wholesomely ignorant of all artificial laws of deportment, she gave to the unrefined spectators a sensation of unreasoned pleasure which a master of the arts and fripperies of the great world would have found it impossible to rebuke. The wonder was, however, not her figure and her airiness of carriage, though indeed both were wonderful enough to people who knew that her parents were poor, wizened, labour-stunted creatures, but her complexion and her voice. That mysterious faculty of nature which prompts her to return upon herself after a lapse of generations, and to revive, in the present, the physical type she had apparently displaced a century ago, had been manifested in this girl. The full, voluptuously-contoured features, the fruity bloom which tinged the cheeks, and contrasted with the pallor of the forehead and chin and neck, should have belonged to one of those fine ladies who, first flinging away their lives at passion's shrine, sat thereafter for saintly profiles to some deathless painter of altar-pieces.

And then her voice! It wanted but that superb touch of education which is communicated by a broken heart to make it an organ of surpassing quality. It had a range in ordinary speech that was as musical as any accomplished singer's, while in laughter it left on the ear echoes so enamoured of their own sweetness that they refused to die. Give it, give her, but soul and refined intelligence, and tune it and her to the key of a gracious life, and she would be a woman of destiny to more than one strong man. As it was, she was but a wood-cutter's daughter; a girl of undeveloped instincts and of faculties which, naturally rude, were coarsening quickly in the soulless surroundings of the bush.

The "chaff" of the snaggers she answered in her glorious voice with zest and vigour; for other homage she could not imagine than the audacious jesting which was the only form of compliment her admirers preferred; and which she relished. Illiterate, barely able to read, and even less capacity in writing, the girl's fancy was at once stimulated and satiated with such incense of gallantry as the crews of the boats and the timber-getters for Echuca saw-mills lavished upon her. Men of that rough mould are never unimpressed by the delicacy of a woman's nature, and make some response to the thousand little intangiblenesses of accent, and look, and gesture with which the woman who is sheltered by her womanliness chastens the angularities of masculine tempers.

When, however, the woman is herself coarse the rough-natured fellows become rougher. Bodily beauty alone does not refine the woman, and she guides him in his defects as well as in his better qualities. And so, instead of Jenny's voice charming away the asperities of these uncultivated spirits with its melody like a throstle's song, they rejoiced the more gladly and applauded her the louder that her golden notes dealt out to them the badinage of their time. And the topics that were discussed! The men did not exchange double *entendres*, for there was no need. Neither she nor they felt under any obligation to beat about the bush. Their speech was Elizabethan in its coarse frankness.

So this smiling Sunday afternoon on which Nature rested and permitted the river toilers to rest also, Jenny sat among ten or twelve snaggers, and jested at them and with them, and accepted their patent homage of jests with appropriate eagerness. The *Ruby* had left the Goulburn with timber for Barbour's mill in one of Barbour's barges, and had left her own barge to be loaded up so that on her return she should lose no time in being dispatched with a second load. And Walmsley's name being mentioned incidentally in the girl's presence had led to her asking, "Why the dickens that Fred didn't get spliced?"

"Why, he's waitin' till yer 'll say yer 'll 'ave 'im, Miss Forbes!" had grinned a rouseabout.

"Oh, Fred," broke in a fireman before the girl could speak, "ses as there ain't a gal alive who'd get him ter give her first place in his 'fecshions so long as the *Ruby* don't get snagged an' ruins him!"

Then the girl had answered the implied challenge by the remark we have reported. "Go 'long! There ain't a chap along the rivers as I couldn't get over if I wanted ter!" And as though these words were not depreciative enough of their class, she added poison to the gall by insinuating her ambition to become a squatter's "laädy." A girl who belonged "o' rights" to the rivers to think of going over to the hated squatterdom! Not to be thought of—even though the squatters would jump down one another's throats to get so fine a piece of womankind.

They attacked her then with a humorous earnestness. "Marry a squatter—she! Throw away the cleanest-cut limbs an' nattiest waist, an' most kissable lips on all the rivers—aye, in all Victoria!—on rascally, dummyin' squatters as was a-stealin' o' the lands? Get out, Jenny!" And after a while they changed the mode of their satire. "A squatter! No bloomin' squatter wants a wood-piler! For yer are a wood-piler, Jenny, an' no mistake! Didn't ol' Capt'n Hill"—Hill, skipper of the snagging boat *Melbourne*, that was—"see yer a-cuttin' down a red-gum tree one day, when th' ol' man was laid up with r'eumatics? An' which o' th' young blokes o' squatters would you be after goin' for, Jenny? Mick of Moira or young Tom of Cannoon; or there's Ewey Mac of up-river? No, no, Miss Forbes, yer stick to th' rivers. You marry Fred Walmsley if he arsks yer—the young Walmsleys 'll come in handy to train up as mates and steermen and to save screws! Nothin' like a lot o' your own youngsters round you, Jenny, to save screws!"

It was their notion of humour to link the girl's fortunes with Fred's, because Fred was distinctly unmarriageable, they thought, and it was by no means unlikely that if any one snapped up Jenny he would be actually a squatter, or at the least a young boss cockie. And the hours slipped away in all their marvellous wealth of colour and scent, till the shadows of trees high up on the western bank dipped into the stream or fell athwart the old *Melbourne*. The girl went homewards then to the miserable hut, standing beyond flood-point on the rise. She refused escort. "Yer afraid o' makin' Fred jealous, or the bloomin' squatter—that's why!" was the parting shot of the snaggers, and, not displeased, she bade them for answer—"Go 'long an' shoot themselves!" The repartee was not without aimlessness, but it provoked laughter, and much keener wit does not always do that.

* * * *

The girl, all untutored as she was, was yet sufficient of the woman to perversely dwell in her spasmodic thinkings upon the possibility of Fred Walmsley giving her a share in his name and in his boat. She really had made up her mind to marry a squatter; but then, till the squatter came along, why not amuse herself with Walmsley? She knew she was "a strikin' piece o' goods"—she had something about her that was pleasing to the men, for on the last snag-boat pay-day had the hands not cleared out Walmsley's stock of jewellery for her? Had not Walmsley himself sold her a length of dress-stuff at less than Echuca prices? Wasn't that an indirect compliment to her charms? Didn't she know that it was her looks that kept the wood-pile going, and not any special need to which the boats were now subjected of obtaining the fuel supplies at her father's pile? And so the thoughts flitted over the surface of her consciousness as the rays of star-shine wavered on the ripples of the river, till she came to a decision that might hold and might not, just as her feelings swayed her when once Walmsley was in her neighbourhood again.

That happened a week later. He came to pick up his own log-laden barge to run it down to Barbour's mill, and called at the pile to pay his fuel account.

"So many cords, so much, Jenny, an' you owe me for the dress."

"Right, Fred. But you kin let the wood stand. Dad ain't short just now for a wonder."

"No—I'll square up now, for I'm not a-comin' this way till the rivers are down again. The snow-water's coming down the Murray, an' as soon's it's safe to get afloat for 'Bidgee up-stream, I'm off. There's heaps of back-season wool waitin' to be collared on wayside stations."

"Oh!" The girl, wondering at herself for the feeling, could not help being somewhat pained at the news.

The skipper did not notice it.

"So here's the damage, Jenny—unless you want something more?" Walmsley simply saw in a pretty girl somebody to trade with.

"No!" Impulsively, knowing nothing of what she was doing, she challenged his admiration with the coquettish arts of which she was ignorant. "I want nothing except—"

"What?" questioned Fred, intent on business.

"You!" With something of coyness, something of hoydenish dash, she muttered the syllable. Blaming herself the next instant, she yet would not have recalled it. All defiant, she had yet become entangled in the delicious meshes of an entangled affection. Thinking much of Fred, she had unconsciously learnt to love him.

Fred did not understand her immediately. Then he disbelieved her. A jolly good joke she was having! But no petticoats for him; so—

"Lord, Jenny! what's made you sweet upon splicin' just now?" He laughed gaily before he resumed. "An' you're pokin' borak at me!"

"I ain't! Look here, Fred—I'm tired o' this firewood bizness. Won't you have me for your gal—an'—an' take me 'way? Oh, I'll make yer a d——d good wife, Fred, I will— an' you'll see how smart I kin be at sellin' thin's!"

She was convincing herself as she proceeded to the point

of emphasizing her newly-born desire for a lover by the oath which was not infrequently on her lips. As for the *Ruby* skipper, he stood for a minute amused and amazed. Then, turning away, he gave her good-bye.

"No wimmen for me, Miss Forbes, even if yer weren't a sort o' jokin' with me. I don't wish for no other kind of wife than my little *Ruby*. So long!"

The girl quivered with the shame of her repulse. She knew now her fate; she really did love this river-man who cared not a rap for anything beneath the sky save his boat; and he—well, he had laughed at her, and would tell the chaps at the public-house bars how Jenny "had given herself away." Hitherto, with much reason to feel ashamed at times, she had never known the sensation, but now she knew what it was to be pricked with the myriad needle-points of a late-born modesty. Till now she had been but a beautiful lissom animal. Henceforth she was a woman, from whose eyes looked, for the first time in her score of years of life, a soul. She had learned to suffer, and to the feminine nature which is deriving that lesson from the Nessus robe of circumstance, all things are possible.

* * * *

Even revenge. True, 'tis an old story how a woman scorned becomes at heart a hell-fury, but all modern art is but the presentiment of the old, old episodes of life in newer settings. And yet this story differs from its prototypes, which speak of the woman's revenge direct upon the man. Not so was the man hurt herein.

The rivers came down suddenly, bearing in their swollen currents the juices of the snowy ridges, and the oozings of lowland hillsides, and the lower streams took upon them-selves depth and breadth, and became alive with fish and fowl, and those creatures of prey, the humans. But only for a few weeks. It was a short rise—a brief foretaste of flood-time, when the great wheels would turn and churn the waters into foamy spray, and take the ore of the yellow water and mint it into precious gold. And the boats enjoyed but a spurt of work. Some were stuck up in the narrow ridges of the Murrumbidgee—two, with their several barges, on the reef near Pental Island—a fourth within hail of Sturt's Billabong, where some day Australia will build a pilgrims' shrine "on those shelving banks." But Walmsley's *Ruby* was fortunate enough to regain the port.

Fred, doubtful whether he should tie up his craft, or join in what, in that state of the river, was the risky work of exploring the State forests on either side of the Murray, was musingly regarding the "State of the Rivers" sheet, posted under the Post Office verandah, when a saw-mill manager hailed him.

"Can you run up to Goulburn at once, Fred, for us? We have a couple of barges ready loaded. They've dropped 'em down from Shepparton to near the junction."

"I was just thinkin' whether 'twas too risky to go up as far as Tocumwal."

"Take my word for it, it is! Better run up for us. You can only get a short job till it's certain whether there is more water to come down, or whether it's run out. What d'ye say?"

"Done!" said Fred Walmsley.

* * * *

Jenny had attributed to him an injustice. He had not told the story of her love-making at the township pubs, for he had, after his first amusement, let the thing slip from his mind in the concentration of his energies upon the day's task. Nor did he recollect the incident until he had brought the *Ruby* carefully to the spot where the mill's two barges were tied up, waiting haulage to Echuca. Then he thought of it, for Jenny stood on the rise, waiting the approach of the boat. She had heard the *Ruby*'s exhaust, and had recognized it.

In the time that had gone since the *Ruby's* departure and her return, the girl had changed. Her colour, once so steadfast, came and went with the passing tempers of her mind. To out-breaks of coarse speech directed towards her parents succeeded moods of pathetic self-loathing, which they understood as little as she did herself. The mystery of sorrow was pressing upon her in all its poignancy. Death—even the uneducated can comprehend his presence; physical disasters too can be understood by the common people; but the finer issues "in clear dream and solemn vision" are perceptible only to cultivated minds. They in whom fortune has not sown refinement cannot recognize but only suffer. Jenny Forbes was such.

She had been crying in dumb, inarticulate fashion for Walmsley to come back, and here he was! Had he come for her? The hope that plucks at straws, and the shadows of straws, was fledged in her heart—and died in the instant she saw him. She knew he had not thought of her.

"Mornin,' Jenny!" He hailed her from the bank.

"Good-mornin,' Mister Walmsley!" she, hugging the pain, forced herself to say. She would never call him "Fred" again till he asked her to marry him.

Unconscious of the wound he was inflicting, and quite unmindful till the response had passed her lips, that the form of his question was identical with that which had led to her curious outburst on the last occasion of their meeting, he called out—"Do you want anything?"

He meant, of course, stores—dress-stuffs, groceries, what-not. But the girl, whose humiliation was ever present to her mind, took the inquiry in the light of a reminder.

She flamed red—then her pulse stopped, it seemed to her, and the pain within her so tightly clenched her vocal organs, that instead of the exclamation rushing forth in the rich throatiness of her voice, it was uttered in a sharp cutting whisper:

"You devil!"

Fred remembered then all the details of the former episode. And he laughed at the recollection—with humorous tones in his harsh laugh.

The girl, holding a clenched fist to her side, ran up the slight hill, maddened. On the crest of the rise she paused and looked back. Through a cleft in the clearing an expiring sun-ray, widening like a blaze of fire, enveloped the pilot-house and the jeering boat-captain.

It must have been from that simulacrum of a conflagration that she drew the inspiration of her deadly thoughts.

* * * *

The *Ruby* was to return in the morning. And because no danger could be suspected in her snug resting-place by the Goulburn junction no watch was kept. Only the great lamps with their hundred facets sheened the placid stream. Walmsley saw they were trimmed for the night before he turned in at ten o'clock.

At midnight there was no sound but the lapping and the wash of the river. The girl who is moving forward makes no noise, you may be sure. She is in stockinged feet.

At sundown there had been stored against the wood-pile keeper's hut, in a lean-to, a great heap of dried wattle-bark. It was so much tinder. And the bulk of it, or at least sufficient for her purpose, this girl had moved to the boat to serve as tinder. Upon it she had heaped wool waste from the *Ruby's* own engine-room. Tinder, all of it! And, yet not content, she unscrewed the cork of a kerosene-tin, and the fluid trickled and covered the waste and the bark.

It had been dead calm. But, an instant before she struck the match, a gentle breeze arose to help her in her work. The decking was set ablaze without trouble.

She had calculated upon ten minutes' burning before the smoke and the crackling would rouse the men. The breeze must surely have been the breath of Erinnys. Within her allotted ten minutes it gave her the advantage of double the space.

The ill work sped as ill work always does. And when Fred, at last aroused by his men, dragged himself to the bank, half-dazed by the smoke, he knew the task of fighting the flames was hopeless. The little *Ruby* was doomed. And, as so frequently happened during the off-season, he was un-insured. He had let his policy lapse with the last wool-trip.

From the west of the rise the girl looked down upon her work and her rival. The boat was gone—that was evident! Neither seriously nor jocularly could Fred avow that the steamer would ever contest his affections with her again. Stark still, save for the trembling that shook her, she gazed, and hated herself for her triumph. Yet she would not have undone the work if she could. Let the consequence of a woman's hate stab herself to death daily, yet, under like conditions, she would so act again.

# SECRET SOCIETY OF THE RING

## THE CONVENING OF THE RING

### I.

CAPTAIN MACONOCHIE, who, with Major Anderson, supplied the non-demoniac element in the reigns of Norfolk Island Commandants, in pursuance of his theory that the convict should be encouraged to hope not alone for an alleviation of his physical condition, but also for "a new moral nature," hit upon an expedient for developing, even in hardened souls, those softening and refining tendencies which flow from a heart-felt solicitude for the welfare of others. By detaching transports into groups, or "sub-gangs," of three or five members, and holding each man of the three or five responsible for the good behaviour of his comrades, an irresistible appeal was at once made to the curiously confused notions that swayed the average convict mind. An argument which had regard only to their own comfort or freedom from punishment would, in the case of nine out of ten "old hands"—the doubly-convicted convicts transported from the mainland or Van Diemen's Land—be welcomed by an oath or a ribald jest. When callousness in infamy was deemed to be an honour—when irons were thought the insignia of chivalry—and "connoisseurs in murder" felt it a privilege to take the hand of a "locked-boot" victim—it was an insult to suggest an immunity from penalties as a reason for right action. Take another course, however, and appeal to the sense of fraternity, which seldom died out even in the "best" men, and that caution in conduct and that eternal obedience to the regulations which a "good" man would never think of exerting in his own interests, would be at once exercised for the benefit of his group-mates. Most of Maconochie's attempts at penal reform sprang from his heart, and were seldom based on a hard, logical apprehension of facts as they were. But, in respect to his grouping system, his heart and his head acted together. His judgment and his experience of the "old hands" taught him that it was literally and absolutely a point of honour with them never to procure punishment for another transport who manifested "spunk." And his heart showed him how to take advantage of this characteristic. What "old hands" would not do for themselves they should do for others. They should respect regulations and official practices, because violation of them would cause the infliction of punishment upon their colleagues of the group.

Between the principal settlement (which was supposed to change its name according to the sex of the reigning sovereign, and, therefore, should have been called Queenstown in the present reign, but which, notwithstanding, was more often spoken of as Kings-town than Queenstown) and the outlying barracks at Longridge, the Commandant laid out, in March and April, 184—, a number of farms of six to ten acres each. On each farm a hut or cottage was erected, and a company of from three to five men was assigned to each hut and farm. For the first year, no rental was demanded by the Commandant. For succeeding years each group of tenants had to contribute a rental of twelve bushels of maize for each cleared acre, this quota being estimated to equal one-third of the average crop per acre raised by labour under direct taxation. And every group was constituted a "mutual responsibility" sub-gang. That is to say, for the misdeeds of any one member of a group, the other members would suffer.

The group tenanting the hut on Section 5B was constituted by some "old hands" whose records were of the very "best."[1] Tested by the official standards of the elder System, they would have been welcomed by Lucifer with a "Hail, fellows, well met!" And thereupon the soft-hearted Commandant resolved they should have a chance to reform. Very much to the amusement of the Commissariat and other officials did he announce this determination.

The sub-gangers were five in number. Osborne, of whom we dare say no more than that it was a daily wonder to his comrades how he escaped hanging; Peake, a small-skulled, thirty-year-old lump of a physical deformity that rivalled his moral nature; a gentlemanly ex-forger who was popularly known as "Barrington" from the circumstance that he knew off by heart the account of that immortal scoundrel's career; a "Swinger"[2]—Felix—less sullen than brutish in feature, and of gigantic physical strength; and Reynell, a former soldier of the "Fighting Half-Hundred,"[3] who had been transported to Norfolk Island by a V.D.L. military court for desertion to Maori-land in a whaler.

A tall, strapping fellow, who carried himself with military erectness, was Reynell, and it was his boast that his parchment record was as long as himself. Of course, the

---

1   At Norfolk Island it was the awful custom among the more hardened convicts to invert the meaning of "good" and "bad." A "good man" was a notorious criminal; a "bad" one was a man who sought to act honestly and purely.

2   Transported for rick-burning—a follower of "Swing," the suppositious criminal who, at the period of the agricultural depression of the Early Thirties, was accused by the peasants of setting farmers' ricks and barns on fire.

3   50th (West Kent) Infantry Regiment, renowned for their conduct and achievements in the Napoleonic Wars. (ed.)

assertion was a slight exaggeration, but Reynell was given to little whimsicalities. A devil when roused, he was, as a rule, a merry soul, who was pleasantly cynical. He entered into crime with the same zest as into a battle-square. "It was but putting the bayonet into the law instead of the enemy," he said to Mr. Pery, Superintendent of Agriculture, one day when Pery asked him why he would persist in setting the authorities at defiance. "I have to let the devil out of me somehow, sir, and as her gracious Majesty—God bless her!—won't employ me against her enemies, I have to make enemies of my own. And the law's a grand enemy to fight, sir! It'll take such a lot of beating!"

Against a criminal of this temper the Law had used everything in its dread armoury, except "the spread-eagle," the gallows, and—a kind word and good faith. These last two instruments of unusual punishment Captain Maconochie now determined to supply. He appointed Reynell leader of 5 B sub-gang at a Sunday morning "after chapel" muster at the Iron Room.

"Henry Reynell, per *Coquette*, colonial transport," called the mustering overseer.

"Reynell, how do you come to be included among 'old hands' when you're a 'colonial'?" questioned the Commandant, with his pleasant resonance of voice, as soon as the man had replied with his "Here!"

"The honourable Court gave me fourteen years, y'r Honour, and as I didn't think it enough I got 'em to make it life." There was a ripple of laughter in the ranks.

"How?" asked the Captain, who took no notice of the demonstration.

"I struck the corporal of the Court guard—and so the honourable Court gave me what I wanted."

"Not the same Court? It could not act at once and without being formally convened by the Colonel-Commanding?"

"As to that, sir, I can't say. All I know is that same Court convicted me—and I came here with a double sentence.

Therefore, Major Ryan thought me entitled, sir, to all the emoluments, rights, and privileges of an old hand. I've been in irons all the time I've been here."

"Will you take a word of advice from me, Reynell?" said the Commandant.

"Will—I—what, y'r Honour?" asked Reynell, with a choking breath in his voice that might have been amusement, or might have been sheer amazement at the autocrat of a penal settlement assuming so extraordinary a tone.

"Take my advice, my good fellow, just to drop that sneering manner of speech." There was a genuine kindness in the words. Reynell drew himself up to his full height and clenched his fist. Those who stood by thought he was about to transform recklessness of tongue into madness of action. The line between a murderer and a hero is often but a hair's-breadth, and this man, who might easily become a hero, might as easily pass the line.

However, other answer than this he did not make. He flung out his closed hand and said—"So easy to preach, y'r Honour! With the iron in the soul, and the cat on the back, and the bayonet-point in the body, what wonder the sneer's on the lip? So easy for you gentlemen to deal with heartless numbers. You say, Numbers 37189—that's me—and 39204—that's Felix—don't feel. God above—don't we! And what weapon ha' we to fight the System with if you won't allow us to use our tongues? Even at our peril we must use 'em!"

He stopped and gathered strength for a last phrase which quivered with the under-thrill of his bitterness. "It's fighting that's our last hope of keeping something of manhood to ourselves, sir! Fight!—I'd die if I did not fight—die or go mad!"

Outbursts of this sort were common enough among the more intelligent convicts, but Maconochie never ceased to be impressed by them. The receptive sympathy of the man—which proved his ruin as an administrator—was always stirred when the note of strength and sincerity ran through the transport's utterances. He listened now to Reynell with a patience that to his under-strappers and to the felons at muster seemed at once wonderful and childish.

With mutual nods and winks (in hearty enjoyment of the joke) the gentlemen of the Commissariat who accompanied him listened to his ludicrously feeble reception of Convict Reynell's attack on the System's amenities.

"Reynell," he said, stepping a pace nearer to the ranks as he spoke, "I am going to trust you—I will give you a farm— you and any four others you may choose to pick out of the old hands!"

"You—are—not jollying—me, your Honour?"

"No—you will find by and by that I never 'jolly!'"

"Then, by G—, sir, I'll be true man to you!"

From the rank of men from which Reynell had been called out came in two or three distinct voices a shout of—

"The Ring'll see 'bout that! The Oath! The Oath!"


## II.


Reynell, instantly flushed with the strenuous hope that had been created by Maconochie's words, paled as instantly. Then—

"I'll take it back, y'r Honour. I'll remain as I am—a 'good' man!"

"That's right, that's right, my man!" rejoined the Commandant, genially. Again, a sibilant chorus from the ranks. The transports were tickled agreeably at what they thought his misapprehension. They had understood Reynell. Reynell, they knew, was simply adopting the vocabulary of the damned, in which "darkness was light and light darkness." But the laughter stopped instantly as Maconochie raised his hand—and did the fatallest thing of his commandancy.

"Men!" he exclaimed, "no more of that! And now listen!"

A rubbing and clinking of irons and a shuffling of feet rose on the calm air as the men settled themselves into position. They had heard they had got a "bad" preaching Commandant—and now Fate was about to confirm the report by cursing them with a second sermon on the one day.

"Men, listen! A threat has been used about the Ring. Now, I tell you—Ring members and non-members of the Ring—that I am resolved to crush that society out of existence."

From among the massed men a confused clamour arose. "So other Com'dants have said—and they failed!" "Better not try!" "Ye'll ha' to croak first!" A chorus of defiance in which rumbled an accent of triumph. The System for three generations of Islanders had been trying to kill the Ring, and the Ring was still immutable and impregnable. The men who were of the Ring feared its despotism, but gloried in its traditions and its power. The men whose names were not scored in its mysteriously-kept roll, respected it and admired it, for was it not a rock that withstood the shocks of the Authorities?—an empire supreme over an empire otherwise omnipotent?

Now, Maconochie had meant to say that the only uprooting force he intended to apply to the Ring was that of kindness and justice. His wish was to render the Secret Society innocuous by depriving it of any occasion for the exercise of its undoubtedly enormous capacity for desperate action. But he was given no chance of explaining himself. Though they thought that the loss of their Sunday dinner— deeply cherished treat!—was involved in the uproar, the one hundred and fifty men, moved by a common impulse of passion, which, like a tornado-wave, swept all before it, continued and increased their clamour. They shouted, whistled, clanked their irons. Every sound was an inflection of evil. To the officials inured by years of familiarity with the Island life to such demonstrations, there was nothing particularly alarming—certainly nothing distressing in the storm. To the Commandant, however, sensitive in feeling, exalted in imagination, and subject to a curious persistence of reasoning which convinced him every transport was less an offender against society than a victim of society's errors and stupidities, the noise was a literal shock.

He held his hand up to command silence. A strong hiss from the centre greeted the gesture.

He folded his arms, as though to wait patiently for the cessation of the tumult. The challenge was responded to by shrieks of laughter.

He lifted his cap and passed his handkerchief across his forehead. Fifty hands derisively copied the action. It was an admission that he was beaten, and they delighted in it as their nostrils would have done in the scent of roast meat.

He turned his back upon the ironed men, and motioned to a gaol-warder. Assistant-Deputy-Commissary-General Shanks thought he purposed to order up the main-guard, and for the first time was prepared to confess to himself that the Commandant was something more than a dreamer. And—Mr. Shanks was to be disappointed.

Instead of bringing up at the "double" a file of twelve men—instead of issuing in bloody sequence, incisive commands: "Ready! Present! Fire!" Captain Maconochie had sent to his own stores for—tobacco! The imbecility of that act!s—how it started Mr. Shanks! How it spoilt his Sunday's dinner and compelled him to sacrifice his afternoon nap so that he might write to Governor Gipps and Mr. E. Deas-Thomson!⁴

"Tobacco for rebels! The establishment is going to the devil!" he groaned later to Mrs. Shanks. "Tobacco!—when they should have had lead. If he had made requisition upon me, and not have drawn from his own store, I'd have refused there and then!" For Mr. Shanks' heart was sore within him.

---

4   E Deas-Thomson-colonial secretary of New South Wales from
    1837 and adviser to Governor Gipps. (ed.)

As for the gentry of the Iron Room, their turbulence held till the box of tobacco was placed at the Commandant's feet. And then it faded, with a final hiss and splatter as a breaking wave dies against the shingle. They were stupefied at this unique form of punishment.

"'E's a-goin' to 'eap coals o' fire on our 'eads!" exclaimed some one, but the remark passed unheeded. The mass were too surprised even for ribald comments.

### III.

"Reynell!" Maconochie called.

Reynell looked round before answering. Did the Ring raise objection? If it did, there was no visible or audible sign of its refusal. And he stepped forward; and, to the Commandant's pleasure, saluted.

"Reynell, call out four men to assist you!"

"What for, sir?"

"To distribute that tobacco—half a fig to a man."

Reynell stared at the Captain—then gazed back at the massed men. For guidance—for a hint as to whether he dare take the bride on their behalf? Most likely so. And so near is weak kindness to refined cruelty, there was not one man there in those ranks of ironed, yellow, brown-and-grey garbed felons with the symbols of shame on their bodies and the glare of the human beast in their eyes, but hated Maconochie in that moment of ordeal. Not a man there but would have risked severe penalties to obtain a fraction of a fig; scarcely a score of the one hundred and fifty but what had already gone through the mire of humiliation for a "bit." Therefore their hearts beat with a venomous strength— because he tempted them sorely. For why did they not answer to Reynell's unspoken inquiry?

Those who were not of the Ring dare not speak. In collective action the Ring led the "private" convicts.

And those who were of the Society grew weak with the

temptation. But then—to accept it was to acknowledge Maconochie's supremacy, and to confess a defeat.

For half a minute the two parties stood silent. The surf, half a mile away, drove its monotone over the still air. From the wooded sides of Mount Pitt, on the other hand, travelled, not unmelodiously, the screech of parrots. A wedge-tailed eagle poised majestically over the square, and hoarsely flung a taunt to the imprisoned creatures. Save for these sounds, the parade was as silent as is the lull before the revolt of thunder against its confines.

Then—first one sharp "No!"—next, two or three were joined in the repetition—and finally, in impetuous volume, the fierce negatives rolled from the ranks. Never did monk of the desert make so great a renunciation! In that volleyed monosyllable those outcasts of civilization refused a pleasure for which, under other circumstances, they would have gleefully bartered their souls.

"No!" A brazen, defiant "No!" which epitomized the curses of Tophet.

Reynell marched back to his place; and Maconochie knew, as the storm of curses and cheers burst out again, that the Ring was triumphant.

## IV.

Unless—

Commissariat-Officer Shanks suggested, with a semi-sneer, the application of old methods. "Try, Captain Maconochie, a platoon! There's pretty considerable of a quietening influence in a volley, sir! That is mutiny, and if you don't get the better of them now, they'll have every iron off their ankles in an hour, and then you'll have to shoot the lot, unless you want us all killed."

"No!" replied the Commandant. "Ball-cartridge is the last thing I propose to use on society's wrecks. Mr. Gaoler—this thing has gone far enough. Finish the muster and give 'em their dinners!"

"What, sir! Their dinners!" Really, the gaoler was to be excused for his patent astonishment.

"Ay,—the poor fellows shan't suffer for my blunder in tactics. The mistake was mine—I've taken 'em the wrong way to-day."

And with this remark, so subversive of all the conventions and principles of the System—for whenever before did a penal commandant admit he was in error?—Captain Maconochie touched his cap, in graceful acknowledgement of the salute of his subordinates, and left the muster-yard.

* * * *

The whole of the Iron Room transports enjoyed their dinners the more for the sauce of triumph. For dessert they were gratified by another delicious morsel.

The Commandant sent an order to the gaoler to despatch by 6.30 a.m. on Monday, Henry Reynell, per *Coquette* (Colonial), and "four other men that the said prisoner should nominate," to Farm 5B, therein to be installed as "sub-gang in charge." The proceeding was, it is needless to say, altogether exceptional. But then the Island owned an altogether exceptional commander, and it had proved a day of exceptional occurrences. And it was, doubtless, in accordance with the spirit of the joke that the gaoler, as he communicated the decision to Reynell, mocked him by doffing his cabbage-tree, and addressed him with a scoffing irony.

"Would it please Mr. Reynell to nominate the gentlemen who were to accompany him?"

Reynell took the jest admirably. He craved five minutes to make his selection, and within that time had informed the officer that Osborne, Peake, Barrington, and "Swinger" Felix would form his comradeship. For the committee of the Ring had raised no objection. "'Twarn't going out to the farmsteads, Reynell," said a high ruler of the league—a

Three—"that we complain of, but your promise to be a true man! No chap in the fellowship shall go 'bad' without permission. It's breaking oath!"

And consent being thus obtained—we translate the "flash" language habitually employed in Ring business—the choice was, as we have said, made, and 5B group constituted.

On Monday, when the dormitories turned out at 5.30, the first thing done by the new sub-gang was to present themselves at the "blacksmith's shop" and have the rivets driven from the bazils.

Felix was last at the low anvil. As the bazil of his left leg fell to the ground he expanded the massive brawniness of his chest with long draughts of tonic morning air; and then clutched Reynell with a wrestler's grasp.

"Why, lad, I be tha' man for ever an' a day. I never 'ud ha' got rid o' them damned clinks but for thee until the day I wed the worms. Felix is tha' man for ever an' a day!"

## V.

And now let us gather up the links of the story.

Monday was formal court-day, and, therefore, none of the group saw the Commandant till the evening. Muster had passed over—the mutual responsibility farms were mustered only by their leader, he answering for his group—and the men were busy preparing their "tea," and rejoicing in the novel sensation of what was virtual freedom, when the Captain walked up to the hut.

They ceased their preparations and saluted. The spontaneity of the movement was plain, and it thrilled the "old man's" heart to notice it. Something, he thought, of that voluntary respect for just authority, which is an accompaniment of manhood, had been generated in the men by that one day's liberty, and surely his experiment was about to be justified? He smiled gaily as he returned the salute.

"Now, men," he said, "don't mind me! Get on with your tea—I am sure you must need it after all this day in the fields!"

In forty years of the System never had Osborne heard the like. He bent his eyes to the block of stone which did duty as a temporary table, and fumbled with his tin maize-meal dish. The others, with the exception of Peake, were also affected; Reynell to the point of turning his head away so that neither the Captain nor his group-mates should discern the tear that scalded his cheek.

"Men!" continued the Commandant, ever deeper touched by evidences of gratitude than by testimonies of insult, "I wish you would trust me! I want to be a friend to you—to every man of the 1600 souls in prison here! Come, sirs, forget I'm the Commandant—the 'old man.' Think of me, for the time being at all events, as a man—one who deeply sympathizes with your sufferings, and who will only be too glad to alleviate them in every way he can without violating his duty to those who sent him here! Come, what do you say?"

Peake was the first to speak. "Reynell, y'r Honour, is our leader!" A dogged resistance to any softening influence was easily to be understood from his manner.

"Then, Reynell, speak for yourself at least—for the others if you can."

The ex-soldier drew his under-lip in, and bit it till blood came, in the severity of the struggle between the Past and the Future that might be. Then he gulped rather than uttered his answer.

"I take back—the insult—of—yesterday, sir. I'll be true man to you—so help me God! And the—Ring may do its worst."

Maconochie knew that, come what might—disdain from Privy Councillors and Secretaries of State, cold water from Governors, and sneers and insubordination from smaller officials—yet still he had plucked one soul from the pit.

After a few more words of friendly tenor he returned to Government House.

Upon his going, Peake dropped his thin mask of hypocrisy and looked what he was—the child of the devil his father, and the System his mother. Other parentage had he known none. When, as a hunchbacked boy of eight, he first understood a little of the meaning of life, the System was already nourishing him at her breasts. And because of this must we excuse him somewhat.

Peake, when the Captain's steps could not be longer heard, pulled off his waist-strap.

"Hold!" He threw out an end to "Penman Barrington." "Barrington" paled—but grasped the leather.

"Reynell, you sneakin' cull—come here!"

And Reynell, too, obeyed the strange command. He took the other end. The strap was pulled taut. Then Osborne and Felix each laid hold upon it in the centre, standing on either side of it. The four thus formed a cross. Sometimes in the cross of the Ring the hands touched and clasped; but never in the cross of denunciation—as this was.

Three—five—seven times Peake walked round the group, and as he moved he recited the Convict Oath.

At last, he stopped suddenly—at the end of the third repetition.

"Osborne, you're a 'Sevener'?"

Osborne, hoarse with suppressed fear, muttered "Yes."

"And you're a Sevener, accused?" Reynell was thus addressed. He nodded assent.

"What are you, Bill?"

"A Niner!" answered Felix.

"Barrington?"

"A Fiver!"

"And I'm a Three. We're all denominations. All denominations necessary to convene when it's a Sevener as is to go up before—Do any object?"

Silence. Only Reynell shuddered.

"Then, the Niner shall bid the Niners, and the Sevener

the Seveners, and the Fiver the Fivers, and the Three the Threes to Ring lodge on Sabbath next if the One ratifies, and the business shall be to try Sevener Henry Reynell, for that he played our noble Society false, and promised to be true man to an Establishment officer, and defies the Society! So the Devil help you all!"

And some trembling lips muttered a low "So the Devil help us!"

## THE SESSION OF DENUNCIATION

### I.

The Ring had been convened. A "session of denunciation" had been called in the manner provided by the traditional statutes of the Society, and Convict Henry Reynell, "Colonial" transport per *Coquette*, had been duly apprised that on the Sunday following, at three in the afternoon, he was to be charged with having violated the "laws." He, an initiate, had defied the Ring; he had told Captain Maconochie that "he would prove a true man to him"; and this after the Ring had ordered that in season and out of season the new Commandant was to be thwarted—not so much disobeyed as thwarted.

When, within a month of Maconochie's arrival, it had become plain what sort of a man he was, the "One," on requisition from the "Three," had convened a "Council of Order," at which it was enacted that the new Commandant was an "enemy."

The business of a "Council of Order" was to enact "laws" and adopt "regulations." It was the least potential[5] of the three descriptions of Ring gatherings.

---

5   "Potential" is used in an unusual way here to mean "powerful" (ed.)

The second was that known as the "Session of Denunci-ation." It was convened only when a formal charge was to be laid against some member ("initiate" or "uninitiate") of the Society, or when some person not of the Society was to be denounced for his treatment of a member.

The third was the "Conclave of Doom." At this meeting the fiat went forth for punishment, the executioner was appointed, and—if the doom was a capital one and the victim a member of the Society—the vacancy would be filled up.

The "Council of Order" could be attended by any member of the Ring—whether he belonged to the initiated twenty-five, or to the uninitiated, "the novices," whose number was practically unlimited. It was invariably held during a meal-hour, for then only could a large muster be depended upon.

The "Session of Denunciation" was attended by the "circles" only, or as many of them as could be present. It was usually held on the nights of Sundays or holy-days, in the Iron Room. The "circles" were, as a rule, in irons. "Clinks" and "Trumpeters" were rather regarded as Ring insignia. Occasionally it was held in the day-time; Reynell's was to be a day-session.

As for the "Conclave of Doom," it was constituted only by the "One" and the "Three." If the "One" was in gaol, or in such other position that his attendance was impossible, then a majority of the members comprising the circles of "Three" and "Five" could proceed with the business. The convening of this culminating assemblage, however, rested absolutely with the "One." The "Three" could not constitute the Doom-session without his consent; and in this circumstance consisted the "One's" power of veto. The twenty-four men constituting the "circles" might pass a unanimous vote of "Death!" or other penalty, and by his simple refusal to convene a Doom-session within the period indicated by the law and custom of the Society—which period, in Maconochie's time, was three months—the presumed victim would go free.

At the Doom-session, the proceedings were, of course, controlled by the "One"—the Centre.

At the other sessions, the president was one of "Three" circle, who acted as leader. The "One" might be present, or he might not, at a "Council of Order," or a "Denunciation"; but, if present, he would not take charge of the assemblage. Such a step would have been tantamount to revealing his identity to the "Ringers" generally, and would have been a violation of the fundamental law of the Society, which ordered that none but the members of the "Three" should know who was the "One." To have torn away the veil of secrecy which shrouded his personality would have deprived him of his power. The Unknown is always terrible.[6]

From the circle of "Nine" to the circle of "Seven"; from the circle of "Seven" to the "Five"; from the "Five" to the "Three"; from the "Three"; to the "One": so ran the grooves of communication.

What, pertaining to the business or the safety of the Ring, a member of "Nine" circle heard, it was demanded from him, by his sworn duty to the Society, that he should communicate to his colleagues of his "circle." And the circle, or a majority, should decide whether the facts or the suspicions should be passed on to "Seven" circle.

Reaching the circle of "Seven," the intelligence, if the circle by majority so decided, would pass to the "Five." In like manner, the "Fivers" would transmit it to the "Three"; and so the "Centre"—the "One"—would hear of it only after long process of filtration and examination.

---

6   The theory of the writer as to the personality of the "One" will be disclosed in the story which follows, "The Conclave of Doom." The question of "One's" identity baffled Marcus Clarke, and the writer might, therefore, have been excused for attempting an answer; but he will venture to propose a solution.

At any stage of the routine a "circle" might send back a "report" for further evidence and information; or, by refusing to pass it on, veto and quash it. The complaint could not be again made by the lower circle till after the lapse of so many weeks.

Should a matter be first set in motion by an intermediate circle, that circle would communicate the essence of the business to the lower rank, but the latter had no voice in referring it to the final judgment of the "Centre." All vetoes were similarly communicated, so that the effect was this: Every initiate member knew the nature of all business which by ultimate transmission to "One" became the concern of the Ring; but every member had not a voice in its determination. No initiate could aid in the settlement of a matter originating in a higher circle than his own.

The exceptions to this general law were two. For the denunciation of an initiate member, the consent of the circle lower than his own was necessary, as well as that of his own and the higher ranks. Such cases were considered urgent, and the vote of one member of the lower circle or circles was regarded as sufficing for the whole of that denomination. And a "Three," invested with scarcely less awfulness than the "One," could act independently of his co-"Threes" by "One's" authority. It was this latter circumstance which originated the belief amongst many uninitiate Ringers that there was no "One." They did not necessarily believe that because the "Centre" was invisible, therefore he did not exist, but they doubted his existence when they saw that attributes they supposed to attach only to the dreaded "One" belonged also to the "Three."

Doubts, however, of this kind belonged to the uninitiates—or novices. The men of the lesser circles—the Nines and the Sevens and the Fives—knew of the "One," and the Three knew him.

They were sufficient, these degrees of knowledge, for they sustained during long years of maleficent working a dreadful society within an accursed community—an empire of evil within an empire of horror. The character of the System alone did not explain the System. You had to take into account also the Ring, which constantly battled with the System, and frequently defeated though it could not subjugate it.

* * * *

It could not subjugate the System, but then neither could the System destroy it.

The battle was a drawn one: the Ring ceased to exist as the animating soul of all evil things on the Island, only when the System acknowledged itself defeated by the "paralysing stroke of circumstance,"[7] and abandoned the spot which, designed by Heaven as an earthly paradise, the Englishman had made into a hell. Yet, one thinks, the result should have been different. There was the might of England behind the System—the majesty of her law, the sanctity of her State religion, the wisdom of her administrators. On the other side, there were—what? Twenty-four felons, and the "One"! A feeble handful of yellow-and-grey-garbed prisoners, most of them habitually in irons, scarcely one that had not shivered as the curling "cat" kissed him! Why, the System could have hanged them all any morning and not been put to the slightest inconvenience other than doubling the number of coffin-makers for a week!

Notwithstanding, for fifty years the Ring held its own. Its heads or "Centres"—the "Ones"—must have been changed four times at least; the "circles" were re-organized again and again as death came along, and touched some "Niner" or "Sevener," or "Fiver" or "Threer," on the shoulder, and gave him his passport of freedom; the "uninitiates" were decimated by shootings and the Battle of the Bloody Bridge, by escapes and hangings. Still, the Ring lived on. And it would have been living today had the System survived.

---

7    Mr. Gladstone thus alluded to the cause of the breaking-up of the Island penal establishment.

## II.

The ceremony of convening had been gone through, as we say, and the "Centre" had approved of the conclave. So the Threes told the Fives, and the Fives passed the notice on to the Sevens, and Sevens to the Nines. Each "Niner" controlled a body of "novices," and to such of these as, in all likelihood, would be in the exercise-yards on Sunday afternoon, he "passed the word" for picket and guard duty.

And to one other person was the intimation conveyed that a Ring session was to be assembled. The Commandant was so informed—by a note pushed under his office-door! Young though he was in supreme authority, he was at no loss to understand the significance of the pen-printed letter:

"WE MEET ON SABBATH NEXT, THREE IN THE AFTERNOON, IN THE IRON YARD. YOU ARE INVITED TO BE PRESENT TO CARRY OUT YOUR THREAT OF BREAKING US UP."

It was the boldest challenge to his rule, and that he should not doubt its authenticity, at the foot of the missive was stamped (in candle-smoke) the symbol which formed the official signature of the "One"—the four concentric circles surrounding the double-triangle over the broad arrow.

* * * *

Over the broad arrow—that stung Maconochie as it had stung Wright, Fyans, Anderson, Ryan, and every other Commandant who had been similarly challenged. For, interpreted, the signature meant that the Ring was supreme over the System. Let the System order, it would be for the Ring to say whether it should be obeyed.

The Commandant consulted the gaoler and such of the overseers as he had divined were not quite enamoured of the old methods of brute force which he was seeking to supersede with kindness, and showed them the message.

None could enlighten him as to what would eventuate at the meeting.

"A Riot?" No; that was unlikely. The Ring had other methods of working than to precipitate an outbreak unless it was thoroughly prepared, and the chances were now against anything of the kind being contemplated.

"Shall I stop it?" Well, his Honour might try, but it would be useless. It would take the whole military force of the Island, and the armed civil guard as well, to break up a Ring meeting; and even then—

"What?" They would communicate their business all the same, and rob everybody of a night's rest.

"How?" Because the signalling would go on the whole night through. The night-guards could hear the signals distinctly from cell to cell; every Ringer keeps awake and passes on the signal to his right or left as the case may be, though he might not himself understand the significance of the signal.

"But how could the Ring, some members of which were in the gaol-cells, others in the dormitories, others in the Iron Room, communicate, seeing that the three classes of buildings were separated by yards?" Heaven knows!—and the principal Ringers; nobody else!

"It surprises me!" So it did everybody else, the gaoler said.

"Do you think, Mr. Gaoler, the Ring would consent to my making an experiment?" Perhaps so; how?

"If I wished for an illustration of their facility of communicating, would they grant it?" No doubt; and laugh in his Honour's face while communicating. "Would his Honour like to see a Ringer?" Every officer nearly knew most of the outside Ringers (the uninitiates)—no secrecy was maintained as to that class of membership—but really those fellows knew next to nothing of the Ring proper. The men who formed the outer circles were known also; but the actual participation of each in the working of the Society, why, that could never be proved.

"Were there many regulations in force against the Ring?" Dozens!

"Any definite attempt at suppression?" Yes; and the Battle of Bloody Bridge was the result.

The Commandant sickened at the reflection that here was a force never taken into account by Right Honourable Secretaries of State and honourable members of the House of Commons, or by Judges and Governors. The System might rule by terror in one direction, and by coarse and licentious favouritism in another, but here was a power that defied the tremendous penal organization "created by British justice and British apathy." Buoyed though he was by his intense belief in the truth of his theory, and inspired by his faith in the essential goodness of human nature, he could not, for the moment, resist the awful doubt which now assailed him as to whether it would not be better to let the System proceed on its old lines. A power that continued its machinations under the eye and in the teeth of Authority, surely the only way to deal with it was to crush it by force! These were his thoughts.

Fortunately, however, for his fame, Maconochie resisted the reaction. When the Lady of Despair, whose breath fanned him for that instant, had passed him, he felt it would be at least wise to wait and see what Sunday would bring forth. He intended to accept the challenge.

### III.

*"O Day most calm, most bright.*
*The week were dark but for thy light—*
*Thy torch doth show the way!"*

Thus had quoted the Rev. Thomas Taylor in his sermon at morning chapel to the Protestant prisoners. His words had been in praise of Sunday as a day which relieved for them no less than for their more fortunate fellows in other places the labour of the week. Their irons might still clank, but they did not fret and jar so painfully, for the movements were those of rest and change, and were not demanded by task-work. Their hands might still require to describe the salute, but the obligation would be less frequent. And the freedom from labour meant opportunity for reading and thought—for recollection of dear ones far away—for indulgence of bright hopes for the future—and for something of that intercourse with their brother-man which, in its unrestricted and unreprieved fulness, would be the principal delight to be conferred by freedom. Something after this manner spoke the tender-natured chaplain, whose spirits had been greatly invigorated since the advent of the new Commandant.

The chaplain's words had touched not a few hearts and had moistened many eyes. Unlike his predecessor, A——, who was for ever throwing "The Prodigal Son" at their heads; or Parson Ford, of Hobart-town, who was chiefly solicitous that his hearers should prove the value of his teachings by making a decent ending at the gallows rather than in reformation of their lives, Chaplain Taylor invariably impressed the prisoners by dwelling upon the few bright things of the present, and the brighter things their earthly future might still have in store for them. His tribute to the Sabbath was consequently highly appreciated, and more than one out of the six hundred transports in his congregation determined to spend the rest of the day peacefully—if the Ring would let them. That contingency had to be faced, for the knowledge was now general that it was a "Lodge Sunday."

The morning muster after chapel passed off without incident—unlike the previous week's, when Convict Henry Reynell—the same who was now accused by the Ring—had, at the bidding of that body, refused to accept, for his comrades of the Iron Room, Maconochie's bribe of tobacco. And the mid-day meal, of 16 oz. roast-meat, 12 oz. baked potatoes, and the extra Sunday relish—to them who had not been under punishment for the week—of 4 oz. of wheat and barley bread, was unmarked by a quarrel. When the final "grace" was said, and the Almighty thanked in mumbling, parroted parodies for the mercies so amply showered upon them, the mass of the men in the yards felt they were, indeed, deserving of the pleasure which was to be theirs that afternoon. Not a single prisoner had been felled to the cobbled floors, and not one had rushed to the warders with a complaint that his cheek had been gashed open because he had been indiscreet enough to object to the theft of his ration. The peace of the beautiful Sabbath-day brooded, dove-like, on the resting throngs.

There were five yards, but we are concerned only with the one on which the Iron Room opened, and the adjacent enclosure. These were the pleasure-grounds of the aristocracy of crime; and the Ring membership was most largely represented in them. A doorway, sometimes closed, but on Sundays usually left open, furnished a means of communication between No. 3 yard and the space devoted to the fettered fraternity. From the elevated sentry-boxes— the "perches"—at the corners, armed guards watched or patrolled the broad-"leafed" walls. Within the radius of a biscuit-throw, two sentries of the military main-guard moved, this one this way, that one the opposite way, from their post at the entrance of a passage leading to the gaol.

At two o'clock the sentries were relieved, and a careful observer might then have seen that a new interest was taking possession of the throngs in both yards. Those who were reading closed their books, talkers became less in earnest, laughers and jesters—these were not wanting, for some men will laugh in hell—abated their merriment, and others who had been nursing their thoughts in abject solitude, shook off their taciturnity and joined one or other of the many knots. All, seemingly, began to count the time.

At a quarter-past two the sentries changed beats. The movement was noticed by the prisoners.

Fifteen minutes later, the soldiers rechanged. The

prisoners knew the half-hour had expired. Without any apparent concord of movement, the men in either yard formed themselves into larger groups.

By the next change of "Go," talk had nearly ceased in the two yards. Such laughter and sound of chat as were borne on the breeze were from the other enclosures. And the careful observer aforesaid would perceive that now the movements of the men were taking something of the character of marching and counter-marching. He would have heard no word of command; and yet he should have understood that some supreme will was giving directions, for, in the two yards, though no more than a few men in each could see what was going on in the other, there was a simultaneity of movement and likeness of manoeuvering.

And by three o'clock, as the guards were re-adjusting themselves to their original path, the 140 men in the ironed yard, and the 200 in No. 3, were disposed something in this order.

Close to the north wall in the former enclosure stood two men. At three paces distance from them, so placed that, had a cord been passed through the hands of each to the others, a circle would have been described, of which the first two men would have formed the centre, stood three more transports. At five paces from these last were another five prisoners. Connect these by a cord, and these five would have surrounded the three. At seven paces, again, from the five transports were a second five, likewise ranged in an imaginary circle order. Nine paces away from this latter five was gathered a group of twenty-two or twenty-three—an outer envelope, as it were, of the inner rings. The mass of the ironed men stood by the south wall—and their faces towards it; but a weak line of communication was kept up by a string of pickets extending to this numerous group from the outer circle.

Thus was arranged the Ring in day conclave. The central two men represented the circle of "Three"; the three, the circle of "Five"; the first five, the circle of "Seven"; and the second five, that of "Nine." Each circle was separated from its next lower one by as many paces as there were members in the lower circle. And the twenty-two or twenty-three "uninitiates" were divided by nine paces distance from the "Nines." The pickets were recently admitted "uninitiates." If the Ring had a message for the convicts in general or for the "uninitiates" who, for purposes of intimidation, were thrust amongst the transports who had refused or not been permitted to join the Society, it was transmitted by the pickets.

The circles of the Ring, it will be seen, were short of their proper number. It was seldom possible, indeed, to constitute a full Ring at a day conclave. Of the twenty-four men making up the circles, fifteen only were in the ironed yard. Of the rest, five were at the "mutual responsibility" farm, and four were in the next—No. 3—yard.

In the latter yard, allowing for the smaller number of the Ringers, the arrangement was the same. No Threer was included in this enclosure, but a Five, three Nines, and a dozen uninitiates were ranged at the proper gradations of distance. The convicts unassociated with the Ring were crowded under the south wall, with their faces turned from the Society group. Between the twelve uninitiates and the mass stretched, as in the other yard, a line of pickets.

On the stroke of three o'clock, then, this was the order of array in both enclosures. Save for a cough, a clearing of the throat, a friction in the "irons," there was no sound among the transports. The sentries walked to and fro and looked to their primings. The armed civil guards on the perches quickened their senses, but yet refrained from directly scrutinizing the proceedings. They could see every face, and yet no guard had ever been found who could, on a formal demand, identify any leader of the Ring. That is to say, none since Major Anderson's time. A warder then had declared to the Commandant he would swear to a score of the inner circles. And within a week he lay on his bed, a shattered lump of carrion. A thirst for information is not always judicious.

## IV.

The soldiers by the gaol-passage exchanged. And at that instant a sharp, curiously-modulated whistle shrilled from the Threes in the ironed yard, and was instantly answered by another whistle from the next yard. "Lodge" was opened.

A Five broke from his circle, and passed to the group of uninitiates. He paused a second before each man, who stooped and whispered something into his ear. Then, from the uninitiates, he passed successively to the Nines, the Sevens, to his comrades of the Five, and finally, to the Threes. From all he gathered the password save from the representatives of the innermost circles. To them he gave it. During his progress there had been countless slightly noisy movements among the massed transports, yet the tension of feeling was so extreme, that many would have sworn there had occurred no sound except that caused by the clink-clank of the irons.

When the Threes received the approving signal, one—Johnson—began to recite the Ritual; the other—Gooch—to lead off the antiphonal responses. Sometimes both the words of the reciter and the response were in vigorous, resonant English; other passages were partly English and partly in the Ring's own variety of the "flash" language; sometimes both were in the argot. It is unnecessary to say the secrets of the Ring were conveyed in the last form of speech.

Very solemn the liturgy sounded. If the words were sometimes ribald, there was nothing ribald in the manner of their utterance. Except in a Catholic service, no such respectfulness of tone and decency of demeanour were ever voluntarily exhibited by the transports as in a Ring meeting. Any unseemliness was visited with a punishment the more to be feared that its precise measure was unknown to the culprit till the moment of its infliction, but the solemnity of its proceedings was at once the cause and the effect of the Society's influence. The portions of the Ritual which were recited in the vernacular were resonantly worded specifically for the purpose of impressing such of the convicts not enlisted in the strange companionship who might be in hearing. Singular though the statement may appear, it was the religious character given to its ceremonies that made it the weapon it was in the service of the devil. Appeals to occult powers, the element of mystery in gesture and language, the measured intonation, the employment of symbolism, the frequent invocation of dread punishment upon men who violated their oath—all were calculated to inspire awe of and devotion to the Society that used it.

The temporary leader of the Ring, who was reciting, reached that passage in the blasphemous liturgy:

Is God an officer of the establishment?

And the response came solemnly clear, thrice repeated:

No, God is not an officer of the establishment.

He passed to the next question:

Is the Devil an officer of the establishment?

And received the answer—thrice:

Yes, the Devil is an officer of the establishment.

He continued:

Then do we obey God?

With clear-cut resonance came the negative—

No, we do not obey God!

He propounded the problem framed by souls that are not necessarily corrupt:

Then whom do we obey?

And, thrice over, he received for reply the damning perjury which yet was so true an answer:

The Devil—we obey our Lord the Devil!

In a corner, by the south wall, a youth of twenty, in irons for a freak, dropped his face on his hands and stifled a sob. He had been trying since sermon-time to fix indelibly on his memory the sweet melody of George Herbert's hymn:

*"O Day most calm, most bright.*
*The week were dark but for thy light—*
*Thy torch doth show the way!"*

And now that music was jostled from his mind by the demons' Litany. Johnson had arrived at the "prayer":

Render us, O Satan, always flourishing in thy work, always happy in obeying thy law, thou who art eternal, who art always young, who never lackest worshippers and servants to do thy will, who art always rich, and never forgettest those who place their offerings at thy altar—

when from No. 3 yard came a long, involved whistle: and in the instant following a murmur ran along the line of pickets.

Captain Maconochie had accepted the challenge.

## V.

He walked through No. 3 yard unattended. His predecessor had never entered it on a Sunday afternoon without an escort of two soldiers. As he passed he acknowledged pleasantly the few salutes he received, and gave no sign that he noticed the majority of the enclosure's occupants declined to recognize his presence. They were waiting to see what the Ring would do.

And the Ring? Save for that murmur of the pickets the session expressed no consciousness of the visitor. The reciter finished the prayer in an even tone:

"Render unto us the rewards of them who obey thee always and God never."

And then suddenly changing his tone from the key of religious solemnity to a simple announcement, said, "The Com'dant!"

In the same instant he saluted and smiled—smiled derisively in Captain Maconochie's face, as the latter, appalled at the abominable import of the Ritual's words, stood still, showing his distress very plainly.

"Good heavens, men! Did I hear aright? Did I hear you blaspheming your Maker so dreadfully?"

"Wot, sir?" asked Johnson. "This is the first degree of a Ring meetin', y'r know! We but say wot we're tol' to say. It's all in the Ritooal, sir!"

"You are in Ring Lodge now?"

"Yessir! First degree!"

"And you blaspheme like this in all your degrees?" Maconochie stammered and stuttered in his horror.

"Wud yer like to know, sir?"

"Yes."

"Then that's jest wot yer won't get to know from me, y'r Honour!" replied Johnson, and the retort provoked a roar of laughter, half-timid, half-defiant, from the circle. Sunday or no Sunday the laughers would have been tied to the triangles by any other Commandant for that outrage, but Maconochie, albeit severely tempted, overlooked the insult.

"When do you hold your other degrees?"

"In present session, at wunst—unless yer a-goin' to break us up!" Again the fellow laughed.

"I am not going to break you up to-day—"

"Nor any other time!" exclaimed the leader.

"'Ear, 'ear!" seconded some "Fives" and "Sevens."


## VI.


"Go on with your Ritual!" said the Commandant, after a pause.

"That's wot we intend to do, yer Honour," Johnson, with measured insolence, responded. "An' d'yer mean to stop and 'ear us?"

"I do!"

"I 'opes as yer Honour'll be vastly interested!" And once more the Commandant was compelled to listen to a laugh that was a jibe. He let it go by, like the others.

Then the leader resumed his devil's business, and gave, in the next half-hour, the Captain a lesson as to the ingenuity of felonry that he never forgot. Better versed than any Penal Commandant, before or since (save Price), in the "flash" slang or thieves' language, he yet scarcely comprehended a word of the many concluding parts of the ceremony brought to his ears.

For, as there were grades in the Ring, there were varieties in its speech. There was the variety understood by all novices as well as initiates—the variety known to "Nines" and all above—another familiar to "Sevens" and "Fives" and "Threes"—one in which only the "Fives" and "Threes" were educated. All these forms of argôt were used that afternoon, accordingly as the "Three" in charge addressed himself to a higher circle or a lower.

And, not content with that patent offence to the Spirit of the System, the Ring perpetrated yet another. It held communication with its gesture language—when a movement of the limbs or head expressed a number, and the number indicated a word or phrase in its "initiate" code—and in its dumb-talk and its whistling vocabulary. These two last were provisions for use when the legs were ironed and the hands in "bracelets." And of all the "talk" and signalling, the Commandant understood next to nothing. All he knew was that the proceedings shaped themselves something like those in a court of justice.

There were addresses from the leader "Three" and his colleagues—slowly and impressively delivered; there were steppings forth from the outer rings of men who evidently gave testimony of some sort with right hand uplifted; and there was a brief and apparently impassioned speech from a "Seven"—the prisoner's feelings prompted him in his excitement to drop into a phrase of plain English, which he corrected instantly upon being checked by Johnson. And, finally, there was the pronouncement of a verdict. Amidst a grim silence, broken only by the shuffling and rubbing of the second "Three's" irons as he moved from rank to rank of the Circles to gather the judgment, the decision was come to. The whole mass by the north wall heaved a sigh of relief as Johnson lowered his head to receive the announcement.

By the laws, to condemn a "Nine" a bare majority of all present sufficed; to "settle" a Seven, an absolute majority of the Circles present or absent was necessary; for a "Five" or "Three" was required a majority of his own circle as well as the majority of the lower ranks. Proxies were used for absentees, if the latter knew of the business. Reynell was represented by proxy.

Now, of the fifteen chief Ringers present in this Iron Yard but seven voted for Reynell's condemnation. On that vote he would have been discharged of the accusation, for it required thirteen to convict him. But, as we have said, five (including the accused) were at the "mutual responsibility" farm, and four were in Yard No. 3 adjacent to the Iron Yard. Two out of the five voted, by proxy, "guilty," making nine! Would the other four go the same way?

There was a lull in the "talk" and dumb show, while "Threer" Johnson pondered an ingenious—but quite satanic—notion that came into his head. He guessed Maconochie would wish for some indication of the Ring's mysterious power to communicate at long distances. That singular capacity had irritated and defeated his predecessors, and naturally he would think with them on that point, however he might disagree on others. Johnson communicated his notion to his brother "Three" in a whisper, and the other applauded it. Whereupon, "Wud yer like to see, y'r Honour," Johnson questioned very respectfully, "'ow we send messages?"

"Yes!" cried Maconochie. If he could but gain some insight into the Ring's methods he would defeat them, he thought. "Yes—yes!"

"Then y'r Honour'll give us yer word as a gen'elman that yer won't use the knowledge yer gain wi'out formal information on oath from other parties?"

The Commandant felt he was justified in saying he would not.

"Then, sir, there are four Ringers in nex' yard standin' by this 'ere north wall. I'll send 'em a message so you can see 'ow it goes, an' if yer like, sir, yer can bring the answer!"

Should he do it? Was it a trap for his dignity? The Captain reflected, and decided to take the risk.

"I will bring the answer!"

"Then, sir, I'm going to send this message!" Johnson clanked to a foot's distance from the Commandant, and lowered his voice: "Do yer vote as the majority 'ere? The reply, sir, as yer'll get 'll convince yer jest that question and no other's gone through. Now, sir, watch!"

The pickets, we have mentioned, stretched from the cluster of the novices to the south wall. At a sharp word from Johnson, they moved, as quickly as their irons would permit, to continue the line to the gate opening into No. 3.

"Now, sir," went on Johnson, "that there message is a-goin' to the end of that line. Yer follow it from man to man. Then, sir, do you, please, join this line to the picket inside No. 3. They will pass the message on, an' yer'll get the reply!"

Anxiously Maconochie watched the procedure. Johnson, in dumb-talk, "spoke" to a Nine; the fellow passed the message to a novice or "uninitiate" by a gesture; he, turning, repeated it in their slang to a picket. So it went to the line's end. Each man, as he received it, revolved on his heel, and transmitted it to the next, the Commandant pacing by their side down to the last picket. Some of these novices trembled because of his proximity; others simply grinned; the sentries and armed civil guards, in their amazement, grew more positive than ever that the Commandant was "looney."

The Commandant—and the message—entered the next yard. The pickets took it up. Man by man, with repetitions of slang, passed it to the group of uninitiates, and then to the three "Nines." Then the solitary "Five" in that yard received it. Maconochie would have sworn that nothing passed from man to man save a few syllables of gibberish. And yet, within a minute, he had been given the reply.

"Yes, sir!" said the "Five," saluting, "we four here votes with the majority!"

* * * *

Grieving deeply over this misapplication of ingenuity, and wondering how he should meet it and defeat it, Maconochie walked back to where the leader of the Ring awaited him in silence at his proper station.

"Well, sir?" questioned, as deferentially as one could wish, Johnson.

"The prisoner said the four would vote—"

"How—how?" came in hard-breathed exclamations from among the circles.

"With the majority!" The Commandant finished the sentence.

Some laughed at the news; some laughed at the exquisitely humorous notion of making the Commandant the bearer of the fatal decision; and one man—a "Niner," a friend of Reynell—said snarlingly (to his own hurt at a later time), "Yer've given Reynell over to his doom!"

Indeed he had done so, though in all ignorance. How the doom fell we shall tell you later.

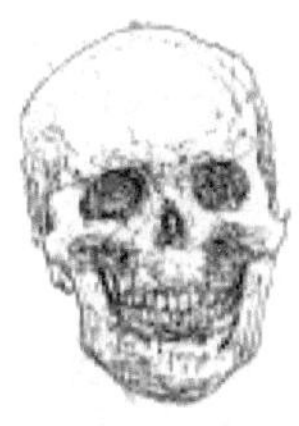

# THE CONCLAVE OF DOOM

## I.

Night in the Iron Room. The majority of the men we saw in the Ironed Yard on last Sunday, when at the "Session of Denunciation," are lodged here. Perhaps a hundred seek the phantasm of repose on the low platforms of its floors; the rest, some forty or fifty, are privileged to slumber in a smaller dormitory adjacent. And, save by the utterly reckless (ever, alas! all too numerous among the ironed men) the privilege of sleeping in the smaller room was highly valued for several reasons, only a few of which, however, dare be stated. The transports there accommodated were the first to be let out in the morning—that was one reason; consequently they enjoyed the earliest use of the towels—this was a second reason. And a third, and even more important one, was that they were not liable to be disturbed after midnight by a Ring conclave. It was one thing to enjoy the solemnity of the Society's proceedings in the daytime; a lodge broke the tedium of the monotony; but it was quite another to lose the superior distraction that came in the shape of sleep, simply because the "One" and the "Three" desired to pursue with adequate rite and ceremony their machinations against the System. Sleep, so precious to all, was trebly precious to the "Black Norfolker." To the felon denizens of the Iron Room sleep was almost as welcome as his "twin-brother," death.

And so, when it became known in the Iron Room the Wednesday evening after the Sunday of Denunciation, that in all likelihood a Ring conclave would be held that midnight, the members of the outer circles and the novices of the Ring, no less than the miscellaneous criminals who were not associated with the Society, were somewhat troubled. The day had been marked by one of those hurricanes which, springing with suddenness from the surface of the Pacific, die as suddenly after spending their tropical rage disastrously upon every object within their scope; and most of the men, having been exposed to its violence, were suffering from bodily exhaustion. Maconochie had excelled himself and desecrated the sacred traditions of the Island by ordering warm tea to be supplied to every man engaged in outdoor employment, and in some cases, indeed, he had granted hot rum, and had, further, shortened the evening muster by withholding "prayers," so that the prisoners might seek their blankets the earlier. And now the Commandant's solicitude was to be partially neutralized by the mandate of the "One." Yet remonstrance, audible and overt, was never once thought of. Had the cases been reversed and it had been the authorities who had with apparent wantonness interfered with the transports' poor comfort, a disturbance would have arisen that would not have been readily quelled. Almost the solitary remark uttered with reference to the Ring's action was that of a wretch, Sam Ward, who from a certain eccentricity of habit—he was for ever speaking to himself—had been refused the greatly coveted honour of admission to the Circles. When the signal went round that a Conclave was to be held and that their rest would be disturbed, he said— "Ah, well—'tis a pity, Sammy! You're always free when you're asleep, and you're so tired to-night, Sammy, freedom'd be all the sweeter!" Beyond these words, the mandate of the Ring met no impediment.

## II.

At six o'clock, when the last padlock clinched its hold on the doors, and the bolts shot in the iron shutters of the two windows, the hundred men ceased communication with the outer world till twelve hours later. So the System judged and ordered.

But at twelve o'clock the Secret Society intervened. A careful grinding of a key in a padlock was followed by an almost noiseless drawing of bolts and the dropping of chains. And then the door the System had closed and virtually sealed was opened by the authority of the Ring. The "One" entered—followed by Peake, the accuser of Convict Henry Reynell per *Coquette*, the prisoner lying under condemnation of the Ring.

The night's conclave was to pronounce Reynell's doom. You may remember that Reynell had been appointed by Captain Maconochie leader of the "mutual responsibility" sub-gang attached to 5B farm, and that Peake had been one of the four hardened, reckless criminals whom Reynell had selected to accompany him. "Barrington," an ex-forger; Osborne, a gentleman who, to his brother felons' surprise, judges resolutely refused to hang—all rules have exceptions—and Bill Felix, a stubborn, country-bred half-brute, were the others of the gang. And you may remember further that Peake had denounced Reynell to the Ring because the latter, an ex-soldier, had been so impressed by Captain Maconochie's unforced kindliness of heart as to defy the Ring and promise "to be true man" to the Commandant. According to the canons of the Society, Reynell had thereby grievously offended, and at his resulting trial had been condemned, Peake and Osborne alone of his colleagues of the farm voting to remit him to the "Conclave of Doom."

On this Wednesday night, then, Reynell's fate was to be decided, and Peake, being a member of the dread innermost circle of the "Three," had resolved to be present. There was no difficulty in the way of his attendance. The "mutual responsibility" gangs were free within limits. By eight o'clock (instead of six as in the dormitories and cells) they turned in. To be out of their hut after that hour was an offence against the Regulations, and a violation of the conditions on which they held the farms. But Mr. Peake reflected that no one would be likely to know of his breach of good faith except those who would not "peach." The essence of Maconochie's mutual responsibility plan was that for an offence of one member of a gang all the other members suffered, the idea being that while a man would not be deterred from wrong action by fear of his own punishment, he would be restrained by regard for his fellows. Even over rascals of Peake's stamp this idea held sway, and that lump of moral and physical deformity, under ordinary circumstances, would have gone to the death rather than have brought Reynell under the whip of the authorities. A defiance of the Ring was, however, another matter, the wretch reasoned, and notwithstanding his personal debt to the man he denounced, who had obtained for him freedom from irons and comparative immunity from supervision, his stunted intellect perceived but the one duty of denouncing the fellow who had insulted their noble Society, and of pursuing him, if the "One" permitted, to the doom. It was for this he was present.

And if you ask how the "One," and Peake the Three, obtained access to the Iron Room when the keys were under lock and key in the Superintendent's office, all we can tell you is that there were but few prison-locks the "One" could not open.

* * * *

The great chamber, as the chief rulers of the Ring entered it, was curtained in darkness that might be felt. In some of the other dormitories a light was permitted after lock-up, but by virtue of their superior distinction the gentry and nobility of the Iron Room were left without a glimmer.

Undeterred by the darkness, the One and his companion passed from the doorway down the middle of the room, as though they were familiar with every inch of the planking. Nor was it till some moments later that a strong, vivid flash from a bull's-eye lantern shot, meteor-like, from the end furthest from the door. The brilliant beam projected its penetrating stroke through the massy blackness, to the distant corners and along the walls that were decorated only with "Abstracts of Regulations," and Forms of Prayer. For a full minute it played on the occupants of the room, and then, apparently satisfying the person who held it that all was right, the light was closed again by the lantern-slide. The mysterious business of the Four might be proceeded with, for there were no eavesdroppers or unauthorized persons near enough to hear.

The bulk of the transports were crowded together in the corners nearest to the doors, with their faces turned to the walls, and between them and the upper end of the room the members of the circles of "Five," "Seven," and "Nine" patrolled noiselessly in stockinged feet and "blanketed irons."[1] These guards, sentries of a very hell, crossed the room from bed-place to bed-place. Not a soul was asleep; and, save the guards, not a body was in motion.

A short space of twelve paces separated the nearest line of guards—the "Fives"—from the group of four men who supplied the infernal motive power to the machinery of the Ring. Thus, as the "One" and the "Three" communicated only in their "cant" or "flash" dialect, excepting in the rare cases when the subject matter of their deliberation passed beyond its far from narrow vocabulary, the Conclave was held practically in private. Shut in the Four were, by the conditions which exalted them to their "bad eminence." The "One" was masked. It would have been the easiest thing for the transports generally to have discovered his identity.

---

1    "Blanketed irons."—Pieces of blanketing were wrapped round the fetters to prevent noise.

They had but to rush in a body from the lower end of the room, and, overpowering the guards, seize the man who exercised over them an authority less questioned than that of the System. An inclination to such an act, indeed, had more than once been expressed by a more than ordinarily defiant spirit among the outsiders, but it had never found general favour. The mass of convicts felt that the Ring, though occasionally a hard taskmaster, gave them ample compensation for the tribute of obedience it exacted. It furnished material for their cramped imaginations and ambitions to work upon—it supplied an outlet for their sense of natural justice so consistently outraged by the authorities—it checked and thwarted the System—it had revenged many of the System's wrongful acts. Nothing to weaken or endanger the rule of the Ring would ever spring from the transports generally: of that the "One" and the "Three" felt quite sure. And so they did not hesitate to exact penances and institute forms which the legally-constituted authorities dare not have imitated save at the risk of rebellion. Had the System sent a masked man into the muster-yard of the ironed men and declared that death should be the lot of the bold villain who tore the mask from the face, a score of hands would have clutched at it. What odds the yard had been turned into an Aceldama[2], if the System had been defied? Yet the Ring sent its masked leader, whom nobody but the "Three" knew, and for the secret of whose identity the System was prepared to pay the price of an absolute pardon, kept all ready signed and sealed in the Commandant's desk: no paltry ticket-of-leave—not even the desirable conditional pardon which conferred liberty within Australian boundaries; but an absolute gift of freedom and a present of money besides to carry the informer "home" and to start him in a new life—the Ring sent this man into the midst of vassals, and they, burning to

---

2   Aceldama—the place purchased by Judas with the money he received for betraying Christ. (ed.)

know who he was, and tacitly demurring oftentimes to his rule, yet crushed their curiosity and obeyed him. "The Ring is wonderful!" exclaimed Dr. Ullathorne to Major Anderson, who had just described the Ring (from less information than we have) to the young priest. "Wonderful, sir!" ejaculated the choleric but conscientious Commandant. "It's damnably annoying besides being wonderful!"

### III.

The masked man knew the "Three"—Johnson and Gooch, inmates of the Iron Room, and Peake, of 5B farm gang. Nevertheless, from each he demanded the password of his circle and the sign of his membership of the supreme rank but one. At the word being given in a low murmur that stirred the darkness like a witch's spell, he began the brief Liturgy of the Conclave.

"For whose service do we meet?" asked the "One."

"In the service of the Devil—the Devil our Lord!" responded the "Three."

"But the Devil our Lord is Invisible!"

"Aye, as invisible as death!"

"Yet is death visible?"

"Aye, to those who can see!"

"Then, is our Lord visible?"

"Aye, to those who can see!"

"Then how appeareth he?"

"In thee, O One! O Mighty One! O Thrice Mighty One!"

"Turn thou then, O men of the Circles, men of the mighty Ring, whose meaning is Unity in Infinity, and do homage to thy chief, to the viceregent of thy Lord! Turn thou! Turn thou!"

The men of the Circles, the noiseless patrol, faced the Conclave, and in the next instant cried as with one voice:

"To thee our Lord Satan do we homage!"

As they cried their hands were upraised. That much

could have been observed, for in that same moment a lurid illumination blazed suddenly upon the scene and hung a garland of flame upon the brows of these human demons.

Through the eye-orbits of a human skull apparently suspended in mid-air, through the opened jaws, through the nasal cavities, and from every fragment of the bony box that had once held the secrets of a human brain, grinned a phosphorescent glare. A mere bit of theatrical mummery, it had a diabolic effect upon weakened nerves already prepared by an incantation muttered in the solemn hush of midnight to be sympathetically impressed. It stamped the seal of supernaturalism upon the ceremonial, and in the perversion of moral sense which characterized the "Black Norfolkers" as it has marked no other community these hundreds of years, it was welcomed with a thrill that had more in keeping with a sensual pleasure than a retributary terror.

## IV.

With the fading of the light the Conclave passed into its most secret stage.

The formal report of the voting in the "Session of Denunciation" was delivered to the "One" by Johnson, the leader who had presided. And the "One" required of the "Three" by their oath to him and the Ring, whether the condemned Henry Reynell had had a fair trial according to the Society's usage?

And two of the "Three" affirmed that he had. Peake, the third man of the "Three," as the accuser, was silent.

"Had the accused been notified that he had been condemned after the trial and in due form?"

Peake affirmed he had borne the message of condemnation "with truth, without prejudice, without fear, and without favour." The message had been of necessity sent through Peake, although he was Reynell's prosecutor, because Peake was the "Threer" having earliest access to the condemned.

"And the condemned! Does he appeal?"

"No. By his oath to the Society, admits he forfeited allegiance by promising to be true man to an Establishment officer, but craves, if the doom be death, one favour."

"What?"

"That he may not be drowned or strangled, but that having been a soldier, he may be shot or stabbed."

Then, after a pause, which held possession of this temple of damned souls as does the tragic interval before the anathema claim the vast spaces of a cathedral of the Church in the hour of excommunication, the "One" pronounced the Doom.

"By the power that is mine, by the authority conferred upon one by our dread Society of the Ring, do I issue my fiat to and make order of doom upon Brother Henry Reynell under bond to the Crown, upon the Crown's register No. 37-889 per colonial ship *Coquette*, and upon the roll of the Society for this year current, No. 12 of our Circle of 'Seven.'

"And the Doom is, That he shall die the death!"

"So be it, O One! So be thy fiat obeyed, O Mighty One! So be thy order of Doom completed, O Thrice Mighty One!" Thus, in their argôt, responded the "Three"; and when their murmur had been swallowed by the silence, the "One" went on:

"Who, of his brethren of the Ring, stands nearest to the condemned Henry Reyne'l in brotherly affection—to whom is he most dear?"

Quaking, shiveringly, Peake made answer: "William Felix, under bond to the Crown, and on the Crown's register No. 39-204, on our roll No. 20 of Circle of 'Nine,' stands nearest to the condemned."

"Speaketh the deponent truly?"

"The deponent brother speaketh truly within our knowledge," confirmed the others of the "Three."

"Then let the warrant of doom go forth to Brother William Felix, No. 20 of our Circle of 'Nine,' that he shall do the deed of death within the circling of a moon's orbit upon his brother the condemned by act of shooting or by act of stabbing, though the testimony be true that the condemned is near to him and dear to him—aye, though the condemned be bone of his bone, blood of his blood, flesh of his flesh, let him do the deed, on peril of his suffering like doom. And from this fiat shall there be no appeal, because—"

The "One" waited for the antiphon. It came solemnly from the "Three":

"Our Society has been wounded, and it heals its hurt by blood."

"So cut we off all traitors! So doom we all that ally themselves to the Law which persecuteth us—the Law which hath given us over to the living death!"

"So cut we off all traitors! So doom we all that ally themselves to our persecutors!"

## V.

Then proceeded to its conclusion this mummery. Its rites and ceremonies—the devices of ingenious and fertile minds compelled by Fate to that most Sisyphian of all tortures, the working upon themselves for want of an outlet for their inventive and imaginative faculties; or of souls capable of forging thunderbolts and of venting forked lightnings, but condemned by society to the unrelieved, hopeless misery of petty taskwork—were, as yet, incomplete.

The "One" had to travesty in blasphemous syllables the prayer commonly used at Norfolk Island executions when a Protestant was to be hanged. The original prayer was this—

"Oh, Almighty God, who according to the magnitude of Thy mercies dost so truly put away the sins of those which truly repent, that Thou rememberest them no more, Open Thine eyes upon this Thy servant who most earnestly desireth pardon and forgiveness. Remember him, most Loving Father; whatsoever hath been declared in him by the fraud and malice of the Devil or by his own carnal wilfulness, do Thou forgive."

The infamous parody of that pathetic appeal as recited by the "One" dare not be quoted. Invert every petition of the original; substitute the name of the Adversary for that of the Deity; invoke as the cause of the victim's ruin and death the loving-kindness of God and the benignity of British Justice, and you will have a faint idea of the prayer he used. The parody was the richest fruit of the System. Were you to clothe with literary form the mouthings of the creatures led by Hébert, as they danced round Lais and Phryne enthroned as Goddesses of Reason on the desecrated Church altars of Revolutionary Paris, you would scarcely parallel it in point of blasphemous horror.

The recitation ended, the "One" and "Three" commended themselves and the Ring to the care of the Lord of Evil, and finally—the Circles being once more bade to do homage—the Convict Oath was chanted in chorus. With foot against foot and palm meeting in palm, the Bond of Obligation was renewed.

Only, there was no drinking of blood from one another's pin-pricked veins. Was it because of the darkness that the libation was omitted? Was it because time was passing?

No; the blood was not drunk because, in the presence of a superior infamy, an inferior shame is superfluous.

* * * *

A "Conclave of Doom," at which was marked the period of some Ringer's life, fulfilled yet another awful function. It at once elected some one to the newly-created vacancy. There were always waiting aspirants for admission to each circle from the grade below it. The man eligible for promotion from the novices or uninitiates was almost invariably in attendance, but if his presence could not be secured—say, because he was in gaol, in Longridge Barracks, or at the Cascades—he was admitted by proxy, the proxy, one of the initiates, being compelled to administer the rite to the newly-elected at the earliest opportunity.

Now, Reynell being a "Sevener," the vacancy in "Seven" Circle had to be filled by the appointment of a "Niner."

Felix, the nominated executioner, was chosen. This step followed the usage. The executioner, having at supreme risk obeyed the Ring, was worthy of promotion if the deed of death created a vacancy.

To fill Felix's place and thus complete "Nine" Circle, a novice was called up by name from the silent, wearied, but docile throng by the door. As the wretch stumbled in the darkness up the length of the uneven boards towards the first line of patrols, his movements were followed by a plaintive wail from Sammy Ward.

"Ain't you going to elect me? It's my turn!" And he was hardly stopped by the smothered exclamations which burst from those equally unprivileged with himself. "Hush, you fool! Hush!"

The newly-honoured convict reached the first patrol. There he was stripped and passed on.

When he came within arm's reach of the "Three," the flash of the bull's-eye blazed into his face, and, for an instant, blinded him. This was done to identify him. Once, two years before, when a man had been called from the outsiders to be graced with his new honours he grew, at the last moment, craven. The man next him whispered that he would go in his stead. He did so, and—up to that night the lantern had not been used for that last flash of identification—was initiated beneath the cloak of darkness. The next day he claimed, as he was entitled to do by his rights of admission, instruction in the "cant" language from an elder member of the Ring. Then he stood revealed as one who had fraudulently obtained admission to their mysteries. The morning following he was found dead in his bed-place; obviously strangled. "But what was the use of an inquiry?"

questioned the Acting-Commandant Bunbury. "To hang the murderer we should have had to hang one hundred and twenty men!" So the flash of identification became necessary.

The man passed the scrutiny—he was the right one, the one who had been called and chosen, and he was initiated.

Gagged in the moment when the light blazed in his face, he could but writhe in the grasp of two "Fivers," and utter throat noises as the "One" thrust a hand against his chest, and punctured its skin with, it seemed, a hundred needle-points. In the shock of pain the neophyte scarcely knew what followed. Into the hundreds of minute wounds, as soon as the needles had been withdrawn, was rubbed a handful of gunpowder. When healed, the scar would describe a solitary circle. Thus was the symbol of the "Niners" impressed upon its new member.

The impression of the symbol was, however, only the first part of the ceremony of initiation. What completed it may not be described, nor even hinted.

Suffice it to say that if by any lucky chance—it was all a business of pure chance—the neophyte had not to the moment of his initiation into the Ring committed any capital offence, the completion of the ceremony placed the rope round his neck. Every member of the Ring was, by virtue of his membership, liable to be hanged. It was really an organization of the condemned. And so absolute was the moral ruin of "Black Norfolkers," that that terrible fact was considered the most brilliant trophy wrested by the Secret Society from the Law.


## VI.


It was three in the morning before Peake reached the hut on 5 B farm. His hut-mates—Reynell, Osborne, "Barrington," and Felix—were waiting for him in a weird, Rembrandt-esque half-light—waiting for the news of the doom. In his walk from the Iron Room to the farm he had passed three sentry-posts; but the "One" had given the countersign at each, and the quiver of trepidation with which Peake had come within range of each soldier's musket had proved quite unnecessary.

Not so, perhaps, the spasm which shook him when he re-entered the hut. The exhilaration of the ceremony had evaporated, and his sense of duty to the Ring was overlain by his awakened remorse that he had betrayed to the death the man who had become surety for his good conduct, and had thereby obtained for him comparative freedom. From the remorse sprang the dread that Reynell—already on his way to the grave—might avenge his betrayal on the betrayer. What would Reynell do?

For some moments after Peake entered no one spoke. Then the condemned broke silence.

"Is it—doom, Peake?" he asked.

Peake nodded.

"Who," stammeringly questioned Osborne, "who is the Ketch?"

Peake, with a trembling forefinger, pointed to Felix.

Felix, great hulking lout, bent himself in the shadows, and covered his face with his gnarled hands.

"An' I'ad promised to be true man for ever an' a day, 'Arry! Yo brought me here, 'Arry, an' rid me o' the domned clinks, an' it's me that's to kill tho. I'udn't do it!" He half said, half groaned these words.

"Then, if yer don't, it's yer doom too, yer know!" breathed Osborne.

"An' I'd take it 'fore I'd break my oath to 'Arry yonder. I'm his sworn man."

"Yer the Ring's man first!" insisted Osborne.

"Ay, that war I; but there's a way to obey th' Ring an' keep my oath to 'Arry too!"

## VII.

On the morrow—rather, at a late hour the same day—while the sub-gang were absent at maize-hoeing, an Establishment officer visited the hut. Save him, no man entered the hut between the time of the gangers leaving it and their return. Yet when they came back for their noon-tide food, one and all of them—fellows who would have laughed at death had it come from Law and the authorities—changed colour as they saw on the stone table a scrap of folded paper.

On the outside of the paper was inscribed a single circle, with the figures "20" in its centre.

On the inside there was no word; only there were inscribed two circles, so—

In the common centre of these was the roll-number of Henry Reynell—"No. 12."

And below this symbol of the personality of the condemned was, stamped in candle-smoke, this—

It was the "One's" signature to his order of doom upon Henry Reynell, "No. 12" of Circle "Seven," and the warrant was addressed to "No. 20" of Circle "Nine"—William Felix. It was his roll-symbol which was marked on the outside of the paper.[3]

* * * *

How Felix obeyed the warrant, and yet kept faithful to his vow to be sworn man to Reynell, will be told presently.

---

3    For these illustrations of the symbolism of the Ring—indeed, for almost the whole of his knowledge of the Secret Society's ritual and ceremonial—the writer is indebted to a venerable (using the word in its literal sense) man, who, though an ex— "Norfolker," was an esteemed correspondent of the late Dr. Ullathorne, R. C. Archbishop of Birmingham.

# THE FALLING OF THE DOOM

## I.

The Secret Society of the Ring had, in regular conclave, ordered that Brother William Felix, No. 20, of "Nine" Circle, should, within one lunar month, stab or shoot to the death Brother Henry Reynell, No. 12, of "Seven" Circle. Reynell's offence was (as already related) the promising "to be true man" to Civil Commandant Maconochie. Convict Bill Felix was a member of the sub-gang of which Convict Henry Reynell was the leader; and, inasmuch as Reynell had chosen Felix to be a member of 5B farm sub-gang, thus freeing him from the constant wearing of fetters and conferring upon him a desirable degree of freedom, Felix had sworn to be his (Reynell's) man "for ever and a day." The tie of fraternity which linked Reynell and Felix thus was sadly complicated with the obligation of obedience which bound the latter to the Ring. Let Felix obey the Ring, and he would have to enact the doom upon the one soul for whom he cared. Let him refuse to execute the death-warrant issued under the seal of the "One"—the dread head or "Centre" of the Society—and the doom he refused to Reynell would be his own. The Ring having given over some one to the doom, would demand the life of the appointed executioner if he failed within the specified time to complete his task. In rare instances a regulation or law of the

Society might be modified or altered in effect. But never in its history had there been known a case where a death-warrant had been left unfulfilled and the stated executioner had continued to live. The idol would demand appeasement for its lust, if not in the person of one victim, in another's.

There is an impressive story as to the working of this Medean law. Before the existing "One" it is believed three men had filled the awful office. The second in the administration had been ordered to murder the then Commandant, Captain Wright. He had acquiesced in the need for the crime—otherwise the order would not have been ratified. And, as the "One," it was his duty to perform the doom on the Commandant. It was a minor but still immutable law of the Ring that the "old man" should only die by the "One's" hands. The honour was accorded to him as a privilege of his dignity. Yet Captain Wright lived to be Major and to give evidence before the Select Committee on Transportation of the House of Commons. How was that?

Wright had been suddenly recalled to Sydney. The vessel which brought the summons of recall could not lie off the harbourless island in the storm season for longer than a week, and instant preparations for his departure were set on foot by the Commandant. The news spread—and twice within the week was his life attempted in vain. He got on board the vessel safe; thus unknowingly he committed the "One" to the wrath and vengeance of the Ring; and the Ring demanded its vicarious sacrifice.

Three days after Wright's sailing the body of one of the most intelligent of the "free" constables was found suspended from a tall pine. The dead man was supposed to have been in pretty general favour with the transports and his fellow-officers; hence it was not believed that he had been murdered, and his death was attributed to suicide. The military surgeon, who made an examination of the corpse, drew the attention of the subaltern of the guard to a curious symbol burnt or tattooed into the flesh of the chest and freshly cut across with a knife. The scarification was, however, only skin-deep, and had been done after death. The officers did not recognize at the moment the significance of the scar.[1]

It was the symbol of the "One."

Not even the dreaded Head of the Society was free of its penalties.

## II.

Civil Commandant Maconochie, it will be remembered, had, in his anxiety to acquire a knowledge of the Ring's methods of communication, been trapped into conveying the report of how certain Ringers had voted at the trial of Reynell. "Condemnation or Acquittal?"—the question hung thus in the balance when Maconochie had appeared in the yard where the Ring Lodge was in "Session of Denunciation." Nine were for condemnation—for sending on the accused to the "Conclave of Doom"; but thirteen votes were required by the law of the Secret Society before the condemnation could be passed. And four votes Maconochie had been trapped into conveying.

Without knowing the precise bearings of his action, he

---

1    It is supposed that the incident here related was the origin of an order once issued by John Price by which every "bond" and "free" constable was required to present himself stripped for examination by a medical officer at certain periods. The "bond" constables had no alternative but obedience, but the "free" officers, almost to a man, refused to submit to periodical inspection as degrading. They appealed to the Governor in Van Diemen's Land, who upheld the objection, in their case, "till Mr. Price could show specific reason for the proposed course in the interests of discipline." Price replied in (for him) a remarkably indiscreet manner--in what was known as a "Semi-official communication"--by alleging that it was necessary to find out from time to time "whether officers' personal marks varied." Thereupon Mr. Price received one of the few snubs of his official career.

had learnt enough to understand that he had given Reynell over to the doom. An interjection by a Ringer who was a loyal friend to Reynell—strange, how in this accursed community of felonry, which a noble member of the House of Lords stated to be deficient in every human attribute, feelings of affection refused to absolutely die out, and thus prove his lordship right!—had informed Maconochie of so much. What was the doom: death, mutilation, or a simple "sending to Coventry"? Maconochie asked several of the officers of the Establishment, but could gain no satisfactory answer. "Most likely death!" he was told by the gaoler. "The Ring didn't think much o' death!"

Herein the gaoler was subject to that tendency to error which infected all thoughts and beliefs, of whatever nature, held in the University of Depravity.[2] The Ring thought a good deal of death when that Mighty Leveller was enlisted on their behalf. It was only when Death acted for the authorities that they snapped their fingers in his face and jested pleasantly with him. When the Ring used him, he was to its members an instrument of terror, and they surrounded him in their imaginations with every ghastly, every agonizing, every horrific attribute of which the distorted culture of the Society's founders, or the dark fancies of the most ignorant Ringers—such as those who ever trembled at the verge of madness—could invent and adapt. But, so momentous is the alteration in human feeling, which can be effected by changing the point of view, Death had but to draw his fees from the Establishment to be sneered at, ridiculed, and derisively welcomed. Black Norfolkers went sardonically to the grave at the Establishment's orders, just because the Establishment wished them to do differently.

---

2   "University of Depravity."—Archbishop Whateley, in his speech to the House of Lords, of May 1840, on his motion for the abolition of Transportation, thus described Norfolk Island.

### III.

Maconochie sent for Johnson, leader at the "Session of Denunciation."

"Have you any objection, sir, to relate the precise significance of the condemnation which you understand the Ring has passed on prisoner Reynell?"

"'Eaps!" was the laconic rejoinder.

"I beg your pardon! What did you say?"

"'Eaps! I sed I 'av 'eaps of objecshuns."

"Oh!" Then, after a pause, "I believe, Johnson, you have been a prisoner under the Crown for many years?"

"More'n can count!"

"Yes? Then you must have heard read many times the regulation as to answering truly and explicitly, and without prevarication or evasion or denial, all questions put by persons in properly-constituted authority?"

"Can't say as I 'av, yer Honour!"

"Johnson!"

"Yes, yer Honour?"

"I mean to deal fairly and kindly with every man on the Island—but I will have truth-speaking. I never forgive a lie, except it is uttered under the influence of terror!"

"In wot 'av I lied, yer Honour?"

"You said you had never heard the regulation enforcing—"

"Savin' yer Honour's presence, I said nothink o' the kind! Yer arsked me 'ad I 'erd it read. Well, I never did! I've 'erd it mumbled ev'ry Sunday since I was a kinchin—but never 'erd it read wunst. There ain't no 'Stablishment orf'cer as can read—unless it's yerself." The rascal grinned in enjoyment of his own satire.

"You know the meaning of the regulation—what it enforces—however?"

"O'course: to answer th' truth, th' 'ole truth, an' nothink but th' truth w'en 'terrogated by 'Stablishment orf'cer."

"Then answer me, sir." (Not imperatively, but with a

studied politeness, did Maconochie now speak.) "What judgment—what 'doom' as you call it—has your Society ordered upon Reynell?"

Johnson gazed reflectively at the ceiling. He passed his right hand over the corrugations of his forehead, and drew it down the scarred and weather-blighted cheeks to the stern, square jowl that had gripped numberless groans of agony in their utterance, and bid them be dumb. Then he said:

"Mr. Com'dant, Pa'son Taylor tells us that w'en th' higher law conflicts wi' th' lower, we must allus obey th' higher—allus th' higher. Do th' pa'son's views meet wi' yer approval, sir?"

The Commandant, already once trapped by Johnson, was dubious of the fair seeming of the interrogation, and declined to answer directly.

"Answer my question!"

"Wi' orl respecks, y'r Honour, I can't till I know wot to obey—that as is th' higher law or that as is th' lower!"

"There is no question of higher or lower law here, my man—none. It is merely a matter of answering my question. What is Reynell's doom?"

"That's w'ere yer an' me jest differ, y'r Honour. 'Tis orl a matter o' higher an' lower law. If I answer th' question, I obey th' law o' th' System. If I don't answer it, then I obey th' law o' th' Ring, an' I'd 'av y'r Honour know as fur me an' sech as me 'tis th' Ring's law as is highest law."

Again the fellow's lips parted and his cheeks wrinkled in a gleeful defiance of authority.

"You're talking foolishly," rejoined the Commandant, bearing the implied taunt with a patience of tone and manner that, if he had only known it, was more likely to penetrate to Johnson's better nature than any number of authority-phrased words; "you're twisting Mr. Taylor's sayings to suit your own purpose. Mr. Taylor meant, no doubt, that when human law conflicts with the moral law of conscience or revealed law, then the latter, as the higher law, must be obeyed."

No more unfortunate admission could have been made by a System's officer; and the ingenious Johnson, whose naturally sharp wits the attrition of adversity had ground to remarkable keenness, while wearing away the moral part of him, eagerly seized the opportunity thus offered of making an embarrassing criticism on the System.

"That's jest it, y'r Honour—that's th' very identical thing as I mean. Now, th' System's laws an' reg'lashuns is th' lower law, an' our laws an' reg'lashuns—th' Ring's laws, that is—they're th' higher, 'cos—but will yer 'ear th' reason, yer Honour?"

"Go on—though you are talking insubordinate nonsense. I will hear what you have to say!"

"This is th' reason. Th' Ring's law is th' moral law 'cos it's founded on justice!" He stooped, and, placing his hands on his knees, crooked his head so as to glare impishly into the Commandant's face to watch the effect of his words, or rather of those he left unsaid.

For not what the wretch said but what he left unsaid stung the Commandant. The implication was clear. The System was not founded upon justice. And in his heart of hearts Maconochie knew the accusation was true. Penalties British law justly provided for those who offended against it, but then British law proposed only to punish, and not to give over the offenders to "unusual punishment" and utter corruption. The System did this, however—and the taunt went home. But, what could Maconochie do? Argument imperilled his authority, and, after all, he did not invent the System. So—

"You decline to answer what is Reynell's doom?"

"Aye, y'r Honour, 'cos th' Ring forbids me!"

"You know I can inflict penalties upon you for refusing to answer my plain interrogatory?"

"Short o' puttin' me into an 'oss' necklace, yer can, sir. But yer won't punish me!"

"Why?" Against his judgment, the Commandant put the

inquiry. Similar remarks had been made to him before by men up for punishment, but invariably they had been uttered in suppliant or cringing tones. This fellow, however, spoke with the confidence of knowledge.

"W'y? 'Cos yer know wot I ses is true. An' 'cos, although yer an orf'cer o' th' Systum, yer 'art ain't in the Systum's way o' doin' things. That's w'y, sir. Yer ain't been long 'nuff 'ere to 'a changed th' 'art o' a man fur th' 'art o' a beast. Yer know who said that, y'r Honour?"

Maconochie nodded.

"Yes, o' course yer do. It struck th' 'ol man, 'im as was jest a-chuckin' o' us into Jack Ketch's mouth like so many sweeties—lor, 'e did love to keep th' carpenters an' gravediggers a-goin', did Billy Burton!—it struck even him orl o' a 'eap! But 'e was wrong 'bout it—an' so is Taylor, an' so are yer, an' everybody else as 'erd o' wot poor Kavenagh said!"

"Wrong—how do you mean?"

"Wot did Kavenagh say? 'When I landed 'ere I 'ad th' 'art o' a man, but yer 'av plucked it out an' planted a brute's 'art instead!' That's wot he ses, an' th' jedge an' everybody thinks it's true o' th' pris'ners only. But, man"—he gathered breath to hurl at Maconochie, with greater emphasis, a bitter conclusion—"them words war truer o' th' 'Stablishment orf'cers. Th' System finds orl its orf'cers men, an' leaves 'em orl brutes! Orl o' we don't get 'ardened, but there ain't one o' yer wot doesn't!"

## IV.

Foiled by Johnson in his attempt to discover the fate in store for Reynell, Maconochie met with no more success when he interrogated the members of the farm sub-gang to which Reynell and Felix belonged. Peake, Osborne, and "Barrington" each frankly enough declared he knew quite well about the order of doom, but as for telling his Honour—well, the

Ring wouldn't allow him.

"If anything happens to Reynell, I shall charge you as an accessory," said the Commandant to each. And the threat was laughed at. Better the vengeance of the System than the vengeance of the Ring. The former could only hang them— the latter could do more: it could kill them after a ceremony of execration. They were frightened of the last.

From Felix the Commandant received his one fragment of consolation. "I be 'Arry Reynell's sworn man, y'r Honour! An' no harm 'ud 'appen unto him if Bill Felix can stop ut wi' life nor limb." And, somewhat reassured, Captain Maconochie went then to Reynell himself.

The man was hoeing. He had stopped for a moment to rest, and stood gazing towards the sea and over the township, which was semi-veiled in a lustrous mist, as though Nature would hide from the eye of Heaven the halls where the devil and the System held their joint revels. On the soft earth the Commandant's steps were inaudible, and the transport did not know of the official's approach till he was addressed.

"Reynell!"

The convict started, and turned round. He "capped" instantly, and, in the same gesture, Maconochie saw that he had dashed away a tear from his eyes.

"Good-morning, Reynell! The gang making satisfactory work?"

"Yes, sir. I think so! With a fair crop, the Com'sariat 'll have to pay them a good many marks."[3]

Them—why not "us"? Maconochie was quick to notice the substitution of the word.

"Why 'them,' Reynell? Why don't you, who are the leader and director of the gang, join yourself with the

_______________

3   "Marks."—Any surplus crop over the rental paid to the Establishment by the mutual-responsibility gangs for their farms was bought, in Maconochie's system, by the Government, and paid for in marks. The marks went towards the purchase of absolute or conditional freedom.

others?"

"Oh," with a marked hesitation, and a quivering of the lips that told of an inward agitation, "'twas a slip, sir!"

Maconochie stepped forward and laid a hand, with kindly pressure, on the transport's shoulder.

"No, Reynell, it was no slip! It meant that already you are separating yourself in thought from your fellow-gangers—it meant that you are under doom of death from the Ring!"

The condemned flamed out into sudden anger. Such strange tricks does the fancy play with a certain order of superstitious minds, that he was jealous that the secret of the Society he thought so much of as to submit himself quietly to its fatal will, should be thus known to an outsider, and that outsider one of the accursed Establishment. "Who told you that?"

"No one. I inferred it—partly from what passed last Sunday—you heard I was present?—and partly from what you say was a 'slip.' Come, Reynell—Harry—"

All the patience, all the forbearance, all the tenderness that it was possible for one man—a superior—to extend to his inferior, Maconochie caused to vibrate in his voice. The prisoner, bringing himself in the sudden impulse of surprise to face the Commandant, showed in the workings of his features how the "Harry" had stirred him.

"Tell me," Maconochie went on, "if not the doom, how I can help you to escape it. Remember, my friend, that I brought this on you!

"No!" In a low, choking guttural.

"Oh, but yes! I cannot forget that it was because you swore to be a true man to me, and thereby helped me nobly in what I regard as my mission here, that you are under the ban of the Ring. Therefore, as through me you broke, it would appear, the Society's law, it is only right that through me aid shall come to you."

"There can—be no—aid, sir! All's up!" Reynell let his head fall on his chest. The action was that of a tired man, of an over-wearied bearer of a burden; there was nothing abject in it.

"No. I pledge you my word, Reynell, that I will get you out of this trouble."

"'Tis no trouble, sir!"

"Listen, sir! I brought you into this quarrel with the Ring because I wanted—well, I wished to count you as one of the trophies of my new methods—"

"Beggin' your pardon for interruptin' y'r Honour, an' it's good of you to put it that way, but it's not true—an' it's no use! I'm doomed—doomed!" And then, with something of that saucy contempt for life which had made him before Maconochie's advent a centre of insubordination, he went on: "It's not that I'm afraid of death—not a bit of it! No Ringer is—few of us are!" He waved his hand so as to embrace in its sweep the whole group of Kingston buildings—the dormitories, the gaol, and the exercise and work yards. "None of us are! But no one likes death at the hands of the Ring, for it's disgrace—and besides—"

"What?"

"Yer won't think me a softy, sir, will yer, for saying it? but I've of'n thought of late—" Again he paused, stumbling for an expression. Maconochie waited.

"I've thought that, p'r'aps, life wouldn't be such a bad thing—if one only had—a chance to keep square!"

Maconochie's heart leapt within him. Here was proof that he was in the right! Bring a creature, however hardened to all seeming, within the circle of human interests and brotherly charities; re-clothe him with manhood and individuality; refuse to treat him longer as a mere Number, as a Thing to occupy a line in returns, as an Object of offence to the Law, and, therefore, to have his badness whipped out of him by the Law's agents; let the unforced music of a kind word sound in his ears; do these, and the fountains of a vigorous life would burst impetuously and imperiously from the core of his nature. This was his theory—here was the successful application of it!

He clasped the transport's hand. "You're right, Reynell—you're right, Harry! Life is worth living—the struggle to make yourself a better man will make it so to you! I'll help you all I can, by removing you out of the reach of pressure from the Ring—"

"You're very good, sir," muttered the convict, "but it's too late!"

"It's never too late to repair the past, Harry!"

"Yes, 'tis—in my case. For—look here, sir—can I trust yer Honour—yer Honour's honour to keep this secret what I'm about to tell ye?"

"If you insist upon it—yes!"

"I do—I do! Why 'tis too late is this—if I don't die, the chap who's to settle me will. That's Ring law!"

"Reynell!"

"'Tis gospel true, sir! An' that's why I've got to bear the doom!"

"I will send you up to Phillip Island yonder till the brig arrives, and then I will despatch you to Sydney," Maconochie said, confronted with this new revelation of the Ring's potency.

"No use, sir. If I don't die, the chap 'll who's to settle me. An' besides, they'd reach me there!"

"I will take you into my household and give you a special guard!"

"The cooks'd poison my rations!"

"I'll send you food from my own table!"

"To reach me they'd poison you and your family."

"Are they devils?" burst out the Commandant, losing self-restraint for the moment.

"Aye, they are that! But who made 'em so—who made us so?—for I'm one o'them, sir. The System!" And then, after a pause, while Maconochie rocked himself on his heels in acute distress at these ever-recurring assaults upon the administration of which he was the head, he resumed:

"No, y'r Honour; I joined the Ring wi' my eyes open. I was eager to make a break in my life—it was all work an' punishment, an' sleep, an'devilry, an' then devilry, an' sleep, an' punishment an' work over again—an' the Ring makes a change. An' I'm not goin' beyond Ring custom, especially as my breakin' away would let another chap in for the doom."

"Tell me who he is, and I'll send him away too!"

Reynell laughed. "You don't know the Ring, Captain Maconochie! Twenty years off, if that chap's a true Ringer an' met me, he'd do for me then! No, sir, let it be. P'r'aps I'm better dead than alive. I can't do any more harm dead!"

## V.

Maconochie, with the taste of ashes in his mouth, left the farm, but instantly despatched an overseer with an escort of a sergeant and four men, and had Reynell locked in a cell, pending his despatch to Phillip Island, where it was his intention to send him. As the escort passed into Pine-lane— a pine-framed avenue leading from the Settlement to Long-ridge—Bill Felix met them as he was on his way to the hut. As he stood aside and saluted the overseer, he glanced inquiringly at the prisoner. Reynell read the glance, and in the Ring language assured Felix to be under no alarm. "If Felix could not execute the order of doom before the twenty-eighth day (a fortnight had still to elapse), he, the condemned, would perform the 'cross-road trick."' Which was—suicide. The Ring should be obeyed; the idol should not be disappointed of its victim.

* * * *

A week passed. Under the supervision of two soldiers— one for day and the other for night duty—Reynell was lodged in the solitary hut on Phillip Island. And Bill Felix, appointed executioner, knew that his own—or Reynell's— time was drawing near. Peake, Osborne, and "Barrington"— none had spoken to him of the imminent event; to have done so would have violated a regulation of the Society; and yet he knew it was an hourly question with them as to the manner in which he would perform the doom. He smiled to himself at the way he would obey the Ring while disappointing it.

Several more days passed. Maconochie himself was on the alert with his telescope at seven o'clock in the morning and five in the afternoon when the sentry on Phillip Island would fire off his musket and thus give the "all's well" signal. Although the distance between Norfolk and Phillip was but two miles and a furlong, the surf fringing either island made the boat-passage dangerous, and as the Commandant did not feel justified in despatching a boat to the rock save on every third day, he had arranged the gun-fire signal. The report could not be heard, but with a spy-glass the flash could be seen. Flag signals from Phillip's had been discontinued since they had been worked by convicts to destroy a boat's crew.

For seven days the report-speaking musket was fired morning and evening, and Maconochie felt hopeful. He had got it into his head, in spite of what he had learnt, that if the month would pass without the violent death of either Reynell or some other prominent villain being reported, the doom would pass also. And to-morrow would end his suspense. He would send a boat over in the morning.

But on the morrow he himself missed the observation of the musket-fire. He was busy investigating the cause of death of William Felix, No.39,204 per *Coromandel*, shot dead by the sentry at the outer gaol-tower.

## VI.

Bill Felix, with no room in his head for two ideas at one and the same time, had been at first strangely confused by the conflict of the obligations to which he had subjected himself. The Ring held by grips of steel which would not relax, and yet his vow to Reynell tugged at his heart. Reynell had chosen him, Felix, from among seven score of men in irons, and had freed him from "them domned clinks," which, encircling his ankles, bit with their subtle corrosion also into his vitals. Most prisoners chafed physically under the compression of the irons; but others—and curiously enough these were not exclusively the naturally refined class—fretted savagely under it both in body and soul. Men who, before exile, had spent their existence for the most part out of doors, in the delicious enfranchisement of wild nature—men who had been shepherds and farm labourers, poachers and gamekeepers, gipsies of the land, or those gipsies of the sea, the merchant-sailors—were fettered doubly. And ex-farm hand Felix—"an incendiary monster," Sir William Follett called him at Manchester Assizes—who had been one of a crowd which burnt a farmer's ricks, and who had as much evil in his nature before transportation as he had intellect, refused to love his chains. They tortured and burnt him. "Oh, Mister," he had said to Major Ryan, Maconochie's predecessor, "tak' th' domned clinks off, an' yo can flog me week in an' week out, an' yo 'ud!" What Commandant Ryan had refused to do, Transport Reynell had virtually done. Therefore, with the best elements of him, he thanked Reynell—adored him—was prepared to sacrifice himself for him. And in his case, as in most others, affection cleared the wits, and enabled him to perceive the paramount duty.

To the Ring he was bound by respect, fear, terror. To the condemned, he, the executioner of the Ring, was linked by love and gratitude. During that four weeks' reprieve, the debate went on between his poor, dulled brain and his quickened heart. And as the day of doom drew near, so did his apprehension of how he should satisfy the doom become the more distinct. At last he saw his course of action.

It was midnight on the last night but one. Within twenty-four hours must the doom fall, or he himself be condemned and for ever accursed in the annals of the Ring. As he rose from his bunk in the hut on 5B farmstead he quivered superstitiously in the ghostly darkness. The moon was not yet up; and he had a long—oh, so long a way to go in the myriad-shaped blackness of the night. "An' he war terr'ble afeard o' th' neet!"

"Be you sleepin', Peake?" he whispered to the hut-mate who slept on the same side as himself.

"No!"

"I be—off—t' do ut, Peake!"

"That's a good cove, Bill, an' ye shall come up higher in the Ring quicker for it!"

Was it fancy alone that thrilled Peake's ears with the words, "Gord forbid!" or did Felix really breathe them? The scoundrel fell asleep again while trying to solve the problem as to whether his hearing had deceived him.


## VII.


Along the pine-bordered lane—a tunnel to hold in the bleak blasts—passed Bill Felix. Gibbering shapes walked with him, "t'owd squoire an' pa'son, an' mither an' feyther from th' whoam village," and dead and gone brother Ringers, and at least one of the three constables to whose death he had been an accessory. They shrieked at him in the gusts that shook the branches of the tall pyramidal pines, and he heard their sobs plainly in the sound of the sullen surf. He could have sworn some of them laid hold upon him; and great drops of perspiration beaded his forehead and soaked his peakless cap. The wonder was that he did not turn back in sheer affright. But the blind mute impulse which not rarely wins men to heroism when their wills bid them act the coward, held him to his path.

By Government House, the sentinel's shadow silhouetted by the door-lamp on the white garden-wall as he stood in front of the thirty-two-pound gun on the slope, startled him afresh. "O Gord!" he gasped. He had forgotten that by his oath to the Ring he should have called on Satan.

Past the Deputy-Assistant-Commissariat-General's cottage he stumbled, the scents of rose-tree, spiceplant, and magnolia from the carefully-tended garden banishing for a second some of his dread. He would have liked to have plucked a banana to refresh his parched lips, but dare not jump the fence. He did not want a bullet before his time.

Over the culvert by the Commissariat offices, creeping down by the low wall fearful that the soldier posted there might see him cross the fanshaped beam of light from the one unblinded window, he reached the Grass-plot. He paused then, leaning against the palisade that surrounded the flag-staff. He heard, rather than saw, the balled flag rustle softly as it hung suspended against the foot of the mast. He would have spat upon it could he have reached it. But he could curse it. Tomorrow—nay, this very morning—the ball of bunting would run up quickly to the truck and would reveal itself magnificently as the Union Jack at the precise hour, perhaps, the requisition went in for his coffin. So he cursed it, beneath his breath.

At last he stood within a yard's length of his goal. See that narrow stream of light, shooting outwards from midway up that great rim of massy blackness? It projects from the loophole of the guard-tower at the north-eastern angle of the gaol. Six feet above the loophole stands, as Bill knows well, a soldier, with firelock ever ready; mute himself, save at half-hour intervals when he hurls into the night a grim, ironical "All's well!" or, more rarely, when he issues a challenge; and his old Brown Bess is mute too—till there is occasion for her to speak. A pace and a half, and Bill would be visible in the flash of light. Thirty-six inches this side of Eternity! And he had always calculated that it would take a drop of ten feet to dislocate his neck. Decidedly death was nearer this way than from the scaffold—by six feet or thereabouts!

Would Reynell do him justice? Would the Ring? Would the Ring, after all, think he was shot by mischance, instead of from his own purpose? "God!"—again! He had never thought of that! Would his sacrifice be all in vain, then? Suppose that the Ring still held Reynell to his doom? "God!"

In the agony of doubt he must have exclaimed aloud. Suddenly the challenge parted the darkness.

"Who goes there?"

He did not give himself time for another thought; he stepped boldly into the light.

"Who goes there? Answer, or I fire!"

"Fire, an' be damned t' tha!"

He challenged Fate as well as the soldier. And both answered.

* * * *

When they bore him into the guard-room he was still alive. He gasped two sentences. "Yo'll tell—Pe—ake—this be th' doom. An' give my lo—ave t' 'Arry Reynell, 'ull yo?" and in a little while passed out of the ken of an aggrieved System.

Maconochie, bending to view the wound, saw that the ball had entered between the rims of two circles described on the man's chest. One—the larger—was an old scar; the other—the inner circle—was still of a festering newness. The latter was the symbol of Bill's recently gained membership of No. 7 Circle.

"Bony" Anderson[4], from the signal-station on Mount Pitt, came down to report that there had been no gun-fire from Phillip's at seven o'clock. A boat was despatched, and returned with the body of a suicide. Bill Felix's sacrifice was in vain, after all. Harry Reynell had anticipated the doom.

---

4    "Bony" Anderson: the ex-man-o'-war's man whom the System chained on Goat Island, Sydney Harbour, as a warning to his brother-transports, and a source of pleasure to Sydney Sunday excursionists. Maconochie made him a signalman.

# THE PEGGING-OUT OF OVERSEER FRANKE

## THE PRELIMINARIES

### I.

PHILIP FRANKE WAS his name, and his grade was Overseer of the Outer Domain Gang. Originally a drummer-boy in the 73rd Regiment, he, by much musical beating of the tattoo and reveille, and by a fine enthusiasm in the use of the cat when a comrade was lashed to the halberds in Barrack Square, had achieved promotion in the regiment. He had won the sergeant's stripes, and with them the commendation of his superiors, and the hearty, undisguised hatred of every one—"Government labour," soldier, or lower class "free"—over whom at any time he exercised authority. A pleasant fellow to look at, save that he was rather undersized, he had a round chubbiness of feature which was suggestive of Primeval Innocence and Uncorrupted Virtue. No man could look more un-Systematic or more cherubic; and when Mr. Lewin, the distinguished botanist and artist, was searching for models for the group of angels he was painting for the lady of his Excellency Governor Macquarie—Mrs. Macquarie favoured Mr. Lewin with many commissions—it is not surprising to learn, firstly, that Lieutenant-Colonel O'Connell promised to send him some one from the Barracks who he thought would serve Mr. Lewin's purpose; and, secondly, that Sergeant Philip Franke was, in consequence, depicted by the artist as reposing on a remarkably neat arrangement of snowy cumuli.

The incident is mentioned here as demonstrating the regard in which his officers held Franke, and also as indicating the foundation for the widespread convict belief that Franke would never get any nearer heaven than those pictured clouds would carry him.

Truth to say, the qualities which were most generally manifested by Philip Franke were not such as to commend him to the loving appreciation of the "Government labour," or of the rank-and-file. And when on the 19th day of March, 1814, it was known that Sergeant Franke had received his Excellency's special permission to remain behind when his regiment was relieved by the 46th under Colonel Molle, there was a wild break-out of hilarity in Barrack Square, and a corresponding depression of spirits among the out-labour passports. For in the same breath that it was made known that Franke had received Governor Macquarie's permission, it was announced that he retired on pension to the Overseership of the O. D. Gang.

His Excellency the Major-General's farewell proclamation to the 73rd was read out by the Brigade-Major at morning parade. When the paragraph—

*In adverting to their Services in this Colony, although unhappily Events have occurred which must always occasion the deepest Regret, as well to the Corps as to the Major-General, it must be recollected that the Odium attending those ACTS OF DEPRAVITY ought in Justice only to extend to the Perpetrators of them*—was reached, a murmur rolled through the ranks—"Acts o' depravutty! Th' spyin o' Sargeant Franke, th' measley sot!" The files on parade had memories that at that particular moment were not to be appeased by rounded periods of glowing eulogy. His Excellency went on to express his opinion that—

*This Station has not afforded the usual Field for Military Glory, but, in as far as the industrious Exertions of those Non-commissioned Officers and Privates who could be spared from Military Duty have been concerned, this Colony is much indebted for many useful Improvements, which, but for the soldiers of the 73rd Regiment, must have remained only in the Contemplation of those anxious for its Civilization for a Length of Time.*

He might go even beyond that magnificent tribute—he might go to the length of averring that—

*The Comforts enjoyed by the Colonists in Consequence of the zealous and laborious Exertions of the Soldiers of the 73rd Regiment will long be remembered with their grateful Recollections.*

But even balm of that sort could not heal the wound Macquarie had inflicted when he had given Corporal Franke an extra stripe for playing the sneak and turning barrack-room and parade-ground into subdivisions of hell.

Healing for that wound came only when it was known later the same day that Sergeant Franke was to stop behind, having obtained fifty acres of land and an overseership.

"But, O Lord, boys, what'll life be worth now for them convicts as he's over?"

This was the barrack-room sentiment. And it was not thought merely and kept in the thinker's own mind, but spoken openly without reserve as a soldier should speak. And it was applauded bravely when spoken.

For with the sergeant would pass away the chief spy of the regiment, and the lesser spies feared the rank-and-file more than they were regarded by the officers. None of the lesser spies were gifted like Phil Franke with sweet manners and a cherub's face, and consequently none could get the ear of the Colonel and the Major-General. With every disposition to emulate Franke's career as a reporter to the High Powers of barrack and guard-room discontent, two or three non-coms. and several privates had been unfortunately deprived by Nature of the qualities necessary for success.

Which circumstance, if looked at in the proper light, will appear a matter for regret, inasmuch as in the barrack-room of the 73rd rebellion was always in an incipient stage, and the expenditure on a few military executions would have conduced greatly to the prosperity of the country.[1] At any time in our colonial history up to 1825 it would have been an easy thing for our Praetorian Guards to have wrested the control of the colony from the Constituted Powers, and more than one such plot had been in course of incubation within the quarters of the 73rd. That the eggs were addled was largely due to our hero, Franke.

## II.

Overseer Franke was installed in office the day after the 73rd had marched down to the Cove and embarked for Calcutta. The Outer Domain Gang, as was the case with all low-class labour (as distinguished from the mechanics), were quartered on the west side of the town in the sheds that surrounded the Old Country Gaol. From their squalid living-place to the scene of their daily work was a good three-mile walk, and that distance suggested to the fertile brain of the Overseer an idea. It occurred to him the very day he assumed command, but he was too astute to play the new broom all at once, so he deferred promulgating it in the ears of the Authorities till he had been some weeks in office.

Then he enunciated it to the Superintendent of Convicts, and the Superintendent of Convicts passed it on approvingly to the Chief Engineer, and the Chief Engineer

---

1    Colonel Arthur, in transmitting a return of expenditure to the Secretary of State for the Colonies, remarked "that every item of the expenditure would be found conducive of the prosperity of the colony." The statement included £20 3s. 4d., executioners' expenses.

quietly appropriated it as his own, and strongly recommended it to Governor Macquarie, who was graciously pleased, in his capacity of Head of the State and Deputy-Providence, to adopt it.

Now, the idea, when we come to state it in cold-blooded print at this time of day, does not challenge admiration either by its daring audacity or sublime originality. The defect, however, is not in the idea, but in us. To appreciate an historic fact, you must weigh and estimate it in the light of the day on which it happened. And the day when Overseer Franke generated, and the Chief Engineer appropriated, and the Governor acted upon the Idea, was the Day of Small Economies. The genius of Old Sydney in Macquarie's early years of administration was the genius of lavish expenditure, but in his later epoch, the fine old ruler worshipped at the throne of another God. Things were so skimped that even the hangmen were compelled to be economical in the matter of hemp. They wished to hang twenty Condemned one day in '21 in Lower George Street, and the Sheriff could not succeed in getting together more rope than would suffice to "top off" nineteen. It would have detained the crowd and the Sheriff another hour from breakfast to have hanged No. 20 with the rope which had already despatched No. 1, and so, as the high functionary dare not anticipate his next quarter's advance by purchasing rope on credit, he put back No. 20 for a week.

It is from the circumstance, then, that the spirit of economy was abroad that Mr. Franke's idea derives its importance.

Instead of marching his gang from quarters to the site of their work every morning, and marching them back every night, he proposed that he should camp out with them the week through, bringing them in for muster—and divine service—from Saturday to Monday.

This was his plan. In the light of the Administration, it was Splendid, Capital! For it promised to save the Government, time, sinew, boots, money. If, in the process of economy, it also lost a soul or two, well, that consideration could not be permitted access to the Authorities' judgment for one second's audience.

Mr. F. A. Hely, Principal Superintendent of Convicts, once remarked to Father Ullathorne, Vicar-General of Roman Catholics: "Absurd, my dear sir! You ask us to consider souls. That's your business! The Administration has to consider cash!"

And Mr. Hely was right. He generally was. When, for instance, he sent seventy-three assigned servants—exactly fifty more than he was entitled to—to his estate of 5,120 acres, an estate for which he had paid £16 13s. 4d., there can't be the least doubt he was right. Consequently, being never in error, his opinion as to the folly of giving heed to souls when cash was concerned, must be respected.

### III.

Nevertheless, that heedlessness was the weak spot in Franke's plan, as the sequel proved. It precipitated his pegging-out.

When Franke took charge of the gang there was about five years' clearing work to do on the hilly land which ran from Windmill Ridge to the South Head Road. All the area now known as Darlinghurst was then wooded, sparsely in places, but for the most part the timber was thick. The task of clearing and burning-off with such appliances as were at command of the outer gang was heavy, and the allowance of five years' time was by no means excessive for the undertaking. The Chief Engineer, however, was able to report, two years after the new Overseer had originated his idea, that the marked-out work would be completed by the gang a good twelve months under the allotted period. For this satisfactory achievement the C. E. not unnaturally took the most considerable proportion of credit, but still he did not withhold some tribute of appreciation from Franke. The

Overseer, indeed, should have had all, as it was by his plan that the gang had got through so much work.

The only people dissatisfied were the gangers. The average number of men in the gang was twenty, and the official power which directly controlled them was made up by the Overseer, three soldiers, and a scourger. Notwithstanding this ample manifestation of care by the Authorities, the gang grew discontented, and had to be soothed back at sundry times into contentment and resignation by two hangings, about a dozen of imprisonments, and several score of floggings.

But even gentle remedies of that kind were not potent to keep always within bounds the turbulence of felon-spirits that feel themselves injured by three things which we shall enumerate in the order of their importance as they stood in the estimation of the genial Overseer's protégés.

Firstly, the gangers objected to the deprivation of their daily walk, or rather shuffle—men with single or double irons on could not walk—to and from the town barracks. They would not have minded so much had the time, ordinarily consumed by the out-gangs in passing from the barracks to the working-places and back again, been allowed them for rest. But that was not so; they had to work those two or three hours. Thus their hours of labour were literally from sunrise to sunset, though other gangs worked, say, three hours less.

Secondly, the camping-out system practically gave control of their ration and clothes allowances to Overseer Franke. And Overseer Franke, as became an intelligent officer of the System, was not slothful in the business of deriving a very substantial addition to his recognized emoluments from those same allowances.

And, thirdly, they lost the sweet solace of companionship with minds that ran in other grooves of duty, which they would have enjoyed had they been barracked nightly. "There is no apparent motive for the prisoner's murder of the deceased!" remarked C. J. Forbes, at a later day, in the preface to his summing-up on a capital charge. "Beg your Honour's parding!" interrupted the prisoner, with a courteous desire to set the judge—all things considered, the noblest man who ever sat on a N.S.W. Supreme Court Bench—right, "my motive's plain 'nuff. I wanted a change! I got so wery tired of gang-work—there was no wariety in it at all!" Well, that was just the matter with Franke's gangers. The nightly chat in barracks would have been a safety-valve for their natures, and conveyed some refreshment to their minds; but in camp their speech was dammed-up, and their lips, if they did move audibly after "lights out!" were in danger of being sealed with a leaden seal. "Fire into the tents, sentry, if yer hear as the men's a-talkin' together. They may be concoctin' mutiny!" Thus the seven men who, on the average, were the occupants of each tent (eight by eight its floor area) were dumb perforce.

There is no tyranny like that of the petty tyrant, and there is no torture like that suffered by his victims. The very littleness of the source of authority adds another and acuter pang to the pain. Had the thousand and one miserable restrictions imposed by ex-Sergeant Franke been directly ordered by a nominal gentleman, or by an officer of commissioned rank, they would have been borne the easier. Only a man with vermin-soul could have designed and put into force some of the methods adopted by Mr. Franke for the subjugation of his men, and being what he was, he was not restrained by any regard for the common humanity which the convict shared with himself, such as even a Foveaux or a Rossell affected (if he did not feel) at times. Intoxicate a creature of his low stamp with the absolutism of power, and you would develop a wretch that even Pluto, who, so far as is known of him, has one or two gentlemanly instincts, would surely be loth to employ. Foveaux, after hanging a man in the presence of his wife and child, patted the latter on its back kindly and told it to "Never mind! mammy'll get you a new daddy soon, p'r'aps!" Franke would not have done that—he would have shown the little one its father dangling at the rope's-end, and would have smiled as he did it.

For Franke was the most ingeniously devilish of the low-caste sons of the System that we have come across. To what degree of excellence he would have attained had the Outer Domain Gang not interrupted his official career it is impossible to say.

That thing they did: in the third year of his Overseership they shortened his official career—at least so far as the System was concerned, for there is no saying what use could be found for him other-where—by terminating his life.

Now that was unkind of the gang, it will be admitted. The amount of work done by it under Phil Franke's intelligent direction was so much larger, as we have said, than could have been expected, that the Chief Engineer had marked out for Franke in his mind's eye a wider and still more remunerative field of labour. And of these new emoluments and this deserved promotion, Franke's gangers robbed him.

# IV.

There had come a new man to the gang. Occasionally, though rarely, it happened that a ganger would remain deaf to the wiles of the System, and would refuse to extend his seven years to fourteen, or his fourteen to "life." The men of Old Sydney held out countless inducements to Government men to extend their term of "Gov'ment labour" indefinitely, or till it reached the foot of the gallows, but now and then it would occur that a transport resisted the temptation in the shape of scourgings and starvings to remain on the muster-rolls, and became free.

Such an event had just happened. One Saturday evening

when the gang went into the town for Sunday Chapel and muster, one of the gangers dropped out an expiree, and Mr. Overseer Franke was consequently able to present no more than eighteen at the muster.

"Overseer Franke, how is it your gang is only eighteen?" demanded the Barrack-master; "your strength's twenty."

"Yes, sir, but your Honour has forgotten that one man got his certificate yesternight—"

"That's nineteen!"

"And one is waitin' trial, your Honour, for assaultin' me."

"Ah, that's the score, but you're still one short, then! There, go to No. 2 yard and pick out a likely fellow."

"Yes, sir!"

And in a second, he had passed into the inner quadrangle of the Muster-yard—some of the stone wall is still standing—where one hundred and forty newly-landed transports were huddled, pending inspection.

Up and down the ranks of sickly wretches—they had been seven months on the voyage, and short of water and lime-juice for the last month—he passed, closely scrutinizing the cargo. It was a regulation that the Governor, or, if that was not convenient, the Colonial Secretary, should allot each new-comer to the work for which he was best suited. The regulation had been obeyed in the case of the *Coromandel* cargo. On the previous morning (Saturday) his Excellency had inspected the "indent," and had selected every man who said he was, or seemed to be, a mechanic. Then he had ordered the rest to "gang-labour," and thus left them to the tender mercies of the Overseer. There are more ways than one of carrying out a regulation.

"A crawling, scurvy lot!" commented Overseer Franke to the yard constable. "I want a strong, wiry 'un, an' there don't seem to be one in the batch."

"Try this cove wots over here," suggested the constable, and pointed as he spoke to where a man, under the medium height, but otherwise well-proportioned, stood, the centre of a ragged group. "This chap ain't much muscle to look at, but he's blooded—he's got sperrit, I should say, an' 'udn't prove a shiser. You try him, Mr. Franke, sir. Here, you feller, stand out!"

The "fellow" stood. The grime of confinement did not blur altogether the fine lines of his face, and the delicate nostrils of the long nose, the sweep of the eyelashes, and the chiselling of the mouth, indicated blood and gentle nurture, while the straightforward, lucid eyes spoke equally clearly of a disposition of integrity. It was a mystery how such a man came to be included in the ring of degraded scum, possibly only to be explained by a sudden lapse into a criminal deed, or, as an alternative (of which there are many instances in convict archives), that he was bearing the brunt of some rich or great man's crime.

"Your name, feller?"

"Edgar Allison Mann," was the reply, respectful in tone.

"Edgar Man!" exclaimed the Overseer, aghast at the fancied affront to his dignity. "Man! Do you know as you're talking to a Hoverseer?"

"Mann, sir, I said—M-a-n-n! Edgar Allison are my Christian names."

"Ah, that's it, is it! Now, jest look here, young feller, we ain't a-goin' to put up with your inserlence."

"I meant no insolence! You misunderstood me, sir!"

"Misunderstood yer, did I! Now, wot's that but inserlence, I'd like to know? Ain't it inserlence, constable?"

"It must be, Mr. Franke, sir, if you say so; you have 'ad more experience than me, sir."

"By my lights, my flash cove, I'll have to take your flashness out of yer. A-tellin' me that I misunderstood yer! Wot'll yer say next, I wonder!"

"That—you—are—a—blackguard—who—has—been— invested—with—a—little—brief—authority—over— your—betters!"

The yard-constable held his breath; Overseer Franke let his tongue loll out in amazement; did he hear aright, or had his senses deceived him? Did the audacious transport really mean to call him all that? The only sound to be heard in that yard for some seconds was the half-suppressed chuckle from a transport who was out on his second voyage: "Lord, ain't the swell a-crackin' a whid in prime twig!"[2]

"Wot's that yer say?" Franke, when he had got over the shock, said. "Wot's that?"

Word for word, pausing between each as he had done before, the transport repeated his former speech.

The whole yard looked for a burst of anger, and an immediate presentment of the offender before the Barrack-master with a request for condign punishment. A genius like Franke, however, was above doing what common constables and newly-landed transports expected from him. He knew a trick worth two of immediate punishment.

"Yer'll do, my man! I likes a feller with pluck for my gang, for it gives me som'at to do to break him in! March to the outer yard there—yer are a-going to jine No. 3 Outer, d'ye hear that?"

When Mr. Franke marched back on Monday morning to the heights beyond Windmill Ridge, there went with him Edgar Allison Mann, No. 14,736, as the twentieth man of his gang.

## V.

Mann adjusted himself with philosophic fortitude to the terrible conditions under which he was placed. Reticent as to his past, he strove by whispered word and the example of a manly bearing where the whole routine was carefully designed to stamp out even the physical type of manliness, to encourage his wretched fellow-gangers to look to the future, to bear up under the infinite degradations of the present by forcing their minds to anticipate a brighter and

---

2    "Cracking a whid in prime twig."—Making a speech in a stylish or masterly manner.

happier time. His influence at the end of three months was extraordinary. Even the Overseer could not but notice it, and should have rejoiced at it, as in the quietude of the gang they worked better. But their superior discipline provoked Franke, for it was none of his doing—caused, instead, by a spirit which he regarded as rebellious, and by methods he considered insubordinate, and Mann's conquest over the rude hearts of his fellow-gangers was the more galling as it was a proof that he, the Overseer, had failed to break Mann's spirit in the first week of the young transport's inclusion in the gang.

He had taken offence at the way Mann saluted him, and understanding clearly that nothing was more harassing to a convict of "superior position" than the necessity he was hourly under of "capping" to the penal officers, he put him through a course of instruction. He had permitted the soldier-guard to supervise the labour of the gang one forenoon while he devoted himself to "a-larnin' the gen'elman how to s'lute."

For three mortal hours he kept Mann marching to and fro on a path six yards long in front of the tents. He sat on a stool in the opening of a tent, midway between the points at which the convict had to turn upon his heel, and every time of passing, he ordered the prisoner to salute.

"One, two, three, four—s'lute. Hand to your peak; higher, feller!" Mann would obey and proceed. Returning, it would be—

"One, two, three, four—s'lute. Left hand to left leg, right brought smartly up, an' held there till yer pass the orf'cer as yer payin' honour to—d'ye hear that, pris'ner, a-payin' honour to!"—he would laugh gaily here, as though to accentuate the stabbing insult; then "One, two, three, four." And so to the end of the walk.

After that exercise of three hours' duration, Mr. Franke turned to the transport, and said, with a heavenly smile lighting up his cherub's visage—

"And now, Mann, d'yer think yer'll know another day

'ow to salute properly?"

"I think so, sir!" responded Mann, with as sweet a smile. "I think so! I'll not forget this lesson." And in the self-abasement which dare not groan aloud, he resolved he would not.

He dare not groan at that or countless other insults, because groaning would have provoked the application of the lash to his back. And Mann dare not, for his soul's sake, do that. Like the poor sinner at Macquarie Harbour, who told Surgeon Barnes that once he was flogged he did not care a brass farden what became of him—he'd as soon go to hell as not—for his thoughts were hell after the lash had bitten him (Charles Buller, to whom the Australias owe so much, wept as he heard Barnes' narrative)—Mann knew he was done for once the cat stung him. He would no longer be a man—a human being; he would be an animal that cringed before such a creature as Phil Franke, or he would be a desperate, blood-craving beast. No, he dare not be flogged. Always he held himself up with that hope that he would always keep to the weather-side of the Overseer's mad passion.

But there was no knowing what a day would bring forth in Old Sydney times, when the monarch of the hour was a cherub of the Franke variety. Mann was flogged—forty stripes save one. "That's Scriptooral, pris'ner," grinned the Cherub—forty was Overseer's limit—"an' I'll take care the scourger don't give yer more. Peel!"

"Peel," he, Mann, perforce did; and as he stripped for the punishment, he swore to his Maker that, before the next Saturday, the Cherub should have a chance of seeing what the earth looked like from another sphere.

The cause of the punishment was Mann's championship of another ganger.

The weekly ration of O.D. Gang consisted of four pounds of salt pork one week, and seven pounds of fresh beef the next, the flour-food being, week in and week out, ten pounds of wheat and six pounds of maize, ground by the prisoners themselves, in their own time, mixed with cold water.

But Overseer Franke, having been appointed, by reason of being in "detached camp," a storekeeper, was entitled to make issues from store to himself, as Overseer. And he would not have attained to the eminence he possessed as an official if he had not contrived to turn this arrangement to account.

As Storekeeper, he was entitled to buy, at the rate fixed by the Governor, meat, wheat, and maize, giving an order on the Deputy-Commissary-General for the payment.

As Storekeeper, he would issue to the Overseer (himself) the scheduled allowance of rations, taking his own receipt for the quantity of produce.

And as Overseer, he would issue to his men what he pleased. And he pleased to issue very little. He, as a fact, robbed them of nearly half.

One Monday an elderly transport, a coarse, languid, brutish "First-fleeter," working in the hot sun, fell ill. He was thrust into the shade of the gums till knock-off time, and then carried to the tent, one of the tent-party being Mann.

In the still watches of a moonlit night, the sick man became delirious for want of nourishment or from the sunstroke. Mann rose and, as noiselessly as possible, so as not to disturb the other poor fellows whom slumber mocked, asked him, "Could he do anything for him?" But the First-fleeter, in his delirium, made no coherent answer.

Mann went to the fly-opening, and called: "Sentry!"

The one sentinel on night duty—twelve hours at a stretch—challenged him and ordered him to stand.

"Prisoner's dying!" Mann never would permit himself to fall into the use of the corrupt form "pris'ner," though nearly everybody, from the Governor, Judges, and parsons, down to the children in the streets, made the word a disyllable. "Prisoner's dying!"

The challenge had awoke the Overseer. He came to the mouth of his tent: "What's that?"

"Pris'ner sick in No. 1," reported the sentry.

"Who's that talking?"

"I—Mann—No. 20."

"Back to your bed, Mann! Wot d'yer mean, my fine swell, disturbin' the gang at this hour?"

"The man—Cummings—is dying!"

"Wot's that to yer if he is! The rule o' camp is no talkin' arter 'lights out.' Back—"

"You are a murdering villain if you let this poor devil die!"

"Fire, sentry! Fire!" And by virtue of the authority which reposed in the bosom of the Overseer, the sentry obeyed. He fired point-blank—Mann had thrown himself down on his side of the tent—and First-fleeter Cummings' delirium merged into and ended with one deep, low groan.

In the flapping of a swallow's wing the young convict was out in the moonlight.

"Shoot me, you murderous scoundrel! Shoot me, if you dare, and all the soldiers in the colony will not save you from the dogs. Shoot me as you've shot that prisoner after starving him—he was ill because you robbed him of his rations. You've as much right to shoot me as that other, for you've robbed me, all of us, of our rations."

A minute of silence. Then the Cherub spoke to some purpose.

"No, no, my fine feller—we don't waste powder an' shot on gentles. That's the death they like. It's the cat as yer don't like, an' it's the cat as yer a-goin' to have. Scourger!"

At two o'clock in the morning, on the height of Woolloomooloo, with the soft sea-breezes chanting plaintively through sassafrass and eucalyptus, Mann got his thirty-nine! Thirty-nine was scriptural.

## VI.

From that morning Mann changed bodily, mentally, morally. From that morning he lived only for revenge; he would not even wait to see what justice would come forth at the Sunday muster.

When the gang went out to day-labour, the camp was in charge of the soldier who had gone on duty at daybreak. This day the soldier, instead of taking his usual sleep, was obliged to continue his sentinelship, for he had to watch over the writhing body of Convict Mann and the stiff one of Convict Cummings.

What passed between Mann and the sentry can be inferred by the circumstance that the soldier threw in his fate with the gang when they made their bolt, as they did three nights later—on the Thursday.

On the Thursday night they bolted, under Mann's leadership, and seized a schooner which lay out in the main stream. Overseer Franke, of course, raised a remonstrance as to their going, but they treated it as unpolitely as they did his complaint that they were hurting him, when they pegged him out—alive—with tent-pegs and lines—on an ant-hill in the heavily-timbered gorge between two hills.

Alive—with food just outside of his reach—and a bullet-hole through his right hand, into which aperture the ants were directed by the ingenuity of one Mann, who made a sweet track of the Overseer's ration sugar from a hole in the hill to the hole in the hand.

About eight or nine years afterwards, Mr. Absalom West was clearing some ground in Bark 'Um Glen—now refined into Barcom—when he came upon a skeleton—pegged out.

## THE COMPLETION OF THE DEED

### I.

Overseer Franke, of the Outer Domain Gang, working on the heights of Woolloomooloo, and engaged in clearing (by means of convicts' agony) the wooded ranges of hills and network of gullies, so as to make room for the perfume-breathing plants of civilization, had been rudely interrupted in his slumbers. One of the gang, Convict Cummings, being half-starved, sun-smitten, and overworked, had become delirious in the mid-hours of the night, and another transport—Mann—had set the Regulations at defiance by imploring the sentry's aid for the sick wretch, his tent-mate. Thereupon, Mr. Overseer Franke had awoke from his beauty-sleep and had ordered the sentry to still Mann's rebellious tongue with a bullet. The sentry fired in Mann's direction, but the bullet had found its destined billet in Convict Cummings' body—and Convict Cummings had ceased from troubling. Unfortunately, the wicked Mann, having evaded the shot, did not rest. He upbraided Overseer Franke for having murdered Cummings. He became positively insulting—and was flogged.

At two o'clock in the morning, at a spot somewhere, we take it, about where Liverpool Street of Modern Sydney dips into Womerah Avenue, Darlinghurst, Convict Edgar Allison Mann received thirty-nine lashes.

And Mann was "gently born"; and when the back of a gently-born transport had once been stained with the infamous stigma of the lash-point, only two things, if he were not to become utterly bestial, remained for him to do: to kill his tyrant, and—to die.

And Convict Mann, being at heart a really fine fellow-being, moreover, a firm believer in Shandy's doctrine that a man's name influenced his character; being, in a word, manly, lost not a minute in coming to the resolve to do both things.

"Peel!" had ordered Overseer Franke.

Mann had obeyed, making a remark as he did so:

"Flog me, and by God who looks from the heaven above, you're a dead man, Mr. Franke!" And then correcting himself, as though before he were subjected to the degrading ordeal he would assert his manhood, he repeated the words, but dropped the title. "You're a dead man, Franke!"

"Scourger—thirty-nine!" laughed Franke. He might have made the penalty forty lashes—beyond forty an overseer could not go—but he read his Bible, did Franke—also the Regulations. "Thirty-nine" was Scriptural. And it was one on the safe side of the Regulation allowance.

* * * *

All through the next day when the only living occupants of the camp were the sentry (the one who had shot Cummings) and himself—Cummings was, of course, also there, but though he was a present horror and outrage, he was in the past tense—Convict Mann nourished himself upon the lees of his cup of shame. And the draught turned to the acid of revenge in his mouth. By the time the gang returned to work after the nooning repast, he had forgotten, however, for a brief space, his physical pangs in the pleasure of anticipation.

He had formed a scheme by which to obtain the freedom of the gang and his revenge upon Overseer Franke.

The one recreation permitted to the gangers was a rare plunge into the waters of the inlet since known as Rushcutter's Bay, which was granted to them whenever they visited the Bay for the purpose of renewing the stock of rushes which composed their beds. The sedge at that time not only covered densely the low-lying areas between the arms of the Bay, but ran out in the inlet itself, and to gain a clear plunge the convicts were obliged to advance some hundreds of yards from the proper beach-line. More than one poor devil, having got so far, thought he would go farther, and had sought to dive and swim beyond the military guards' range. If the soldiers missed, however, there were other and still more vigilant guards (the sharks), and these never, so the Authorities believed, missed their man.

On the last occasion, six weeks before, on which Overseer Franke had thought it desirable to refresh his "labour" with a bath and with new bedding, Mann, with another ganger, going out a little further than the others, found that a derelict ship's boat had been tide-borne into the Bay, and had nosed a short way into the spiky sea-growths. Their hearts had laboured mightily at the discovery, for the fates would be cruel indeed if, with such a tool to their hands, they could not win freedom somehow. They had kept the knowledge of the boat to themselves. They had driven the craft with all their might farther into the sedge, and then had diverted the attention of their fellow-gangers from the vicinity by raising the cry of "A shark! a shark!" and by retreating hurriedly from the spot. And all the time that had intervened, the knowledge of the boat hidden in the rushes had soothed the ache of the hearts and hands of the two men. The boat was oarless, that was one disadvantage, but they did not always think of the deficiency. They dwelt upon what they had, not upon that which they had not.

This day—a Tuesday—which Convict Mann spent in camp, brooding over his shame and his revenge, he thought less, perhaps, of the boat than he had on other days—till the afternoon. Then, the recollection flashed upon him, and, all gashed and pain-stricken as he was, he strove to act upon it. He called the sentry.

"Sentry! Can I speak to you?"

The soldier paused in his wearisome walk by the tent-mouth.

"Yes, Mann."

"Will you do me a favour?"

"Ef it ben't agen Reg'lashuns."

There was a moment's silence. Then—

"It's against the letter of the Regulations, but not against their spirit."

"I don't know wot yer mean."

"Well, the Regulation is that flogged prisoners should be turned out to work as soon as possible after the flogging, isn't it?"

"Yes."

"Then I wish to get better soon—to get about the quicker. And a dip in the bay'll heal—the—back—quickly. The salt is good for it!"

"No-a! I'll not let yez go. Yez 'ud drounded yesself!"

"Sentry, what do they call me in the gang?"

"Gen'elman Ned."

"Yes, Gentleman Ned! And though I'm lying here flogged"—then, for a second, the restraint to which he was subjecting himself gave way, and he shivered and sobbed— the wrung agony of a strong man's sob!—in the impotency of his wrath. "Though I'm here under punishment, I hope— I hope—I'm still a gentleman in that I won't lie. I'll come back, sentry, if you'll allow me to go!"

"Yez u'd not get there ef I let yez go. Yez too sick."

"By Heaven, I would, sentry. My will will carry me, and back, if I had no other power."

The soldier—a pock-marked, skimpy-eyebrowed-and-haired fellow, with the irresoluteness expressed in his features of the creature who has always been subject to rule—grew dubious.

"Ef it be th' salt as yez wants, th' Overseer 'ud 'a issued some 'a yez spoken for it. I might give yez some now."

"The Overseer would place you under arrest for stealing the salt, if you did. No; I would not ask you to do that, but the salt of the sea-bath would cure me quickly. On the word of a man who never lied, sentry, I'll come back."

The sentry hesitated. If Mann did not keep his word, or became too ill to return before the Overseer and the gangers came back to camp at six o'clock, then he would be ruined. Mann read his thought.

"On my word of honour, sentry, I will be back before five o'clock. It is now about two. Weak as I am, I can do the distance in the time."

"Strike your breast, an' swear be God that yez 'ud not ruin me."

The crude, childish oath was taken. Mann struggled to his feet, swinging involuntarily round on his heel from weakness as he did so, and then invoking what strength he could, set out. Under some scrubby gums, offending the day with the rigidity of its contorted nakedness, lay the murdered thing. Feeble as he was and blood-exhausted, Mann spent a little of his poor force in breaking off the feathery crest of a young wattle; and threw it on the corpse. There had been no opportunity to bury Cummings before the gang went to labour in the morning, and the interment would have to be performed by the men in their own time at night.

The sound of the breaking sapling directed the sentinel's notice to Mann. He ran up. "Yez mustn't do that, Mann; Overseer left no orders," he said, as he pulled the branch off the dead man.

At no era in its history did the System inculcate respect for the convict dead. The convict alive was carrion; dead, was carrion still.

## II.

Mann dragged himself to the waterside through the scrub and timber. It was awful work—heroic in the endurance of suffering of the acutest kind. But he was whipped onwards by the shadow of the cat. Again and again he fell; and once when he fell he burst out in a wild spasm of anger, and swore by the heaven that smiled upon him and upon the System that he would not move from the spot. He grew delirious for a few minutes and fancied that Franke was chasing him with the sentries. "Come on! Come on, ye devils!" he shouted, but they did not come, for they were not there. And then the rustle of the breeze in the wattles and the gums, while it cooled his brain for the moment, and momentarily banished the fever of madness, played, too, its tricks with his fancy. The interlacing shadows caused by the movement of the branches seemed to him a horrid play of floggers' whips. The air was full of "cat-tails"—they whistled, they were falling upon him, they would lacerate him yet again! In his dread he rose and turned to flee, and in the turning dashed his head against the jagged end of a limb that had been ruptured by a southerly squall. The wood ripped into his cheek, but the gashing of the flesh was his salvation. The inflamed blood was eased through the wound, and he became rational again.

He cursed his fate that he had become clearer in head, though his weakness of body had increased with the outflow of blood. And he cried against the God that would not let him die in a blessed unconsciousness of dying. But again his mood changed. He remembered his promise to the sentry and addressed Heaven once more. This time it was in prayer. He bent his head, and craved strength to keep his word. "Let it not be said that Gentleman Ned had proved false to the trust placed in him by the miserable wretch of a soldier-guard!" A poor prayer, indeed, and if wholly sane he would have spurned the paltry vanity that prompted it. Perhaps, however, all unknowing to himself the Power whom he approached had Himself framed the pleading. The only evidence the lower-class creature, free or convict, had in those days of the existence of a Power that was true and righteous and just, was a brother-man's word. A broken vow, a violated promise—and away went the betrayed one's faith in God, truth, honour, justice, everything.

Stumbling, staggering, now leaning against a tree for rest, now pressing his lips against the exuding gum on eucalyptus boles, he went on to the rushes, crying aloud sometimes for help and sometimes hoarsely whispering to himself in pity of his own plight—moving while two voices echoed in his ears: "The boat! The sentry!" If he could only find the boat safe! If he could only return to the sentry in time to prevent the man being punished for the breach of good discipline caused by his permitting him to leave the camp! Onward to the boat, back to the tents! Once—he gave up and moved in his return path! And then, the thought of the boat spurred him forward again.

## III.

At last, he reached the Bay. Then his strength come back to him impetuously. He crashed through the reed-beds out to the circle of blue water, and plunged into the shallows. The brine stung him, pricked him—it punctured him in a thousand pores, but it renewed his vigour, and supposing there had been human eye to see, he had been cheered for the boldness with which he parted the waves as he swam towards the point in the sedgy arc where the boat had been driven in by himself and the other convict. With the boat was freedom, perhaps happiness, for the gang; and though the rush-edges cut his back and thighs, he was reckless of the smarts in the exhilaration of the conquest over himself, his weakness, Franke, the System—a victory symbolized by that swim through the cool, foam-flecked billows. He laughed in his sense of triumph as he recognized where his brother-ganger, in forcing his way out again from the dense growths, had broken off short the dagger-points of a cluster of reeds. He laughed again when the outer line of sedges closed behind his own path, as, treading water, he drove himself into the springy mass, and saw the plants which he and his mate had bent and bruised as they had pushed the boat before them. It was a note of mighty exultation that laugh—which changed in its last accents to the dry cackle of a parching mouth.

The boat was gone!

Had freedom, and wealth, and home, and woman's love, and the prattle of one's child, and all other things that make life glorious, been offered to Convict Mann the next hour as a condition of his telling, he could not have related how he reached the camp again. But at five o'clock, just when the clod's brain of the guard was dimly pondering the question as to whether it was not time for Gen'elman Ned to be showing up, he flung himself gaspingly on his rush-bed. He could have told to an interrogator nothing but the one thing—that the recollection of the sentry waiting for the fulfilment of his vow had alone kept him from there and then throwing away the life so ridiculed of fate. To march through an Inferno to reach the boat—and then to find it gone! God!

Now, the sentry could not know of this disappointment, of course. All that the stupid fellow saw was that Mann had returned, and, diverging a yard from his "go," he strove to make himself as pleasant as it was right for Authority to condescend to when the person to be patronized was only a transport. .

"Yez a-got back then, Mann? 'Ope as yez 'ad a raal noice swim, now!"

"Oh, blast you, blast you! Go away!" the tortured wretch exclaimed, and turning his head upon the rushes, recked nothing of the anger of the insulted soldier. Which, nevertheless, was not to be despised, for was he not the representative of the military power, and the civil power, and every other power on that hill-side, pending Overseer Franke's return.

## IV.

At five minutes past six that personage came back to camp, closing with his two soldiers the procession of ironed labourers. He was affable, and, as the sentry saluted, asked him how the "gen'elman" had passed the day.

"'E war inserlent to me, y'r Honour—blarsted me!" reported the soldier.

"Mann!"

In his tent, the transport heard the command, and dragged himself to his feet to obey it.

"Mann!"

Haggard with his shame and with the horrible recoil from his hope that had acted as a new blister upon his hurts, Mann went out, and saluting, faced his tyrant.

"Yer've bin inserlent, Mann?"

The transport looked towards the sentry. And the sentry then remembered that, after all, it was Gentleman Ned who had cursed him—and Gentleman Ned had kept his word— and once upon a time Gentleman Ned had doubtless enjoyed the right to swear at common people like himself; and so—

"Mister Franke, I don't wish to press th' charge!"

"Oh, very well! Then we'll let yer orf this time lightly. An' so yer'll jest dig that stiff 'un's grave for punishment! I won't flog yer agen—yet!"

Mann's first impulse was to refuse—the next to strike Franke, and he had actually stepped a pace nearer to the latter when another and wiser thought occurred to him. He would dig the grave, for by so doing he would obtain a shovel which would serve the fell purpose he had in his mind. The hand he had raised to strike Franke he carried to his forehead in salute. Franke noticed the transition and laughed.

"That's right, Mann! Yer a-gettin' broken in, I see! There's nothin' like the cat for gentles arter all—it breaks the spirit so purtily."

At 6.30—the gang had returned from labour at six o'clock—the evening muster was held. "Tea"—12 ounces of maize meal (reduced by the Overseer's peculation to 10) mixed with cold water—was rationed out, and then two men were told off to dig Cummings' grave.

"No. 20" (Mann).

"No. 7." This was a feeble old fellow, one of the "passengers" by the fatal "second fleet"—"built in the eclipse and rigged with curses dark"[3]—whose constitution had never regained vigour after the terrible privations of a voyage that had been one long feast for the sharks which followed the vessels' wake.

"Nos. 20 an' 7—no, we don't give no precedunse to gentles in this 'ere neighb'rood. Nos. 7 and 20 'll dig th' late Mister Cummin's' grave—an' make a tidy job of it—an' sink four foot!"

Mann and his co-sexton limped towards the scrub where the dead body lay. The Overseer followed them to mark out the grave. He ordered Mann to take from the heap of tools thrown down by the labourers a pick, and No. 7, a shovel. "Ye're the younger man, No. 14,736"—when Franke was unusually genial he would address the convicts by their register numbers, and not merely by those of the gang-roll (and when Mr. Franke was genial the scourger was busy and happy)—"Ye're the younger man, an' jest yer take the pick, an' begin 'ere. Oh, it's the pick—an' the cat—as is good fer yer gentles. Oh"—the jeer changed dreadfully—"oh, help! Mutiny—"

The crashing of the pick closed the sentence. Well was it for Overseer Franke that the torture of the forenoon had drawn the strength from Mann's limbs and the oil from his sinews. The smooth handle of the tool slipped round in the transport's hands as he lifted it, and the pick struck the official's head with the side instead of the point. It was well, we say, for Franke; for the blow did not kill but only stunned him. Perhaps, though, it was ill that he survived.

---

3   "It was that fatal and perfidious bark,
    Built in th' eclipse, and rigged with curses dark,
    That sunk so low that sacred head of thine." *Lycidas*, John
    Milton (ed.)

The Overseer's cry had roused the guard. The few minutes that they could call their own of the whole twenty-four hours were those immediately following the muster for "tea," and before the nightguard was set. It had been always a thought of Franke's that at that time of the day the convict-mind was less disposed to study the whys and wherefores of a "bolt" than at any other period, because the gangers would then be suffering from the lassitude of the day's severe labour, and the inertia which comes from stomachs filled—such filling!—after long fast. Consequently, he had never objected to a brief relaxation of military discipline. For a few minutes their muskets would be laid down by the three sentinels—their pipes would be lit—and they could feel themselves a trifle freer than the transports they guarded.

Now, by this circumstance—this illustration of his own magnanimity—was Overseer Franke undone. Had he permitted no relaxation of sentry-duty then, his cry would no sooner have reached the guards' ears than it would have elicited the speedy aid of a bullet—and it is quite unlikely that Convict Mann would have been missed a second time that day. As it was, though the three soldiers heard the sharp appeal for aid, they were some yards away from their muskets, and before they could reach the weapons, several of the convicts had rushed between them and the guard-tent. In the passing of the eye-gleam in which they saw Mann's deed, some of the wretches apprehended the consequences of the act, and, on the instant, became—men. Sottish they were one moment with the debased cravings of the creature that exists only to work, and be fed, and to sleep sleep that gives no rest; but they were men the next, under the influence of that blow for mastery. It wooed their manhood back to them.

And the guard were powerless to help the Overseer.

## V.

Mann, having struck Franke to the earth, threw the pick down and strode towards the startled but pleased transports. One or two of the more adventurous of them, in that rebound towards mental independence, abandoned all caution, and cheered him. "Well done, Gen'elman!" "Well done, Mr. Mann!"

"I don't think I've killed him, coves," said Mann, hardened into a vulgar familiarity of speech by the very deed which had strengthened the others' respect for him, "he'll come to, presently. But I'll kill him then."

A soldier—one of the two that had formed the gang-guard—at this, thought to withdraw himself quietly from the group. Instantly the action was noticed, and a ganger stopped him. "No," said the fellow, "you don't get to the town. We've got a chance to bolt now, and we'd be fools not to use it. What d'ye say, pals?"

Then Mann knew his task was easy—even without the boat. Unless he could tell them of the boat, he had not thought to win the assent of every member of the gang to an attempt to escape. Now, he understood that they had responded to his rebellious act as tinder to the spark.

"Yes," he exclaimed, "hold the lobsters."

"You won't murder me, Mann?" entreated the soldier.

"No—but we will bind you till we have made our run."

"'Ear, ear," was gasped by some of the transports.

"We'll tie 'em up!" And, in a second, two tents were on the ground, and the lines were being cut for the pinion-cords for the military guard, who, once assured of their lives, made but slight resistance.

The whole camp of transports was now seized with semi-madness. They were a long way from being out of the wood, for, as yet, none (not even Mann himself) had the least idea of how they were to effect their escape. Inland, or over sea? None knew. All they cared to understand for the moment was that their oppressor, who was to them the only Visible

Authority, lay senseless—destitute of life apparently as he was of power. In their wild burst of licence some rushed on the store-tent, others sat down to "oval" their own or their comrades' irons. Nearly all whistled or sang. The soldiers—two tied to tree-trunks, the third supine on the grass—were amazed at the antics; Overseer Franke did not remonstrate; and was it fancy altogether that suggested there was a grin on Cummings' face?

Mann, as befitted the leadership which he had assumed without dispute, was the first to recover himself. His back was torturing him. The pain reminded him of his vow.

"Coves—mates!" he cried. "Silence! we have business to do!"

Instantly they stopped their clamour. Two or three, however, went on "ovalling," and the ring of the hammer as they forced the anklet-bands out of their true shape so that the feet could be withdrawn, disturbed, with a singular sharpness, the suddenly-created silence. Disturbed also Mr. Overseer Franke. He came to himself.

The gang heard the rustle as he turned on the gum-leaves where he had fallen; they heard him moan and his cry for a drink; they heard—and for answer looked at Mann.

And Mann made due reply.

* * * *

He walked up to the prostrate official and asked him did he know him—him, Mann. He put the question courteously—oh, so courteously—"May I have the pleasure of this valse?" was the style of it. And Franke nodded a "yes," and prayed for a drink.

"Cummings craved for a drink—and you gave him a bullet!" said Mann.

Did Franke respond to that retort? Not that Mann knew, for with that insight with which the gang, inspired by sudden liberty, had been endowed, the transports who had handled the sentries' muskets seized the weapons once more and rushed simultaneously to tender to Overseer Franke the cooling draught he had proffered Convict Cummings.

"Don't kill him, boys!" said Mann; "only wound him!" Then—

"Stay!" he continued. And motioning for help he erected the still half-dazed Overseer against a tree, and called for more cord. They bound him to the bole, but at Mann's order left the wretch's right hand free.

Free—for a second it was. Then Mann himself took it (as limp and nerveless as Cummings' own) and stretched it outwards by a piece of line, the other end of which was fastened to another tree. The cord was tautened, and thus the hand of the Overseer was between two trees.

Mann went to the camp fire-place and, lifting a charred bit of fuel, returned with it and inscribed a circle, and, within the circle, "a bull's-eye," on the palm of the suspended hand.

"There!" he exclaimed, as he threw away the charcoal. "There's a target. Fire away!"

The second shot riddled the hand, and the third smashed the wrist.

Then the leader stopped the musketry practice.

"That's enough for the present," he said. "We may want these bullets for living men. And this one is as good as dead!"

## VI.

Thereupon Mr. Franke—whose portrait may be seen in Government House, Sydney—realized vividly his fate; and banishing all weakness—even a tyrant may be strong when pleading for his life—cried out for mercy.

"Yes!" replied Mann, "the mercy you showed Cummings and myself and all of us!"

"Wot d'yer fight fer Cummin's fer?" moaned the Overseer. "He peached on yer!"

"Yes?" Mann could not restrain the note of curiosity in his voice.

"Yes, 'e did. 'E tol' me 'bout yer findin' the boat. An' I gave 'im two figs of chaw-stuff fur a-tellin' me!"

Mann turned, as though he would have spit upon the dead body. But his better self was not yet dead. He thought that, after all, the System had made Cummings a traitor—and to a meanly-endowed creature such as he was, two figs of tobacco in the hand were worth a dozen boats in the sedge.

"Where is the boat?" he demanded.

Between the groans and the tears his wounds were wringing from him, Overseer Franke tried to effect a bargain.

"Will yer give me my life if I tells yer, 'an 'ow yer can get orf?"

The gang waited breathlessly for the reply of their leader. When it came, after a moment's deliberation, it was "Yes!"

"On yer word as a gen'elman?" bartered the infamy.

A lump rose in Mann's throat. Still, he confirmed his previous answer.

"Yes!"

And the gang breathed freely. And so did Overseer Franke.

* * * *

Then the Overseer told Mann and the others how he and Cummings and a soldier had gone to the Bay, upon Cummings' betrayal of the boat, after dark one night, and had removed the boat to another part of the inlet. And Cummings had kept that new secret, because he was to have a fig weekly till the boat was sold. For, needless to say, being a representative Government official, though the boat was properly Government's, Mr. Franke intended selling it for his own profit.

"And how will we get off?" questioned Mann.

"Ter-day's Tuesday. Ter-morrer the coaly-town (New-castle) schooner's due, an' the night arter she comes in, skipper an' crew go 'shore. There ain't a soul on board. Thursday night—yer can go—an' I'll not report yer till Friday."

"'Ear, 'ear!" applauded the gang. But Mann remained silent.

"Yer won't break yer promise, Mister Mann?" pleaded the prisoner.

How the gang enjoyed the "Mister!" But Mann's face clouded the deeper.

"What promise?" he exclaimed, at last.

"Yer promise to give me my life."

"I made you no such promise!"

The gang shrank into stupid silence.

"Oh, yer a gen'elman—an' break yer word!" The misery of that expostulation from the Overseer!

"Blast you—yes! You cut the gentleman out of me with the cat. You die!"

And in the late-fallen dusk there mingled, curiously, the rapturous applause of the transports, and the alternate prayers and imprecations of the doomed officer.

## VII.

That was on the Tuesday evening. On the Wednesday the gang had a merry day. They found the boat in the morning, and stored her with provisions from the store-tent. And in the afternoon, they pegged-out Overseer Franke. On an ant-hill, on a wooded gully-rise, they fastened him down with tent-lines. His right hand was stretched out with tightened cord again—this time to a special peg. A track of sugar was made from the orifice of the ant-bed to the hole in the hand, in case the industrious little creatures should not otherwise perceive so appetizing a banquet as that shattered fragment of official humanity.

Before they pegged him out they flogged Overseer Franke.

After they pegged him out, they placed some victuals and water—just outside of his reach. It was Mann who suggested that last refinement. In fact, it was the gentleman whom the cat had robbed of his gentle-hood that devised the means for keeping the latter-day Tantalus busy while he lived. And it was not Mann's fault that he did not make Franke immortal.

* * * *

The soldiers threw in their lot with the convicts. Such a thing happened as a matter of course, when there was no superior officer of the System to say nay.

And on the Thursday they seized the schooner, and, after a successful trip, reached a South Sea island.

Sydney heard of them later—when the missionary, William Ellis, complained to the British authorities that they were playing havoc with his mission-field.

But Mann was not with them then. Mann, in fact, never left Port Jackson. He committed suicide just as the vessel was stealing out of the Heads in the midnight darkness of Thursday night. His last words were: "I've done all I can for you, coves! Good-bye!" And then he pulled the trigger.

He was privileged to receive an oration over his grave in the sea.

"Damn him! W'y didn't he drown hisself? That shot might be 'erd at South 'Ead Signal Stashun."

Absalom West found Franke's skeleton in 184-.

# PARSON FORD'S CONFESSIONAL

## I.

IT IS BEYOND question that Parson Ford's resolve to keep up the amount of his fee for performing marriages was responsible for the annoyance which visited him on the occasion of our story.

Eight pounds sterling was his fee. Parson Knopwood would do the work for three and take payment in currency; and it was generally the easiest thing for an expert bridegroom to relieve the old man of the money as he was returning home the same evening. When Parson Bob performed the ceremony, he invariably celebrated the event at the "Hole in the Wall," the favourite public-house, where his welcome was always warm and his chalk-score deep, and he would seldom proceed homewards to Cottage Green till the everlasting stars came out in their glory and flaunted their drunkenness in his shame-stricken eyes. At least that was what the cheery old chaplain used to say as he stumbled over Macquarie-street cobble-stones. "Wheresh O-rion? Shure I saw O-rion (hic) jush now!—'sh gone! Shtrange—th' bleshed (hic) stars dansh about so. Tell Gov-en-or!" And then perhaps the bridegroom, who had paid him about eleven o'clock that morning £3 in paper notes or dollars, would take his arm respectfully to help the reverend gentleman along—and himself to the £3. Sometimes, indeed, the bridegroom would not wait to tender his assistance. This was when the fee had been paid in forged notes, as several times happened.

Now, Parson Ford was a steady, pure, and sober man, and was not in the least inclined, when he became Principal Chaplain on Bobby Knopwood's official retirement, to view with aught but displeasure the irregularities which his predecessor had tolerated. He never got drunk; he knew the difference between forged currency notes and general currency by the "feel"—he could tell by the touch, so he said, any one tradesman's notes from every other man's—and he went home by dusk, or if detained after dark by pastoral duty, only after he had emptied the contents of his pockets and his fob into the keeping of a trusty acquaintance or officer of the garrison. Consequently, being possessed of these defects, he was not at this time beloved by the lower, or, indeed, any orders of society. Not till later did even the official classes come to believe in him. A community in which the heads liked to be drunk by mid-day, where matrimonial arrangements seldom were entered into except for the purpose of securing an additional grant of land or a right to other property, and where it was unsafe for a person to be out of doors after nightfall, because of his liability to be robbed, if not by unofficial criminals, by the men of the watch, was not prepared to take to its bosom at once a strong-minded cleric, whose pockets were never worth robbing, who would not drink to excess, whose only vice was snuffing, and who was so much of a Puritan that he had even admonished his Honour the Lieutenant-Governor for having a plurality of paramours. And when Parson Ford was so ill-advised as to raise the marriage-fee to eight pounds sterling, he placed the coping-stone to the edifice of his unpopular life. One and all, high and low, Lieutenant-Governor and lumberyard transport, who would not have married his "jomar" if the marriage-fee had been nothing, indignantly resented the step.

Why people who disdained marriage should have been thus irritated we do not positively know. We can only suppose it was by reason of that perverse trait of humanity which prompts it to value the thing which is beyond reach. If only a few couples could get married, nearly everybody would either wish to go through the ceremony or affect the desire to do so. Perhaps some such consideration had influenced Parson Ford in raising his fee. He assessed matrimony at a pecuniary value far beyond the reach of the mass of persons, and instantly they began to denounce the avarice and the injustice and the wickedness which prevented them from obtaining the blessing of the Church on their very irregular alliances. They forgot they had not rushed to the altar when the terms were only three pounds.

## II.

"I hear, Mr. Ford," remarked his Honour, as the parson paid him the usual morning visit exacted from all Hobart Town gentlemen who drew pay from the Colonial chest, "that you have caused it to be known that your marriage-fee is to be eight pounds in future?"

"That is my fixture, your Honour," replied the chaplain.

"But I do not know whether I can allow it! You know that the Governor in Sydney has fixed the fee at four pounds?"

"Guineas, your Honour," gently corrected the parson. "But that is within two described parishes. I am sure of my legal rights on the matter."

"But the moral effect, Mr. Chaplain—the effect! Have you sufficiently thought of that? A heavy fee is—ahem—an impediment to marriage!"

One great virtue had Parson Ford. He looked over a lot of things in persons of authority, but, when put on his mettle he never winced before a Governor, whether he was only a "Lieutenant," or whether he was the omnipotent "General." He faced his Honour now, and said distinctly, with an uncourtier-like acidity of tone: "Would it have proved so in your case, your Honour? If so, I'll reduce it!"

And his Honour took the unpleasant thrust pleasantly. His wine-reddened face was not unusually flushed as he responded: "Well, well, if you must have it so, you must, I s'pose, Mr. Ford. But don't you think you can make it currency, instead of sterling?"[1]

"With all respect, sir, I do not think I can. My object is to make the ceremony valued in the eyes of the people, and I conceive there is no better way of doing it than to attach an expense to its performance. You have seen, your Honour, that Mr. Knopwood's low charges did not encourage marriages. Now, we will see what my method will do."

"Very well, Mr. Ford, very well, have your own way. I think you are mistaken, but it's your lookout, and not mine. I'm not—h'm—my brother's keeper—of his morals, at all events. That's your duty."

And with this, his Honour bowed his reverence out, helped himself to a glass of Spanish wine from a bottle which, one of a dozen, had been presented to him by his former comrade-in-arms, John Macarthur, in Sydney—Capt'n John had bought it at a sale of certain prize booty in the year '5, and treasured it greatly—and set to work to devise a scheme by which to revenge himself upon the clergyman. Davey was not given to vindictiveness, but he dearly liked a jest, and when by the same stroke he could have both his joke and his revenge, he would have fallen below the level of his drunken, rollicking, immoral old self if

---

1    "Currency" and "Sterling."—The difference in value in Davey's time varied from 121/2 to 25 per cent.

he had refrained from applying it. He had all the qualities of a good Governor except dignity, firmness, purity, honour, sobriety, and magnanimity.

As the result of his reflections he outlined a plan which, in the bosom of his irregularly constituted family circle at Government House, was fairly elaborated that same night. It was necessary, you see, for him to use an intermediary in the business. He rather prided himself on his free-and-easy manners. Had he not made his début in the colony in his shirt-sleeves, excusing himself on the score of its being too hot to wear full regimentals? Had he not established the custom of drinking and smoking in court? Was it not he who had stopped the trial-gang on their way to the wharf, and treated each of the unfortunates to a drink of rum-punch and a churchwarden pipe at Half-Hanged Jack's beershop? Did he not accept kindly their thankful "God bless yer Honour!" and wish them in return a fair trial, and, if God and the Judge pleased, an easy death? And was it not, too, his identical old blackguard self who, instead of enclosing to Sydney with the depositions of evidence against a convicted forger, the forged note for threepence, put the note, and therefore the evidence, into the fire, with the remark that a throat that could give out "Tom Bowling" so well, was too good to be fitted with a throat necklace? As a matter of fact, "free and easy" was an absurdly weak term to apply to Lieutenant-Governor Davey's relaxed manners. Nevertheless, he felt it was "not quite the cheese"—the phrase is not ours but the Governor's—for him to place himself in direct communication with the principal in the plot he had contrived for the discomfiture of Parson Ford. "No, Julia," he said to the presiding madam of the week—his two "ladies" took week about in doing the honours of his private table (his legal family living quite apart)—"it won't be quite the cheese, my duck, for me to see the little dears at the Factory. One of you will have to do that for me."

"Oh," simpered madam—she was the identical pretty piece of frailty respecting whom Captain Colnett, of H.M.S.

Glatton, had quarrelled with Governor King[2], and the twelve years since the row had only matured her charms—"anythin' to please yer, dear Gov'nor—an' really, ye know, none of us leddies like Parson Sniff an' Snuff! Bobby's my 'dea of a parson. Ain't he yours, dear Gov'nor?"

"I'm with ye, madam, in everything, as ye know," replied the Governor—whose gallant speeches were not yet intermingled with hiccoughs. "Ah, old Bobby never interfered between me an' ye, did he, dear? But ye'll attend to the Factory, Ju, without fail before Monday evening? Ye know, 'twould never do for his Honour, the Gov., to be known in the business."

"Oh, lud, your Honour, how squeamish we're gettin' all at once," tittered the sorceress of the week; "why, ye'll be turnin' saint yourself soon an' 'll cry 'Fie!' an' blush when I do this."

And, bending forward, she pressed with her ruby lips the viceregal forehead. Madame Julia knew the ways of Government in early Van Demonian days. Also which side her bread was buttered. She was better off with Colonel Davey than with Captain Colnett, R.N. Immeasurably.[3]

## III.

What the official lights-o'-love achieved the sequel will show. The Governor did, however, make a specific contribution to the plot, but he kept the knowledge of it

---

2    Considering that, as a rule, Rusden, the historian, damns the cause he advocates, it is an unfortunate thing for Governor King's fame that Rusden defends his conduct in the Colnett case. King's action appears, however, eminently creditable to him, even in the light of the superior morality of this generation. Tested by contemporary canons, it reflected infinite honour upon him.

3    She boxed Colnett's ears. He retaliated.

from his Cleopatras. He chuckled mightily as he added his fragment of fuel to the flame which was to scorch Parson Ford. He penned the following—

"Private.

"Government House, THURSDAY.

"REVEREND SIR,—The words that passed between us on a delicate subject have afected me, and have not failed to impres me. As one means of helping to releeve me from his reverence's sensure it is likely that a warm discourse on the subject by which you will understand I mean the iregular connections which your reverence does not approve of, on Sunday coming, would strengthen my hands, for I have come to the conclusion that my honourable position does demand from me conduct which would not remain open to your Reverence's objection.

"Your Reverence's obedient servant.

"(Sd.) THOMAS DAVEY, Lieutt.-Gov.

"To the REVEREND THEOPHILUS FORD, at St. Davids Parsonage."

Like the illustrious Wellington, Colonel Davey was weak in orthography and in grammar, but the Rev. Mr. Ford was too well acquainted with official eccentricities of the kind to dwell upon those features of the document. What impressed him was the possibility it held out of a reform in popular morals. And he resolved to accept the hint, "and to give it 'em warm."

It was on the succeeding Sunday that he rose to the occasion. It was the first Sunday in the month, consequently a muster-Sunday, and pretty well everybody in Hobart Town was crowded into the church or within its precincts. A muster-Sunday for the bond or ticket-of-leave classes was, of course, compulsory, and those who were emancipated or "free" by "servitude" were almost as regular in attendance, for, besides the fun of the thing, there was the gratification of witnessing the subjection of others to a procedure once so galling to themselves. Then the few people who "came free" and the "garrison ladies" came also to witness the spectacle. It was so amusing, you will understand, to note the distress of some poor "ticket-of-leave," as, from some more or less real peccadillo, his "ticket" was withdrawn, perhaps a little home or business sacrificed, and he himself re-consigned to the purgatory of the lumber-yard or the hell of the road-gang. In an epoch when popular entertainments were rare, the Sunday muster was highly valued by all except those who were compelled to attend it.

On this Sunday the muster was before Church. The Muster-Master, as though in anticipation of the coming storm, was righteously indignant in the cases of a couple of dissolute fellows, who, having permission to marry, had gone no nearer the altar than the broomstick. They pleaded Parson Ford's increased fee, but 'twas no use. Their tickets were withdrawn, and they were ordered to present themselves before the Police Magistrate in the morning for sentence.

This incident had so agreeably entertained the "free" people, "irregularly-attached" or not, that they would have been prepared to enjoy even a less thrilling sermon than that Mr. Ford preached to them. Therefore, when he gave out his text from Ecclesiastes vii. and 26th—

"And I find more bitter than death the woman whose heart is snares and nets, and her hands as bonds; whoso pleaseth God shall escape from her; but the sinner shall be taken by her"—they settled down with an unusual zest. They knew by instinct something interesting was coming.

Illustrating his theme by pretty well every Scriptural passage having the remotest relation to it, the preacher denounced the iniquity of "irregular connections." Then, by way of contrast, he painted the virtues of the typical British home, drew tears from many eyes by a description of the conjugal felicity which prevailed in the palace of the Sovereign—he was discreetly silent as to the Regent—and, having insinuated a refined advertisement of his reasons for raising the marriage-fee—"that which costs nothing or next to nothing," he said, "is never valued,"—he concluded with a most touching peroration. With eyes alternately directed to the roof and upon the viceregal pew, he thanked Heaven that he had it from the best, he might say the very best, authority that henceforth the Local Representative of that pure and pious Personage whose virtues added lustre to the Crown of England, contemplated reflecting in his person and establishment the example of his Gracious Sovereign. With so striking an exemplar on the spot, he reminded his hearers that there would be no excuse for their permitting their irregular unions to remain unblessed by the Church and unsanctioned by the Law.

The effect was tremendous. New South Wales and Van Demonia in the early days had, of course, no opportunity of showing how a C—could throw an aristocratic splendour over the gallows, or how a H—could transform by grace of manner a niggardliness of expenditure into a refined economy; but yet they possessed, all things considered, as devoted a regard for the representative of the throne as we can claim to-day. The eye of the congregation seemed fixed upon the broad shoulders of the Lieutenant-Governor as he sat a few yards away from the pulpit. A kindly shadow from a pillar prevented, however, all save those in the immediate vicinity observing that the viceregal form shook as though with suppressed emotion. Frequent applications of a yellow handkerchief to his eyes further testified to the impression the sermon had made upon him. Was the Colonel really going to reform? Was he smitten with sorrow for the past, and moved by passionate desire for better things in the future? It seemed so, indeed, and one portly merchant—a conditional pardon man from Sydney-side—reflected ruefully that, eight pounds or no eight pounds, he'd be obliged to follow the Governor's example, if the great man really meant to abandon his harem.

But the merchant and those who noticed his Honour's emotion need not have been afraid. True, he did wipe tears from his eyes, but—it pains us to say it—they were of mirth. The Colonel of Marines was all the time wondering to himself how Jess and Ju were taking the sermon. He had never gone so far as to instal them in the viceregal pew—the ladies of his family proper would have drawn the line at that—but he knew they were in church. He'd have given a day's pay in sterling money, and not in those rascally rupees which were worth no more than eighty per cent of their nominal value, to have been able to look round and wink at the sweet creatures. But that he dare not do: it would have spoilt the sport, for did he catch their eyes in return he would to a certainty burst into laughter. Accordingly, he had to wait till afternoon.

## IV.

The Parson dined with his Excellency, and received the latter's great compliments for the unstinted and fervid morality of the discourse. The Colonel now coincided with Mr. Ford as to the wisdom of the increased fee, and expressed a hope that not many months would elapse before it would be—er—as difficult to find an irregularly-attached couple in Hobart Town as a needle in the proverbial truss of hay! And the joy which is generated by the consciousness that a good work is meeting with the applause of the high and mighty settled upon Parson Ford's soul as he bade his Honour good-bye, and betook himself to the church for afternoon service. It was a joy undimmed by the least doubt as to the sincerity of the Governor's conversion.

After second service he was asked to tea at the table of one of the two married ladies of the garrison. The garrison was, matrimonially considered, very badly organized indeed. With the exception of two, the ladies who looked after the comfort of the officers, drawing married men's lodging and fuel allowances, however frequently they quarrelled among themselves, had one characteristic in common. They possessed no certificate of marriage—at least, they owned no certificates that sanctified their present relationships. And now, in consequence of Parson Ford's sermon, the virtuous and duly married two were more determined than ever to look down upon their unlicensed sisters of the quarters. Accordingly, as a preliminary, they mutually arranged an applausive tribute to that dear man, the clergyman, who at last had put his foot resolutely down "on the shocking, the really too shocking, state of things that prevailed in the town, and particularly within our brother officers' quarters, you know, dear." Mrs. Lieutenant Bobbin had wished to do the honours, and invited Mrs. Captain D'Ewes, her sister in matrimonial distinction, to take tea with her and the dear parson, but Mrs. Captain D'Ewes, by virtue of her husband's rank, pressed for the privilege of first entertainment, which Mrs. Bobbin at once effusively and affectionately conceded. And so at half-past five o'clock the Rev. Theophilus found himself seated at a table with Mrs. D'Ewes and Captain D'Ewes, and Mrs. Bobbin and her Lieutenant. It may be remarked, by the way, that the Lieutenant's experience of wedded life was rather regarded in the town as strong evidence of the advantages of single blessedness.

Mr. Ford having said grace (the circumstance from its unusual nature deserves to be chronicled), and accepted some of the hospitalities of the table, his hostess lost no time in expressing her congratulations on his proper, very proper, course that day. And did he really think his Honour would alter the disgraceful, very disgraceful, condition of Government House society?

"I am, ma'am, firmly convinced in my own mind he really contemplates a change of conduct," affirmed the Parson.

"Then—then—those women—Oh, really, Mr. Ford, I blush for my sex to think such things are possible! And will his Honour at once dismiss them to the Factory?" Thus spoke the virtuous Bobbin dame.

"I am quite of opinion that he will do so. In fact, I may tell you—in confidence, ladies, of course—that I believe they have already been returned there!"

"No!" exclaimed both ladies in a breath.

"Indeed, I think so. As I was taking off my surplice in the vestry, the matron of the Factory came in and said that the Governor's ladies—you know, ma'am, that the way those low-class women will speak of these disgraces to their sex—"

"Yes, indeed!" indignantly said Mrs. D'Ewes, "this misuse of words ought to be put down! And the matron said?"

"That those sinful women had been driven out to the Factory. The matron, bringing in the rest of the Protestant women for afternoon service as usual, met them half-way. They looked in a fine fluster—to use Mrs. Chubb's words— just as though the consequences of their sin had at last fallen upon them."

"Ah!" said Mrs. D'Ewes, "there comes an end to all wrong-doing sooner or later."

"Why," said the Lieutenant, "didn't the matron stop and ask them why they were going out?"

"Oh, Lieutenant, you don't know what a trouble 'tis to that poor woman to get those drabs of Factory girls to church!—she could not attend to anything else! She has to bring them in two batches—morning and afternoon—for it would take her whole staff to march the lot in together, and she must, of course, leave two or three wards-women behind to look after the sick ones."

"We'd always tell off a corporal's guard to help her," said Captain D'Ewes, flippantly. "Our men would not object to guard-duty there. 'Guardians of beauty, if not of virtue,' and so on, eh, Bobbin?"

Bobbin, with his spouse's eye upon him, dare not acquiesce verbally, but in his heart he approved of his comrade's sentiment. Of course, their respective wives were not aware that among the Lotharios of the camp, D'Ewes and Bobbin were included, even though they were married. Had he wished to reply, however, he would not have found it possible to do so, for Mrs. D'Ewes sharply remonstrated with her husband.

"I think, Captain," she said, "that you should keep your

wit for the low associates of the barrack-room. Remember, a clergyman is present, if you have no respect for ladies. And now, dear Mr. Ford, I should like so much to know whether those—those creatures are really at the Factory! You, I suppose, will find out in due course?"

"Oh, to-morrow, ma'am, is my usual Factory day— Monday succeeding Muster-Sunday, y' know!"

"Oh, yes," broke in that ribald D'Ewes, "tomorrow's your confessional day, is it, Mr. Ford?"

"My what—sir?" returned the astonished Parson, who was nothing, if he was not a sturdy Evangelical.

"That, I believe, sir, is the term given in the town to your—ah—method of interrogating those frisky young madams at the Factory, of whom you're so fond."

"Sir!" exclaimed the insulted Parson, rising.

"D'Ewes!" appealed his better-half.

"Captain D'Ewes!" ejaculated the horrified Mrs. Bobbin, whose husband simply chuckled to himself under cover of the storm.

And though D'Ewes apologized, and handsomely withdrew the imputation, which, he averred, was merely a jocular nothing, the Parson's sense of injury was not appeased until both Mrs. D'Ewes and Mrs. Bobbin had consented to accompany him to the Factory on the morrow. "Then, ladies, I beg you'll interrogate every woman for yourselves. Ask them what questions you like as to my treatment of them, and see if I've ever acted in a manner unbefitting my sacred office!"

As a simple fact, Parson Ford could not have played more nicely into his adversaries' hands than when he extended that invitation. Davey's plan had been merely to suggest a very naughty idea to the frail fair ones in Mrs. Chubb's charge, and to trust to chance for the result finding its way to the knowledge of the townspeople. But here Ford himself had provided the means for his own discomfiture.

## V.

On the Monday afternoon, the Rev. Theophilus, accompanied by Mesdames D'Ewes and Bobbin, was respectfully welcomed by Mrs. Chubb. As the matron made her final curtsey, she said—

"Twelve new ones, your Rev'runce!"

"All—ahem—er—delicate?"

Mrs. Chubb simpered and looked down. "Yes, sir!" she said.

"Now, ladies," and Mr. Ford turned to the garrison ladies, "of course you don't understand what Mrs. Chubb means?"

"No—not exactly, Mr. Ford," said Mrs. D'Ewes.

"Well, I must tell you, ma'am. You know, of course, why so many girls are sent back to the Factory from service?"

Mrs. Bobbin blushed. Mrs. D'Ewes didn't, but replied "Yes."

"Well, in the interests, first of morality, and then of the finances of the colony, I'm determined to put a stop to that sort of thing, ladies!"

"Quite right, I'm sure," said Mrs. D'Ewes.

"Quite right, sir," echoed Mrs. Bobbin.

"Now, there's only one way, and that is to punish the fathers of the children. But to reach the fathers you must know their names."

"Of course, Mr. Ford!" said both ladies together.

"That is why, then, I have what the Captain very improperly called my confessional, Mrs. D'Ewes. I interrogate each girl separately as to the paternity of her child. Now, to-day, I will ask you ladies to pursue my inquiries for me. Have you any objection, ladies? Then you can tell the Captain the nature of my method."

"No objection at all," chorused the gentle beings.

"Then, as there are twelve to be examined, may I suggest you take six, Mrs. D'Ewes, and you the other six, Mrs. Bobbin, and I'll simply look on!"

The twelve girls—they were nearly all on the youthful

side of womanhood—were ranged in a row, each standing by the foot of her pallet. Some were quivering with suppressed shame—or laughter. Others were biting their lips. But all were silent till the interrogation began.

Humming a hymn, Parson Ford walked up and down. His back was to the line of women, and consequently he did not see the startled looks which were bestowed upon him and then upon each other by the two ladies. By the time, however, he turned in his walk, each interrogator had examined her second girl, and as she obtained a reply, she glanced so strangely at the clergyman that he could not help but notice her manner. He put the singularity of the look down, however, to some surprising revelation. "Revelations" under the like circumstances were so common, that they had long since ceased to be surprising to him.

As Mrs. Bobbin interrogated her third girl, Mrs. D'Ewes finished the examination of her fourth. They exchanged a look of horror—then moving simultaneously into the centre of the room, they exclaimed together—

"Oh, Mr. Ford! You wretch!" called Mrs. D'Ewes.

"Mr. Ford, you're a hypocritical villain!" cried Mrs. Bobbin, and she hysterically searched for her handkerchief.

"Ladies!" exclaimed Parson Ford, not believing his ears.

"Yes, sir, I'm glad I came today to unmask a scoundrel! Each of these four girls says you are the father of her child!" cried Mrs. D'Ewes.

"Madam!"

"And—oh—infamous!—these three girls all say—they— owe—their—ruin to you!" gasped Mrs. Bobbin, in tears.

"And I say the same!" said a girl as yet uninterrogated.

"He's the father of my child too!" said another.

"And of ours!" cried the rest in chorus.

Under this terrible avalanche of accusation Parson Ford was dumb!

* * * *

Governor Davey and his "leddies" had calculated only on surprising Parson Ford himself—by bribing the girls with a ticket-of-leave apiece to allege that he, the clergyman, was responsible for her presence in the lying—in ward of the Factory. They had not contemplated so astonishing a success for their little plot, as was achieved through Ford's invitation to the garrison ladies.

Not for many years was Ford allowed to forget this episode. Governor Arthur, fifteen years after wards, referred, at a birthday dinner, to Parson Ford as one of the "fathers of the colony," and was immensely surprised at the uproarious laughter his compliment elicited from all colonists present—save Ford.

# MAROONED ON THE GRUMMET

## I.

RAIN IN TORRENTS, rain in sheets—and two hundred convicts, out in the storm, and in "Church." Huddled together, with heads bent on their breasts so that their faces at least shall be protected from the deluge, they stand in the main barrack-yard as they have stood for 30 minutes past, and will continue to stand for another 120 unless Heaven or its Sarah Island representative inclines to mercy. And the cutting, salt rain dashes upon them and soaks them through and through and leaves never a dry stitch among the lot, as they stand in "Church."

"Grand rain," remarks Captain Bankes, Commandant, as he chalks his cue in the billiard-room thrown out (at His Majesty's expense) from the gable-end of Officers' Quarters.

"Yes," rejoins Lieutenant Darrell, his opponent, as he asks Forger Joe, the marker, for the score and prepares for his shot; "grand rain—'ll do a lot of good. It'll bring up that young wheat in No. Nine paddock splendidly." (He cannons.) "If we get a small harvest on that experimental crop I'd suggest—damn, what d'ye mean, pris'ner, coming in like that?' (He has missed his stroke.) "I've a good mind to give you twenty, sir, interfering with my stroke!"

The intruding convict-servant salutes and makes humble and trembling reply: "I knocked, sir, I did. Thought you told me to come in, sir. I came to tell you, sir, as Church was waitin'."

"Oh, damn Church, and I don't believe you, pris'ner. You didn't knock, and if you tell me so again I'll give you fifty for lying. Now, did you knock?"

The poor half-witted fool instantly impales himself upon the dilemma so ingeniously offered him by Lieutenant Darrell.

"No, sir—I didn't knock."

"Then why did you say you did! You are a liar, then, are you? Come up for punishment to-morrow morning and evening—a 'dozen' each time. D'ye hear?"

The convict-servant retires, knowing he is wronged, and yet understanding, too, that he has blundered some how. Lieutenant Darrell, whose turn it is for Muster and Church duty, throws down his cue grumbingly, and dons his belts. Captain Bankes, glancing through the window, resolves that he won't do inspection-rounds to-day. The grand rain shall not fall to-day upon the Just. It must content itself with the Unjust.

"I won't inspect this morning, Darrell. Give 'em short Church and half the Regulations, and let 'Complaints' stand over. Come back quickly and we'll finish this game before lunch. What's the score, marker?"

"Forty—thirty-eight, sir," respectfully answers Forger Joe. "And, beg pardon; Mr. Darrell, but Birch did knock, sir. I heard him."

"What's that? What right have you to interfere? Out to muster, my man, at once! We don't own any favourites here, and don't permit shirking by the billiard room fire when Church-parade's on."

And out in the storm of rain and sleet, from his snuggery in the billiard-room, went Forger Joe. Though the outer world was bleak and damp, nevertheless Forger Joe should not have come to the resolution which he then and there did. If a man interferes on behalf of truth and justice, he should not be surprised at receiving the reward customarily granted by society for such conduct. Those who bemoan the thorns of the martyr's crown should not commit the deeds which win for them a place in the martyrology. And Forger Joe, though he did not regret that he had made his interjection in the interest of billet servant Birch, lamented in his heart the loss of the warm shelter in which he had expected to pass the Sunday.

For, of course, you will have understood by this time that this particular day was Sunday. Intensely solicitous as the System was for the religious and moral development of its Children, it stands to reason that it could not spare time for prayers except on Sundays. And so devoted to duty were Messrs. Bankes and Darrell that by the time they got through their week-day round of supervision and chastisement, they were, as a rule, too weary even for billiards. Thus their combats with the cue were generally reserved for the Sabbath Day.

Before muster and after lunch on Sundays, the click click of the balls was wont to sound merrily from the square-roofed annexe to the barracks, and Forger Joe had been greatly envied by his brother-felons. The opportunity of witnessing pretty play between the superior officers of the Settlement was an inestimable privilege, to say nothing of the cigar-ends that Captain Bankes—not Darrell, you may be sure!—was so forgetful about; or of the circumstance that the marker was "free of muster." Not that he was exempted by regulation. That could hardly be, inasmuch as billiard-tables and markers were unknown to the King's Regulations. He was permitted to absent himself by grace of the Commandant or the Lieutenant. Which quality generally superseded the Regulations when it was a matter of meeting the officer's convenience.

No, Forger Joe did not feel pleased when, by the fiat of that Angel of Justice, Darrell, he was driven from the Paradise of the billiard-room to the outer world where there was gnashing of teeth and shaking of chilled limbs. And the devil coiled himself down into Joe's breast, and doubtless laughed gaily.

The rheumatic tremors which had seized the majority of the "congregation" in "Church" momentarily gave place to a thrill of genuine excitement as they saw Joe emerge from the billiard-room and slouch over the soddened gravel to join them.

"What's up?" went round in eager whispers. "Joe's in for it!" And a score or two wretches instantly made up their minds to fill the markership, vice Joe, dis missed, if they could.

## II.

The muster began. Under the eaves of the narrow verandah stood a row of soldiers. Behind these the mustering Overseer, other subordinate officials, and that great man, Lieutenant Darrell. Out in the rain, the convicts.

The rain plashed and splashed as the voices rang out in call and answer. By number, and name, and ship, was each convict called, and a simple "Here!" from the man himself, when the man was present, constituted the response. When the man was not present, if his where abouts were known, a warder answered for him. If they were unknown, then the presumption was that he had escaped, and "Absconded" would be pencilled against his name.

The absent prisoner might still be within Settlement boundaries; he might be away on some officer's message, the answering warder being in ignorance of the fact; he might actually be an absconder; but whatever was the occasion of his absence it would be all one in the result. Down would go "Absconded" opposite his name.

Now at this period, and for years after, for that word to be placed over or against one's name was to be literally under sentence of death.

The muster continued somewhat in this way:

"Bond, John, 440. *Asia?*"— "Here!"

"Fulbert, Eric, 12,930, *Marquis of Hastings?*"—"Billet" (from the warder).

"Gordon, Charles, 17,211, *Pestonjee Bomanjee?*"—"Gaol—condemned cell."

"Irvine, William, 163, *Ocean?*"—" Gaol—Hospital." (Irvine was suffering a recovery from a flogging).

"Jones, Robert, 9,439, *Sussex?*"—" Refractory cell, Grummet Island."

"Judson, Joseph, 11,889, *Royal Sovereign?*"—No answer. Only a movement of heads.

"Call him again," shouted Darrell. And once more, overbearing the rush and dash of the incessant rain. Joseph Judson's name was called.

Again there was no answer. Again there was no sound except the falling rain and the rustle of heads craning and moving sideways to catch a glimpse of Forger Joe.

"Call him the third time," said Darrell, "and if he fail to answer, report him as absconded."

For the third time, in a still higher key, the Overseer uttered: "Judson, Joseph, 11,889, *Royal Sovereign?*" and still Joseph Judson, alias " Forger Joe," was mute. Unaccountably so! One would think Joe really desired to entrust himself to the tender mercies and polite ministrations[1] of Brother

---

1  This is not sarcasm. Dogherty, or Dougherty—the former spelling follows the Gazette, the latter his death-warrant—was the most gentlemanly of the many functionaries who, in the Australian provinces, have, politely invited their fellow creatures to step out and be hanged. One man round whose neck Dougherty had just knotted the rope informed (after his reprieve on the scaffold) the late excellent T. J. Crouch, of Hobart, that "a lady couldn't have done it nicer," and this person's judgment should be regarded as decisive, as on two former occasions he had been the recipient of delicate attentions from an executioner. It is pleasing to know that first-hand testimony corroborates the statement of two

Dougherty, the Hobart Town hangman.

"Joseph Judson, absconded," cried the Overseer, and turning to Lieutenant Darrell, he continued:" I report Joseph Judson, No. 11,889, ship *Royal Sovereign*, as absconded, sir. Usual instructions?"

"Usual instructions. Inform the guards. If the absconder is found within the bounds, challenge once, and in default of immediate surrender, fire. If without the bounds, fire."

"And then challenge," said a voice in the felon-throng, "Scarborough fashion!"[2]

"Who said that?" repeated Darrell. For reply, the throng opened, and closed again, and Forger Joe, who had taken his place on the right wing, was now standing in the centre of the crowd.

Darrell stepped into the front—out into the heavily beating rain. His face bore the look which nearly every convict dreaded—the look of irresponsible power mad for the assertion of its rights and lustful of revenge; such a look as John Price used to wear in the 'Forties and 'Fifties—as he wore the day he was killed at Williamstown Pier.

"Who said that?" Darrell asked again. And then a

---

distinguished historians, the Reverend John West and Mr. James Bonwick, respecting this useful and genial official. "There was no amateur gaiety in his (Dougherty's) manner," writes Mr. West; "no harshness in his speech." And Mr. Bonwick says: "It was his trade to give the lash and tie the last knot; but he did the one with gentleness and the other with decent solemnity. . . . He sought to drown the remembrance of his professional duties in the cup of intoxication: the day following an execution he always spent in a drunken stupor. Disgusted with his trade, he contemplated retirement from public life; *but the multiplicity of applications for his position restored his self-respect, and reconciled him to the degradation of his office*." The italics are the present writer's, not Mr. Bonwick's. Dougherty did eventually drop out of public life—suddenly.

2   "Scarborough fashion"—First knock a man down, then bid him stand.

prisoner—one of the aspirants for Judson's billet—whimpered: "Forger Joe, sir."

"Forger Joe!"—the Lieutenant admirably simulated a start of surprise. "Forger Joe—Joseph Judson here? Joseph Judson, the absconder? Ah, I see him!" With that, he drove himself, wedge-like, into the massed convicts, and, seizing Joe by the collar of his coat, pulled him from their midst to the shelter of the ranged muskets. So rapid was the action—it seemed as though it had taken place between the falling of one rain-drop and of another— that the prisoners did not realise its happening till they saw Joe lying in the puddles by the soldiers' feet.

"It was you, was it, Marker Joe!" said the officer. "You found your voice, then, did you? You couldn't answer the muster-call, though! Don't you know, you fool, what your silence means? Don't you know you're an absconder—condemned to death! That's what you've got for sulking, my man!"

Forger Joe tried to rise. He was prostrate in a couple of inches of water, and the overflow from the eaves fell copiously upon him. At a signal from Lieutenant Darrell a couple of guards thrust him back with the butts of their muskets.

"Keep him down!" ordered Darrell; "bayonets to the ground, and, Overseer, proceed!"

They finished the calling-over, Convict Judson cooling his temper the while in the puddles and underneath the steel-points.

"Any complaints?" called the Overseer. A dozen hands were thrust forth.

"Complaints must wait till next week," said Darrell. Then they had prayers.

For, you will remember, this little episode occurred in "Church."

### III.

Half-an-hour later Lieutenant Darrell reported to Captain Bankes, who was seated by the billiard-room fire reading from a twelve-month-old copy of the LONDON MAGA-ZINE.

"Ah, Darrell, back?" "Y'sir. Report, sir—."

"Oh, hang report. Just listen here. It's a letter from that fellow, Elia, to Judge Field. Delightfully rich! Wonder how the 'Mancipists 'll like it!" And Captain Bankes, who was careful to keep up his reading in the interval of flogging prisoners, and who prided him self equally upon his literary taste and his capacity for making the System pay, extracted the plums from Charles Lamb's communication to Barron Field.

*I cannot imagine to myself whereabout you are. Sometimes you seem to be in the Hades of Thieves. I see Diogenes among you with his perpetual fruitless lantern. What must you be willing by this time to give for the sight of an honest man! You must almost have forgotten how we look—*

"That's deuced insulting to the Staff," said Darrell. "That damned scribbler forgets there are English gentlemen holding official positions in the colonies."

Bankes went on:

*And tell me what your Sydneyites do? Are they th**v*ng all day long? Merciful Heaven! what property can stand against such a depredation! . . . Is there much difference to see between the son of a th**f, and the grandson? or where does the taint stop?*

"Splendid!" exclaimed the Commandant. The Lieutenant grinned a "Ha! Ha! That shot'll go home!"

"That's more than, the 'Mancipists can do, then," chuckled the Superior as he ended his quotations:

*Do you bleach in three or four generations? Do you grow your own hemp? What is your staple trade, exclusive of the national profession, I mean? Your locksmiths, I take it, are some of your great capitalists.*

"'Gad!" exclaimed Bankes, throwing the periodical down and leaning back in his chair to laugh more at ease. "That'll do for Field in the old town. He won't write many more 'Botany Bay Flowers' there, I should say!"

"But that's not half a bad hint about the hemp, sir," suggested Lieutenant Darrell, in all seriousness. "And I don't see why we shouldn't make a trial of it here. I feel sure we'll never succeed with grain, and we really ought to cultivate more ground. Now, there'll always be a big demand for hemp in the colonies."[3]

"I'll think of it," replied Bankes, and, to anticipate a little, we may say that in the following year No. 9 paddock was sown with hemp. The crop, however, fortunately for Charles Lamb's fame, was a failure. Nature did a lot to accommodate the System. Tommy Townshend, afterwards Lord Sydney, was quite convinced there was "a Divine leading" in the discovery of the Australias, just when Howard had kicked up such a row over the condition of British prisoners; and, in the words of Colonel Sorell, "Providence must have designed Macquarie Harbour for a prison." Governor Arthur said much the same things respecting Tasman's Peninsula generally and Port Arthur in particular; and John Price and J. S. Hampton were equally as emphatic in their approval of the wisdom which had so completely isolated

---

3    This conversation and its sequel are historic. Noble Mr. Schofield, Wesleyan missionary to Macquarie Harbour, when at Hell's Gates, received a parcel of books, papers, &c., from the Wesleyan Missionary Society's offices, London, some of the wrappers of which consisted of several loose sheets of the LONDON MAGAZINE for 1822-3. On one of those sheets Mr. Schofield read ELIA'S "Distant Correspondents." The "B.F." of that famous essay, and of the delightful "Muckery End, in Hertfordshire," was Barron Field, of Sydney, the hanging judge who was known to have completed a poetic couplet with the same dip of ink with which he had just written, "Let him be hanged" against a criminal's name.

Norfolk Island. Nature (in the opinion of the System) was partial to it, and yet, singular to state, she drew the line at hemp. To this day the Australias are obliged to import their hangmen's ropes.

Commandant Bankes, having thus intimated that he would keep an eye on the desirability of meeting the System's requirements, asked for the Report.

The Report was the document which reflected the "strength" of the Settlement and the disposition of the prisoners and guards.

When he came to the column headed "Absconded since last report," he was surprised into "Hello! Forger Joe bolted! The beggar lost no time. I s'pose that's because you ordered him to muster."

"Look at next column, please, sir," said Darrell complacently. For, of course, Darrell, being a very exact bookkeeper and a model of method, had also entered Joe's name in the "absconders recaptured since last report" column.

"Ah! That's good! You lost no time, either. Now, what shall we do with him? Of course, it's death."

"Yes, it's death. I've put him in the Condemned Cell."

"So I see," the Commandant replied, for he had noticed that the "Condemned Cells" column had been increased by one. The total was now seven; yesterday it was only six.

"Those cells are getting crowded, sir," remarked Darrell. "Shall we hand him over to Skeleton Johnny[4] here, or wait for the schooner and send him to Dougherty? She won't be down for a month yet."

"H'm! Ah! Don't know, I'm sure. You see, Darrell, it doesn't do to hang too many here. An odd one now and then doesn't matter when the *Cyprus* is away and the gaol's full, or even half-a-dozen in an emergency, but we gave Johnny two last month, y'know. No; I don't think we'll hang our

---

4    "Skeleton Johnny"—"Jack Ketch," or the hangman. "To give him to Johnny" was to hand a man over to the hangman.

marker this time. Suppose we maroon him? Three months at the Grummet 'll be a change from his billet here."

"Just as you please, sir." And in this solemn manner, as suggestive of the majesty of law as of the incorruptibility of justice, was the fate of Convict Joseph Judson, alias Forger Joe, No. 11,889, per *Royal Sovereign*, decided.

## IV.

It pains us to have to record that the event was calculated to give the lie to Shakespeare. The Commandant's deed of mercy doubtless blessed the doer, but it certainly did not bless the receiver. The dew of Heaven never fell upon a rock more obdurate than the heart of Forger Joe. He proved himself distinctly insensible to Captain Bankes' magnanimity in reprieving him.

When the constables came on the Monday morning to remove Joe to the boat which was to bear him to the Grummet Rock, the islet in the Harbour where the Administration was wont to lodge "refractories," and informed him of his destination, he stormed and raged. It was just like that —— card Darrell that it was, to revenge himself in that mean way. What the devil did they think he'd shut his mouth for at Muster if it wasn't to be sent to Hobart Town as an absconder under sentence of death? He was tired of this hole, he was, and wanted a change. Bankes and Darrell were afraid of his letting a little light on their proceedings, and that's why they objected to his getting a change to the city. They didn't want the Hobart Town people to know about their billiard room and their women. And more impotent rigmarole to the same effect.

Speech of this kind was not only impolitic, but absurd and wicked. Impolitic, because an intelligent man like Forger Joe should have reflected that Messrs. Bankes and Darrell's administrative proceedings would be certain to meet with approval from the Authorities, and that being so, the two officers need not care the snap of a finger for the trumpery public opinion of the capital. Absurd, because the billiard-table had been charged by the military chest to the Settlement not as a billiard-table, but as a comprehensive assortment of commissariat stores, which included boots and shirts, yellow-and-black suits, leg-irons, handcuffs and basils, Sydney meal and West India rum. (English gentleman on the Staff were given to little dodges of this sort). And wicked, because though Messrs. Bankes and Darrell's liaisons with the female transports were unblessed by the Church, they had nevertheless been favoured with the sanction and example of Governor Sorell.

He was landed on the Grummet at midday—fettered and manacled. The boat, however, carried his handcuffs back to Sarah Island. The stock of "darbies" was rather low, but of chains the Establishment had a very ample supply. It would not matter very much if he did throw his leg-irons into the sea.

With the body of Forger Joe the boat-constable deposited on the rock the material nourishment for its sustenance during the period of the sentence. As follows:

1 bag maize-meal. 1 bag salt. 1 keg of water. 1 blanket. 1 pannikin. 1 Bible.

The bag of meal weighed 69lbs.; that of salt, 11½lbs.: the keg's contents measured 12 gallons. These quantities were to keep the life in Convict Judson for the period of 92 days for which he was to be marooned, and were computed according to the gaol-ration scale of 12ozs. meal, 2ozs. salt, and one pint water daily. You will observe, if you take the trouble to check the calculation of the Settlement commissariat-clerk, that he was liberal in the matter of water. Water at the Settlement cost nothing, or less than nothing, to procure: only the groans and sighs of the whipped cask-carriers; hence the System could afford to be liberal. It was not quite so generous with respect to the meal and the salt, inasmuch as it weighed the "bag in," and the convict was therefore deprived of an equivalent to one day's ration. Which the System, in its peculiarly playful fashion, did not think a point worth consideration. Supposing a prisoner did go for a day without food—if meal and cold water mixed could be termed food—it was only a fast, and fasting was good for the soul; and that the System did not neglect the maroon's soul is proved by "1 Bible." If, on the other hand, he objected to fast, he was at liberty to eat the bag. But then the System would flog him for destroying Government property.

There was one omission from the list of stores. Every convict was entitled to one ounce of soap daily, and there should have been issued to Joe 5¾lbs. of the filthy compound known as "ration soap." But the Commissariat clerk didn't see what Joe would want with soap on the marooning rock, so, to prevent waste, he did not issue it to the Forger. In absence of mind, however, he credited himself with its delivery to the convict. Thereby he pocketed two-pence ha'penny. Commissariat-clerks often suffered in that way.

Furnished with his supplies, Forger Joe waded through the surf and was welcomed by his fellow-maroon, Robert Jones, No. 9,439, per *Sussex*.

"Hello, Joe! old boy, what brought yer 'ere'" "The boat," answered Joe, grumpily.

"So I see. But don't yer think as yer'd better be perlite, Joe? Yer out o' favour with the Com'dant, or yer 'udn't be 'ere, so yer needn't be toffish, Joe."

The new-arrival failing to reply, the affable Jones continued: "We've ter be mates, Joe, for 'nother three months at least—'ow long'r yer fur?"

Joe seated himself on his meal-bag, and, seizing a loose piece of rock, began to "oval" his chains. Mr. Jones' argument was not without force. As they had to be mates, their relations would not be worse for a display of cordiality on his part, so, thawing, he told Jones of the circumstances leading to his marooning.

" Ah! I thought they 'udn't give yer less'n quarter quid.

An' now, matie, I'll do th' onners."

With the graciousness of a well-mannered host, Jones showed Joe over the rock—first assisting to free Joe's feet from his chains. Not a very difficult task when there was ample rock about.

"'Ere's yer quarters, Joe," he said, pointing to a wave worn recess a couple of feet above high-water-mark. " Yer won' be so bad, 'cepting w'en the sou'-wester's on. Then the sea's over ev'ry d—inch o' th' rock. Yer get a 'eap o' sand up, wrap yer toes in yer jacket, an' yer body in th' blankut, an' smuggle down into the sand, an' there yer are as right as tuppence. An' yer kin sleep as long's yer like. There's no mornin' bell. Leastways, as long's the waves 'ull let yer, and there's no sou'-wester more'n three or four times a-week. No mornin' bell, Joe, an', wot's better, Joe, no silunse bell either. Sumtimes, though, w'en the winds off-shore, an' I'm tucked up in the cave, I jist ketch the sound o' the silunse bell. An' then wot does I do, d'ye think?"

"What?" queried Joe interested, and anxious to learn the ins and outs of life on the Grummet.

"I gets up, I comes out, I 'alloos and shouts at th' top o' my voice, I defies 'em ter silunse me, and I puts my fingers ter my nose and tells th' orthorittes ter go to th' devil. Nex' day, Joe, I don't mind th' waves, even if they does go over th' rock. Fur I've 'ed my larf at th' Systum, Joe. And, Joe, m' boy, that's wuth 'eaps!"

## V.

One week passed, two, three in this companionship. The marooned mates had their laugh at the System together when over the waves, sweetly stealing into their ears with the rustle of the fresh land breeze, there came the silence bell; together they bore the heat of the day, and the dreadful burden of the stormy nights when the sea-horses dashed their manes of foam into the sleeping caverns, and when the elements shrieked and roared about the rock as though the lost spirits of that other world so faithfully represented on earth by Macquarie Harbour Settlement had in very truth forced their way through Hell's Gates; together they mixed their cold meal and water, and together they nourished their shrunken caresses upon it: together they rose to salute the pilot-boat as it flew by on patrol duty; together they shook their hard clenched fists at it as it disappeared behind Bloody Point—it was not safe to do so till she had rounded the cliff, for the boat-constable had a good glass, and the Administration was apt to view impertinence with displeasure; together they laughed and sang when they felt their freedom; together they cried and cursed, and together they trembled and shivered when the angry sea drenched them with its spume and isolated them with its horror; together they mocked Heaven, and together they read the Bible.

For three weeks, then—

One night, waking from a dream of love and light—a phosphorescent gleam from a midnight wave had touched his eyelids and brought him to consciousness—Forger Joe, over the bulwark of stones which he had erected in the mouth of his cave, saw the figure of his mate outlined against the grey walls of the sky.

He rose noiselessly, and watched Jones turn over the small rock with which they had closed the recess where they kept their meal-bags, into his—Joe's—bag went Jones' hand; then into his own. Once, twice was this done. Then Jones returned to his cave to sleep the sleep of the innocent.

At least he said he was innocent when, the next morning, Forger Joe taxed him with the deed which was not so much a contemptible theft as a deadly treachery.

* * * *

"We'll soon see," said Joe. "We'll measure!"[5] And ration by ration Joe weighed out his meal in his hands. He emptied the bag on his jacket, and as he balanced each handful replaced it in the canvas pocket.

"Been here 20 days. Twenty rations gone—72 should be left."

There were not 60. Jones must have been at the business of transfer for several nights. Of course he would not take too much at once.

"You've been living well, Jones! I thought you were keeping up flesh remarkably well. You're a nice 'un now, ain't you? To starve me—that was your little game. Or make me signal the boat for more tucker, and get as an appetiser, with each new ration, twenty lashes for extravagance. Now, Jones, the Grummet's not big enough for you and me. We'll toss up who goes over to the white fins."

Convict Jones demurred to this proposition, and declined to submit his precious life to the hazard of the die and the maw of the shark. He put his objection into the shape of a blow. They grappled—wrestled—Forger Joe knew a trick or two with his heels and threw his fellow-maroon on his back. And Jones' back lay on the two meal-bags, which, under the pressure, spurted out their contents over the rocky edge to water-level. Very literally had they cast their bread on the waters! Whether they found it after many days is a matter of opinion.

Joe lifted his knee from Jones' chest. Then he flung the bags after the meal.

Jones was the first to speak.

---

5    "Weighed out:" Old convicts, to whom an ounce of meal or meat was a thing of importance, developed so extraordinary an accuracy of discernment that they could gauge to a quarter of an ounce, by balancing in their palms, the weight of an unboiled ration, and almost to the same degree food that had passed through the hands of the cooks and peculators. A prison cook was always a thief.

"I'll toss now. As well be thrown to the sharks or 'anged, as starve 'ere ter death or be flogged ter bits. My curse on yer, Forger Joe!"

Joe prepared five smoothish pebbles. On one side of each he marked, respectively, with the point of a sharpened stone:

"Why don' yer put figgers? Wot're ye puttin, 'kisses' fur?"

"They'll do. 'Sides, we'll both be kissed shortly by Death."

"Yer funny," said Jones.

"Highest out of the three throws kills t'other," suggested Joe.

Jones nodded.

Jones took his cap and shook the stones together "Draw," said he, "for first throw. Lowest 'as it."

Joe, looking over the sea, dipped his hand in, and drew the three. Jones drew the four.

Joe, with a murmur, clasped the five bits, and tossed them up. They fell, chinking,—three marked, two blank ; 5, 1, 4; total, 10. His second cast was 6 ; his last, four blanks and 1.

"Luck's out," he said, "You'll beat that 17 easily."

"Orter," said Jones. But he threw 9 and 7, and then faltered. "Sixteen, too!" For the first time he quavered.

"You'll throw four blanks—see if you don't," laughed Joe.

Up the stones went propelled by a very shaking hand. And, true enough, four blanks did fall. But the faced stone was two. Eighteen!

"I've won, I've won!" he shouted.

"Yes," replied Forger Joe, "the Devil generally looks after his own."

Joe went into his cave. When he came out again he had his Bible with him, "I'll be ready in a few minutes, Bob." And, seating himself calmly, he read a chapter.

"I'm ready, Jones," he said, when he closed the Book. "Look, the white fins are waiting!"

He spoke the truth. Two vultures of the deep were sheening their fins within musket-shot.

"You're funking, Jones. I've no objection to make it

suicide just to oblige you."

And Jones, evidently disliking the privilege he had won, assenting mutely, Forger Joe "made it."

Nevertheless Captain Bankes hanged Convict Robert Jones, No. 9,439, *Sussex*. But it is doubtful whether it was on suspicion of Judson's murder or for destroying two meal-bags. Most likely it was the latter: Bankes once hanged a man for flattening out a tin-pannikin.

The pilot crew caught a shark a few months afterwards. There was no evidence that the man's jaw found in its interior was Joe's, as several other Children of the System had preferred the white-fins to the Grummet.

# AT BURFORD'S PANORAMA

## I.

"LADIES AND GENTLEMEN," remarked the lecturer at Burford's Panorama, Leicester Square, London, one afternoon in May, 183-, "we will now take you from the Old World to the New. We have shown you the glories of ancient and modern Italy, and have revealed to you the snowy glaciers of Mont Blanc, the monarch of mountains. Now we pass to other regions—regions where, if travellers speak truly, beauties of Nature adorn the scene that rival Italia's, where, though the art wonders which make Rome and Florence the theme of admiring myriads are absent, there are to be found subjects not unworthy of the pencil of Michael Angelo, and where, if noble peaks bedecked in eternal snows do not penetrate the horizon, there are still Alpine heights which are as grand in their cerulean aspect as Switzerland's mountains are in their garb of purity. Ladies and gentlemen, behold the magnificent harbour of Port Jackson, in New South Wales, with the beautifully situated city of Sydney on its shores—nursing, no doubt, in the youth of her existence, dreams of the coming time when she shall rival Carthage, Rome—aye, London itself."

The lecturer paused to allow the panorama to unroll, and his turgid eloquence to sink into the minds of his hearers. They stirred in their seats with the restlessness which is hungry for a delayed delight. This was what they had paid their shillings to see. They knew all about Italy—and they were so sick of Mont Blanc—and Paris on a painted transparency, even when lit up with double-wicked oil-lamps, is no particular wonder. But Sydney! That was something new! Sydney was in Botany Bay, of course, in the land of kangaroos and convicts, where all the bad people went to when the king was too merciful to hang 'em, and was right down the other side of the world, and the people stood on their heads there, and did other sorts of curious things, getting up when we went to bed, and the savages ate them—"they roasted Captain Cook, you know, dear, at Botany Bay!" whispered a prim governess to her charge— and, in short, the ladies and gentlemen in the crowded, darkened auditorium trembled all over with pleasure as the panorama of the finest harbour in the world stood revealed. All of them—except two men, who sat almost the length of the room apart. Both of them were present because they knew something of Sydney in the real, and were curious to see what it was like in the ideal. One, of short, thick-set figure, who sat near to the transparency, gazed stolidly at it, careless of its beauties and alert only to notice its deficiencies. And the other, almost a Jew in feature, sitting near the door, did not look at the panorama at all. His eyes were fixed upon the short man; studying every inch of the profile as intently as the dim light would permit.

The lecturer began his detailed description of the picture of Sydney. As became a loyal son of Church and Crown, he pointed out, first, the Churches of St. James and St. Philip, and then the seat of Government, and became dramatically vivid when he discerned—wonder of wonders—Governor Ralph Darling riding out with his private secretary and aide-de-camp, Captain Dumaresq!

"See, ladies and gentlemen, look at the two brave

dignitaries! They are clothed with righteous power and military costume. And, by way of contrast, see this black man dressed—I blush to have to remark it, ladies and gentlemen—in no more than a blanket and a cocked hat." (The prim governess cast down her eyes, and bade her pupil follow her example.) "See this black man! He is the symbol of the time that is passing away! He is King Boongaree—monarch of the Sydney tribe, and now a pensioner on the bounty of the Colonial Government. If there is, ladies and gentlemen, one thing more than another on which England has a right to feel proud, it is that of her treatment of aboriginal races. Observe how the artist has painted the Savage King—how deftly he suggests the epoch which is passing away before the new era of civilization! See, he lifts his hat to his approaching Excellency! He does homage at once to the Representative of August Majesty and to the Age of Progress!"

The orator paused to recover breath and win applause. And the man near the curtain took advantage of the opportunity to declare in plain, audible tones that "it wor all a cokumed[1] job!" Then, encouraged by the surprise he caused the audience, he went on: "There worn't no Boongaree or wot's 'is name, an' wot th' cove 'ad p'inted out as Saint James's wasn't that at all, but it wor th' old dock church on th' 'ill, an' wot 'e'd called Saint Philip's wor ak'shally Saint James's, only they'd turned it round th' wrong way! They'd got th' —— spire th' wrong end. Th' spire was th' town end—not a-facin' Park-'urds. W'y, for two balls[2] I'd paint a —— better picter myself!" Then, modestly content with the success he had achieved, the speaker sat down.

And, not to deprive the man of his honours, we must say that success was very marked. The lecturer, who had lectured before crowned heads, but who had never been

---

1   Cokumed—deceitful, as of entrapment. (ed.)
2   "Balls."—Convict term for "free drinks."

lectured save by his wife, was dumb with anger. Some school-lads shouted "Hear, hear!" an elderly gentleman hammered the floor with his stick, and the governess was so tickled that she overlooked the necessity of instructing the little girl to put her fingers in her ears at the "naughty words." But had there been any one to notice it, the most remarkable tribute to the effect of the extemporized oration came from the Jewish-looking fellow at the door. He chuckled, and chuckled again!

Disdaining to comment on the interruption, the lecturer proceeded. There was, however, less glibness in his utterance, and he displayed a hesitation that smacked of a doubt concerning the trustworthiness of his information.

"Follow me, please, ladies and gentlemen," he went on, "and notice the points and convolutions of the Harbour—"

"There ain't no conwo-yo'call'ems," interjected the critic, who, unlike most critics, evidently knew what he was talking about. "They're all coves an' bays!"

The lecturer kept his temper to admiration, and proceeded. "Here on this central point jutting out perceive Macquarie Fort, built, as its name imparts, by Governor Macquarie—"

"A good sort, old Locky—"

"But having been designed by a civil architect—"

"I knowed 'im—old Greenway."

"Instead of an engineer, it is erected in such a situation and in such a style that it is rather a picturesque object than a useful defence."

"'Ear, 'ear! Yer've got it right at last!"

"The fort stands on Bennilong's Point, so called from a house having been erected on it for the residence of a chief named Bennilong—"

"Oh, Lord—who's been a-kiddin' o' yer?"

"Really"—the lecturer lost patience now—"really if the gentleman by the wall persists in interrupting in this fashion, I shall be compelled to have him removed!"

"Well, I puts it t'ye, leddies an' gents, is it fair as 'e should be cokumin' yer in a lot o' damned trash, w'en I knows better?"

"Hear, hear!" shouted the boys. "Angcore!" cried the Jewish fellow (in a falsetto). "No, no—certainly not!" said the gentleman with the stick, who ought to have known better. And even the governess ventured to whisper to her charge: "Oh, I wish he would go on—if—if he would not swear so."

The proprietor of the panorama was attracted from behind the screen by the uproar. As a wise showman, he knew it was his duty to humour his audience, and proved himself equal to the occasion by suggesting that his lecturer should be allowed to proceed, but that afterwards the gentleman from Sydney might perhaps, if he would be so kind, favour the audience with—er—a more particular description—er—of the beauties of the harbour—er—of Botany Bay. And the gentleman from Sydney generously agreeing, the professional lecturer resumed, with, it must be confessed, something less of spirit and eloquence, his oration.

"I was saying, I believe, ladies and gentlemen, when I was—when the gentleman from Sydney was good enough to—er—speak to me, that a chief named Bennilong had his residence on that point. I may be wrong, or I may be right, but such is my information. He was the first native to become attached to the settlers. He was brought to England by Governor Phillip, and returned with Governor Hunter. Although he was in a great measure civilized, yet he could not altogether forget his former pursuits. For instance, he would frequently discard his clothes, and pass several weeks at a time with his old companions in the woods—"

"They all do it—they sell their breeches for grog."

The remonstrance of the lecturer was drowned in the roars of laughter from the indecorous. Everybody was indecorous, not excluding the school-girl.

"We will pass on. Observe this point, ladies and gentlemen! It is Dawes' Battery—mounting fifteen guns, and commanding the harbour. It is, however, inadequate to the defence of the town against any respectable force. This place acquired its name from Lieutenant Dawes, who sailed with the first expedition, and being charged by the Board of Longitude to make observations on an expected comet, erected his small observatory on the spot. May I ask the gentleman from Sydney whether that is not correct?"

"I shouldn't be surprised if it wor. But you didn't tell 'em that Black Sam wrecked th' 'Awkesbury passage-boat on that point. 'Owsomever, go ahead, old cove—yer as slow as th' Rosehill Lump, or Jim Hughes, th' angman, wen 'e turned off 'is mother-in-law."

"How slow was that?" questioned the old gentleman, who must have been a disreputable old gentleman, thus to set at defiance the routine of a respectable entertainment. Certainly he was a humorous one.

"Well, I'll tell yer, if so be th' leddies are willin', ven th' lect'rer 'as slung 'is patter. Go on, pal!"

Glowering daggers, the orator proceeded. But, alas! he was an orator no longer. No resonant periods flowed from his lips. If the people wished to be entertained by a vulgarian from Botany Bay, well, they might. But, as for himself, he would no longer cast his pearls before such swine. He jerked out brief, unpicturesque sentences.

"This ship in the stream is H.M.S. *Success*. Captain Sterling, who commands her, has at a late date taken her round to the western coast of New South Wales to found a new settlement."

"New 'Olland, yer mean. The old colony ain't got a west coast!"

"An' this ship, ladies and gentlemen—this ship—or rather the hulk of one, perhaps"—here the speaker infused a palpable malice into his tones—"the gentleman from Sydney would not mind telling us what it is?" He pointed to a black object depicted in midwater off Dawes' Point. It might have been anything from a badly-drawn island to a ship's hull.

From his seat by the wall the interjector peered at the painted canvas. The audience, made more interested themselves by the accent of meaning in the lecturer's question, listened intently—none more so than the Jew-like man by the door. His heavy eyes glistened with his suppressed eagerness, and his nostrils dilated as he held his breath. He knew better than any one there how pertinent was that inquiry.

"Oh!" continued the lecturer, as the other did not answer, "I should have thought the gentleman from Sydney would have been certain to have known that! That is the *Phoenix* hulk—used as a place of confinement for prisoners of desperate character."

In the half-light of the hall it was not possible to distinguish any alteration in the man's features, but there was a strangeness in his voice which went far to convince most of those who heard him that with his voice had changed his features. The shock that dries the throat blanches the cheek.

"That th' *Phoenix?*—that 'taint th' *Phoenix*—th' hulk didn't lay there—she was in Cockle Bay—orf Goat Island!" But somehow the assertiveness was out of his voice, and he was quiet while the lecturer ran over the remaining features of the harbour and the town. Possibly he would not have again opened his lips, but have noiselessly departed, when the lecturer closed the exhibition by a striking quotation from Darwin's "Visit of Hope to Sydney Cove."[3] But the old gentleman and the boys, aided by a falsetto from the back-seats, clamoured for the story of Jim Hughes.

He began to speak from his seat, but the audience called him to mount the form. And so, at last, he stood and gave them the story of Jim Hughes and his mother-in-law.

"Yer must know, leddies an' gents all, as Jim Hughes was Jack Ketch in Gov'ner Macquarie's time. An' Jim, though

---

3   A poem by Erasmus Darwin, published in 1789 to celebrate the arrival of Governor Philip in Botany Bay. (ed.)

he warn't so full o' work as 'e wor later, did purty well week-in an' week-out. Six-pun' ten, in dollars, a quarter 'e got, an' all th' stiff-uns' duds—I mean, leddies, as 'e wor given th' boots an' togs o' th' free people as wor turned orf—o' course, Gov'ment pe'ple 'adn't duds to leave. Well, Jim married, but 's missus died, an' so 'e got 'is wife's mother—she wor a lag, y' see—assigned to 'im, that means, leddies, as she wor to be 'is servant. But it 'appened that th' old woman got drinkin', an' she killed 'nother woman, an' so she wor ordered ter be scragged." As he proceeded, something of the intoxication of public speech inspired him, and he regained part of his former aggressiveness.

"Well, w'en Monday mornin' came, Jim takes 'er out as neat as can be. There wor two men, an' he ties 'em up spick an' span, but 'e leaves 'er to the last. 'Yer slow, Jim!' ses she. 'Yes, mother, I be,' ses 'e. 'Well,' ses she, 'I allus thought as you wor a workman, not a damned codger'—a-savin' o' yer presence, leddies, she wor givin' ter naggin' 'im a good bit, wor Jim's mother-in-lor. 'But,' ses 'e, "tisn't nateral, is it, I should be in a 'urry ter turn yer off?" 'Oh,' ses she, 'I don't know as ter that! Yer never cared much for me or my gal.' 'P'r'aps I didn't,' ses 'e, 'an' I don't say as I did. But I'm slow now as 'opin' th' Gov'nor may 'prieve yer! I axed 'im!' 'Like yer imperence, Jim Hughes,' ses she, 'interferin' with wot ain't yer bus'ness! I don't want no 'prieve at yer 'ands!' 'I don't care wot yer want,' ses 'e. 'I wants yer 'prieved for my own pu'pose. If I turns yer orf ter-day I ain't got no 'ooman to whop!' An' that's w'y, ladies an' gents, Jim Hughes turned his missus' mother orf slow."

"Didn't she get reprieved, then?" asked the old gentleman.

"No, sir!" replied the Sydneyite. "An' 'tis a pity too. Jim 'udn't get a second missus—it 'tain't ev'ry 'ooman as likes Skeleton Jimmy—an' as 'e wor wun o' them sort as must 'av a 'ooman to whop, to ease th' temper like, sir, he took to th' grog."

## II.

A few minutes later the audience filed down the stairway to the street. As the "gentleman from Sydney" was passing through the doorway to the landing a hand grasped his arm, and as he turned with a startled movement at the touch, the full lips of the fellow who had been watching him bent to his ear.

"An' vat is the time o' day with you, Sam Jefferson, alias Dicky Arnold? He-he! the game's up, Dicky!"

The man spoken to stared dazedly at the other. The white terror of the hunted animal at bay was for a moment in his face, but vanished as he strove to carry off the incident in a braggart style.

"Wot's your game, my covey?—I ain't no Dicky Arnold or wot d'yer call th' cove as yer named—er—Sam Jefferson neither. I don't know nothink 'bout yer!"

"Vy, vot a dear innercent chap ve've got 'ere!" returned the other, sardonically. "An' ye don't mean to turn yer back on an old Sydney pal, Dicky, d'yer? Oh, Dicky, Dicky, I'm kevite ashamed of ye!—wantin' to cut an old pal jest 'cos you're so big in yer shoes arter a-lecturin' all these city blokes an' donnas!"

The gentleman from Sydney had now regained his wits and his courage. "No more o' this—nonsense, or I'll call a— trap, an' give yer up!"

"Vy, vat a bold bloke he is to be sure!" admiringly exclaimed the other. "If he ain't a innercent, he is a tiptopper, an' no mistake! S'elp me, I never 'erd of a cove vot vas frightened of th' traps so, a-talkin' so bold! But if so be as ye want to give me up, vy I'm villin'!"

By this time, the couple had reached the street. The Jewish fellow's arm had gradually tightened round the Sydneyite's, and though the latter made one strong effort to escape, his capturer foiled it instantly by twisting his leg inside the other's.

"You bolt, Dicky, an' I'll raise th' hue an' cry! An' vere vill ye be then, my son? Now, don't be a fool, Dicky! I ain't goin' to be 'ard."

A light of hope shot into the Sydney man's eyes.

"Wot d'yer mean, Izzy? 'Ull yer square it?"

"Ho, ho! Dicky, I'd 'a thought better o' ye! Ter go an' give yerself avay, like a born fool! Vy, ye do know Israel Chapman then, arter all, d'ye? Yer ol' friend, Izzy—vat copped ye at Parramatta an' sent ye to th' Phoenix! Vy, o' course ye knows Izzy—yer ol' friend Izzy!"

"An' wot if I does?" growled Chapman's prisoner. "Anywun wot 'as wunst seen yer ugly mug ain't agoin' ter forget it in an 'urry, neither!"

"Vell, vell," quoth the notorious Sydney thieftaker, "ye ain't too compliment'ry to yer old friends, Dicky. But I'm going to do pis'ness, Dicky, pis'ness!"

"Honour bright an' above-board, Izzy?"

"Yes, s'elp me, by Father Abraham, I am!"

"Ye won't take my money an' then give me up, arter all, Izzy?"

Mr. Chapman looked genuinely distressed. "Vy, mine friend, vat d'ye take me for? I ain't Pounce!"

At the mention of old Pounce, the Sydney forger, who did so large a trade in official forgeries of all kinds, Dicky Arnold, otherwise Sam Jefferson, started again.

"D'yer mean ter say as Pounce 'as sold me?" he gasped.

"I ain't a-goin' ter say nuthin', mine friend—until we skevares matters, or I gives ye up at Bow-street perlice-office as a returned from transportation cove."

"Well, Izzy, wot's it ter be?"

Mr. Israel Chapman, over from Sydney on "Government business"—in other words, commissioned by Mr. Alexander Macleay to ascertain the destination of certain Sydney Commissariat bills on the Treasury which had mysteriously disappeared from the Colonial Secretary's office, Sydney, gave the insinuated proposal two minutes' consideration before he replied.

"Vell, y' see, there's a reward for arresting a returned from transportation man 'ere—that's five! An' then there's the Sydney reward for pickin' up a *Phoenix* bolter—s'elp me, Dicky, that lect'rer chap gave it ye pretty sharp, all unbeknowin', though, didn't he?"

"Go on! To—with the lect'rer! If it 'adn't been for 'im, ye wouldn't 'a cotched me!"

"P'r'aps I vudn't an' p'r'aps I vud! But I vas really in doubt till I 'erd ye tell that yarn 'bout Jim Hughes! Everybody in th' old time knew Dick Arnold's story of Jim Hughes' missus' mother."

"Go on! go on!"

"Don't lose yer temper, mine friend! If people vat ought to keep 'emselves low vant to brag an' show off, vy, they've got to pay th' price of greatness, Dicky. Vell, then, besides, the *Phoenix* revard is ten—that's fifteen pun, Dicky."

"I'll give it yer to let me go."

"Stay, stay, not so fast, my son! I never does these little friendly jobs except for double the Gov'nment price."

"That's thirty pun—I'll make it guineas!"

"Ho, ho! Vy, yer must 'ave a nice plant someveres, Dicky! An' then, y' know, there's somethink for the credit— ye must make allowance for the credit, Dicky! Vy, dis would be a brilliant capture! Vot shall ve say for the credit, Mister Arnold? Just a leetle bit of paper for twenty quid? Say yes, Dicky!"

"I s'pose I must say yes if yer insist 'pon it!" cursed the other.

"That's fifty altogether, Dicky. Now, I put it to yer, Dicky, ain't that too low for a service to a friend? Make it double, Dicky—say an 'underd—an' I'm blowed if I don't let ye go!"

"Square?"

"Skevar!"

"On yer honour?"

"On the honour of a shentleman, Dicky!"

And, though Mr. Arnold paid the notes over with a

seeming reluctance, he rejoiced in his heart that his unauthorized return trip to his native land was to cost him no more.

"Tip us another tenner, Dicky, an' I'll tell ye 'ow I heard o' ye being here!"

"No!"

"Better 'ad! The chap vat gave ye avay this time may give yer avay again. An' if ye gets sent out once more—an' ye're bound to, Dicky, when ye're spent all th' mopuses on the gals—th' knowledge 'll be useful!"

The contingency of another voyage across the seas not being altogether beyond the limits of possibility, Mr. Arnold, otherwise Sam Jefferson, thought the outlay of another ten pounds only a precautionary measure. So he made it.

"Vat did ye pay old Pounce for Sammy Jefferson's certificate of freedom?"

Arnold's mouth twitched in angry surprise. "A tenner!"

"An' vat did it cost to 'ave Sammy Jefferson's marks tattooed on your buzzum?"

"Three pun' ten."

"So this leetle trip 'ome o' yours has cost yer wi'out your ship-money, 'ow much, Dicky?"

"One 'underd an' thirteen pun' ten."

"Now, ain't that a nice sum to pay for trustin' ol' Pounce?"

"D'ye mean ter say—?"

"As Pounce gave ye 'vay? O' course I do! He says to me, 'Izzy, ye're going 'ome! Ven ye're in Lunnun look out for Dicky Arnold vat bolted from the hulk. I'm afraid he vent 'vay'—them vas his very verds, Dicky!—'on Sammy Jefferson's ticket. Dick ain't no marks on his buzzum, Izzy, but if ye find a Sammy Jefferson in Lunnun with a mermaid an' a 'nanchor in a true-lover's knot on his buzzum over S. J., that chap's Dicky Arnold!' That's vot ol' Pounce said, Dicky. An' he vanted to go halves in th' revard if I cotched ye! Vasn't he mean?"

"Mean! I'd mean 'im if I'd 'im 'ere for ten minutes!"

"An' look 'ere, Dicky. Ven ye comes out again, an' I'm in Sydney—an' ye vants to make another bolt, v'y, you send for me, Dicky. I'll get ye a whole pardon with th' seal an' all reg'lar for vat Pounce charges for a ticket of freedom only! An' I allus acts skevare, Dicky—I never gives no one avay vat deals honour'ble vith me! Now, let's 'av a drink, Dicky, for the sake o' old times!"

* * * *

Within a week, Richard Arnold, alias Samuel Jefferson, was arrested by a Bow-street runner as a convict illegally returned from transportation. Only Israel Chapman did not appear as the informant. Nevertheless, he fingered the reward.